Ed Buffington

Neil,

Thanks, We'll
keep you posted on
the new films,

Max Bann

8/2004

HEADS OR TAILS

Ed Buffington
Max Bain

Alliance Books
an imprint of
Harlan Publishing Company
Summerfield, North Carolina USA

HAR LAN

PUBLISHING

Heads or Tails is a work of fiction. Any references to real people, events, establishments, organizations, or locales are intended only to give the fiction a sense of reality and authenticity. Other names, characters, places, and incidents portrayed herein are either the product of the author's imagination or are used fictionally. The views expressed in this book are purely those of the characters.

Published by Alliance Books
P.O. Box 397
Summefield, North Carolina 27358

Book and Cover Design by Jeff Pate

ISBN: 0-9747278-3-0

Library of Congress Catalog Number:

Acknowledgements

For all the friends who have read and commented on
everything I have written, I am grateful beyond words.
E.B.

To the people that read the written word,
over and over again.
You make my dreams come true.
For that I thank you.
M.B.

To my wife Carolyn who was abandoned
all those evenings I spent writing.
E.B.

For those few friends that let you stand on their
shoulders when you just can't see.
This one's for Dan and Nelson.
M.B.

CHAPTER

1

CLIENT: Mrs. Wilma Ellman

J ACK WEXLER parked his Honda in the loading zone, unfolded his six foot one inch frame from the small car and dashed into the Mechanical Engineering building. He checked the listed final grades on the bulletin board under his student ID number. Not bad, he thought, as he raced back to his car. An A and a B+ was about what he thought he would score. He had checked his grades in Calculus and Physics the day before. Right on track, he thought, for a grade average in the low A or high B area.

His car was loaded with clothing and a few other personal items he would need for the next five months. Everything else was stored, waiting for his return to Auburn University for the summer term. His Aunt Emily was expecting him to arrive at her Homestead, Florida home late the next afternoon, however, if he drove straight through, he could make it before noon. So, he headed east through Opelika, Alabama and Columbus, Georgia.

He was glad to leave Auburn as the spate of cold weather that came during Thanksgiving had lingered on through his final exams in early December. He was really ready for the warmth of southern Florida.

Jack was one of the rare individuals who had no sense of how incredibly handsome he really was. He was well built but not overly so. He had a friendly nature with a winning smile that was attractive to his male and female friends alike. It was his intensely blue eyes and black curly hair that really set him apart. The only part of his Marine Corps background he changed was opting for a less severe hair cut. There was a strand of curly hair always falling over his forehead.

Aunt Emily was his mother's sister. Now, other than some distant cousins, she was his only living relative. She and Uncle Joe Noonan had moved down from Letterkenny, Pennsylvania when he retired from his civil-service job with the nearby army arsenal. He survived retirement eight years before lung cancer took him away. Now, having no children of her own, his aunt took great comfort and joy with each of Jack's extended visits.

It was just getting dark when Jack turned south on Interstate 95. He set the cruise control on seventy, loaded the CD deck from a stack of disks and settled down to the long drive before him.

Jack was that independent breed of college student who worked his way through. Oh, he didn't work during the time he was enrolled for classes—he just took a quarter or two off as needed to build up his bank-roll. He could have gotten a loan but that wasn't in his makeup. He had learned early in life to pay his own way. After High School, when others were starting college, he had joined the Marines for four years. For him, it was the best move of his life. When he was working, he would do anything legal, moral and not a danger to his health in order to earn money. And now, at twenty-eight years of age, he was making a future for himself.

It was just past noon when he pulled into the driveway behind Aunt Emily's Buick. He would move his Honda to the street after he unloaded his stuff. No sooner had he shut the engine off, Emily appeared at the back door, wiping her hands on her apron.

"Jackie, I just knew you wouldn't listen to me. I figured you would drive straight through. Come on in, I have lunch ready. Fried chicken, mashed potatoes and gravy, buttered peas and the yeast rolls you like so well. Come on in, Lord, I'm glad to see you. You can bring in your things later."

The house was constructed of concrete blocks with a flat concrete slab roof. The yard was overgrown with every sort of ornamental shrub. Jack thought he would try to trim them back when he had some spare time. He hugged his aunt for a moment as he entered the back door. Then, he headed straight for the table. He wasn't surprised that table was loaded down with food—she had made enough for an army.

"Now Jackie, not until you wash up. You just go on to the bathroom and get some of that travel off your hands and face."

She had a habit of doing that—treating him like a child—but he al-ways obeyed her. She reminded him of his mother, now dead five years, they looked so much alike.

After he had eaten too much, he felt glued to his chair. He forced himself to empty out the car and get moved into the spare bedroom. He brought in all the clothes that were on hangers and stowed them in the empty closet. When he finally emptied the last of the boxes and suitcases, he got the boom box out of the trunk and placed it on the desk that Uncle Joe had used for his ham radio station. The transmitter and receiver were still there. Emily really didn't know what to do with the equipment. His wire antennas were still strung here and there across the lot.

"You've had few calls. One was from Carl at the Coral Palms. The other was from a woman. She didn't give her name but she had a New York accent—Bronx, I think."

He got his address book, looked up the number and called.

"Concierge desk please, for Carl. Hello, Carl?"

"No this is Dennis."

"Well, can you put Carl on the phone?"

"Just a sec."

"Hello."

"Hey Carl, this is Jack. It's been a while."

"Hey, Wex, I called your aunt a couple of days ago. How you doin'? Did you keep up the grades?"

"Yeah, I'm doing okay. Mostly A's and a few B's. I'm right on track for graduating in a year and a half. You got any bridges you need built?"

"Guess you're calling about the message I left with your aunt. Well, I got a call from a Mrs. Ellman. She wanted your phone number. You remember working for her last year?"

"Yeah, good money."

"She wants you again."

"You got her number?"

Jack took out his book and wrote the name and number. He dialed as soon as he finished with Carl.

"Hello, Wilma?"

"Yes."

"Jack Wexler here."

"Oh, Jackie, I've been trying to find you. How have you been? How was school—some kind of engineering wasn't it?"

"I'm good. Still on schedule for graduation in a couple of years."

"Jack, are you engaged the next four weeks?"

"No. I've only arrived at my aunt's place this day. When will you be here?"

"Tuesday afternoon at 2:55, United flight 585. Can you meet my plane?"

"Sure, but you know the heap I drive. Perhaps you should reserve a rental car."

"Good idea. I'll have them call you at your aunt's number. Ciao."

After he put the phone down, he suddenly felt tired. He kicked off his shoes and made for the bed. When he woke it was dark. He looked at the digital clock on the nightstand. Ten-fifteen. Where had the day gone? When he started to get up, he felt the weight of the blanket his aunt had spread while he slept. He listened for the sound of the television but all was silent. Quietly, he slipped on his shoes and left the house. As he opened the door to his car, Aunt Emily spoke from the darkness of the front door.

"Don't forget, Jackie, the key is under the flower pot."

"Thank you. I'll try not to be too late."

He drove south on US1 to a sports bar on Key Largo where he knew the owner-bartender.

As soon as he entered, he was greeted by the familiar booming voice of Wally Frontiere. "Hey, look what the cat dragged in. It's been a long time Wex, Semper-Fi buddy."

"Yeah, Wally, Semper-Fi. How's business?"

"This is the best time of the year for me with football and basketball both going strong. I've got four wide-screen TVs with satellite dish to pull in any game of interest. After the Super Bowl, all that's left is basketball. Though we get a little interest in soccer from time to time."

Taking a swipe at the bar in front of Jack with his towel, he asked: "The usual?"

"Yeah."

The bartender quickly scooped up two ice cubes and filled the glass with club soda.

Jack put a five on the bar. Wally waved it away.

"On the house."

Jack raised the glass to the bartender and took a sip. He swiveled about on the stool to check out the patrons. He noticed two girls sitting alone at a table. They had their own drinks as well as several beer bottles in front of them. One of the two girls made eye contact with Jack. Jack smiled and raised his glass in salute.

Jack turned around facing Wally. "The two at the table over there—are they alone or what?"

"The guys abandoned them almost as soon as they sat down. They're with that bunch watching the game."

"Oh."

Jack turned toward the girls again. This time, both were looking in

Jack's direction. Again he smiled and raised his glass.

The girl nearest Jack got up and came to his side. "Would you do us a great favor? We left our car at Moon's and got in the car with those jerks. We want to ditch them. So, could you please take us back to our car?"

"Sure, I'll meet you outside. It's an old gray Honda."

He turned to Wally. "Later, my man."

"Hope you get lucky."

"You can never tell."

Jack drove his car to the entrance and opened the passenger's side door. As the girls raced to the car, he opened the back door for one of the girls to sit there.

"My name is Jack. Yours?"

"I'm Robin and this is my sister Dove. We're twins."

"You don't look like twins, but I do see a strong family resemblance."

"Silly, we're not identical but we're still twins."

"Your accent is Midwest. But you may be transplants. Are you from around here?"

"Detroit. I work at Ford and my sister works at PSK Accounting. She's the smart one—a CPA no less."

They soon arrived at Moon's. They could hear the beat of the Latin band from the parking lot. All three left the car and made their way to the entrance. They found a table far enough from the band so they could hold a conversation. As soon as they were seated the waitress came by.

"What'll you have?"

Robin quickly ordered a screwdriver and Dove chimed in with her order for a lite beer.

"And you, sir?"

"Club soda on the rocks with a twist. Tell the bartender that I'm driving."

When the waitress left, Robin asked: "No alcohol?"

"Not since I got drunk one night when I was a senior in High School. That was it for me. Never again will I feel like that."

"Do you dance?"

"Try me."

With that Robin, Dove and Jack headed for the dance floor.

For the next two and a half hours, they danced more or less continually. At two in the morning, the crowd began thinning out. The band was packing up their instruments with the music coming from the house sound system.

As they were returning from the dance floor, Dove grabbed Jack about his waist and gave him a long kiss. Robin gently pulled her away and kissed him herself. It too was a long kiss, full of passion.

Dove whispered, "Let's take him back to the room, I want him now!"

Robin was still holding him about the waist. "Seriously, Jack, since we've both been drinking, would you please drive us in my car back to the motel? It's the Blue Dolphin across the road."

"Sure, let's go."

Dove got into the back seat with Robin sitting as close to Jack as possible. From the back seat, Dove began kissing Jack on the neck and ear as Jack drove the short distance to their motel.

As they pulled into the driveway, Jack asked, "What room?"

"One forty-three. It's around the back."

As soon as they stopped, Dove got out of the car and entered the motel room. Robin and Jack continued kissing as they walked to the open door. As they entered the room, Dove was removing the last of her clothing.

Dove looked up. "I'm first," she said, as her sister locked the door.

Jack woke when the light from the window pierced through the narrow slit between the closed curtains. The two girls were tightly against him like nested spoons. He rolled out of bed to the floor. He went to the bathroom and urinated. His watch said six. He quickly put on his clothing. Before leaving, he took a last glance at the nude sisters, still asleep.

As he walked the hundred yards to Moon's to get his car he noted that the marina and parking lot were alive with fishermen getting ready for the day. When he arrived at his car, he searched his pockets for his car keys. When he found the keys he also found two business cards—one from Robin and one from Dove. There was a note on the back of Robin's card: 'Call me anytime—you will always be welcome.'

Well, Jack thought, it's nice to be appreciated.

I T WAS FULLY LIGHT with the temperature rising when he reached his aunt's house. He entered the back door to find her putting the finishing touches on a magnificent breakfast. Coffee, orange juice, eggs, bacon, sausage, ham, biscuits, gravy, cantaloupe, French toast, maple syrup and three kinds of jelly and jam. He made for the bathroom to wash up. He was very hungry.

When he sat at the table, Aunt Emily commented with a smile, "You missed a place. There's lipstick on your ear and neck."

Jack smiled back.

Emily joined him at the table.

"A call came for you about ten minutes before you arrived. Trumpet Rental. They have a Town Car. I have the number. They said they would deliver."

After breakfast, Jack took a shower and placed his laundry in the washing machine.

"Now, Jackie, you don't have to do that. I'll be glad to do the wash for you."

"But, Aunt Emily, I'm used to taking care of myself."

"I don't mind if you just call me Emily."

A horn sounded. "That must be the car."

Jack went to the front door. A maroon Lincoln Town Car was parked in front. A beautiful young lady, tall and very blond, got out.

"You Mister Jack Wexler?"

"Yeah, that's me."

"If you're ready, let's go. We need to fill out some paperwork at the office. Be sure to bring your driver's license."

Jack disappeared in the house a few seconds then returned and got into the car.

The driver drove the few blocks to US1 and turned north. The sound system was on low with some pretty good jazz. He recognized the CD but asked nonetheless. It was bebop guitar.

"Who's the guitar player?"

"Bruno."

He had known it was Jimmy Bruno.

"Does it come with the car?"

She smiled. "Fat chance. Get your own."

"I will. What's your name?"

"Doris Day. Now don't laugh!"

"Why should I laugh?"

"You know, Doris Day the actress? Back in the sixties? My mom named me after her. Thank goodness when I get married, the torment will be over."

"Never heard of her."

"You're kidding, right?"

"No. Really, never."

"Finally a guy who has never heard of Doris Day. I think I'm in love."

They pulled into the parking lot of Trumpet Rental. Twenty minutes later, he was driving the Lincoln back to Homestead with the address and phone number of Doris Day in his book.

On his way back, he stopped at the insurance office to renew his personal liability bond. Then he stopped at the Sheriff Substation, a low gray concrete block building with two flagpoles in the front.

"I need to see Colonel Reynolds, please." He told the officer at the desk.

"Your name?"

"Jack Wexler."

She pushed some buttons on a complicated looking phone. "Jack Wexler is here to see you." She paused a few moments listening. "Go on back. It's the last door on the right."

Reynolds met him at the door. "Wex, it's good to see you again. How did Engineering School go?"

Jack's hand met the Colonel's as they shook hands. "Good to see you too, John. I'm on track for graduation in a year and a half. The more money I make, the longer I can stay in school."

"Come on in and sit down. Got any leads on work?"

"Got an escort and bodyguard job working for a lady from New York. I start this weekend. Should last a month or so. I have the usual feelers out with people I know at a few hotels."

"Jack, I can't tell you how much I appreciate your work for us last year. When compared to what DEA gets, it was small potatoes. But for us, it was a good bust."

"Thanks, Colonel. Oh, here's my liability insurance and bond." He took the papers from his hip pocket and pushed them across the desk."

"Carmichael!"

A female deputy appeared at the door. "Sir?"

"Make a copy of these. Front and back—all pages."

He went to a file cabinet and spun the dial on the combination lock. "You've been promoted. You are now a Special Investigator."

"Do I get a pay increase too?"

Laughing, "Sure, twice as much as before."

"But I wasn't paid before."

"Right."

The officer returned with the copies. "Wait a second, there's something else I want you to do."

Turning to Jack, "Sign here, here and here." Looking in the folder, "Let's see, your photo from last year is still okay."

He handed the papers to the officer. "Laminate this ID card for me, please."

Back to the filing cabinet, he extracted an automatic pistol. "This one should be just right. It's a 380 automatic. Small size—easy to conceal—extra clip. You'll have to buy your own ammo, though. All we have is 9mm. And you get a badge too."

"Okay. Is that it?"

"You were sworn in last year so I guess that's it. Keep in touch. Oh, pick up the ID card on your way out."

When he left the Sheriff Substation, he felt like speeding just so he could flash his badge at any officer who pulled him over but kept the car at a legal speed. After he pulled into the parking lot of Shooter's Heaven, he put the pistol in his hip pocket and entered the store.

"Help you with anything?"

He flashed his badge. "I need two boxes of ammo for a 380 auto."

He retrieved the two boxes of fifty and placed them on the counter. "With your discount and tax that'll be twenty-four-thirty-six."

"Can I use your range?"

"Sure. Targets are fifty cents each. We'll just round off your bill to twenty-five even."

"And here's the twenty-five."

He called after Jack as he started descending the stairs to the basement shooting range. "There's ear protection in the cabinet and the light switch is at the bottom of the stairs."

Jack found the earmuffs, attached one target to the carriage and cranked the handle that sent the target out to twenty five feet. He attached the second target to the adjacent lane's carriage and cranked it out as well.

He heard a humming noise and the sound of gurgling water from the corner of the room. It was a sump pump. He had forgotten how high the water table was. It was a wonder that the basement wasn't flooded.

After shooting sixty rounds he was confident in his ability to handle the weapon. He got the broom and a dustpan and swept up his spent brass. There were two cans labeled 9mm and 38/357 plus a third one tagged 'other'. He dumped the brass in 'other'. Before he left, he loaded both clips with eight rounds each.

He paused at the counter, taking the clip out of the pistol. "Do you have any leather to fit this weapon?"

"How do you want to carry it? At your side, the small of your back or under the arm or perhaps attached at your ankle."

"I think the small of my back. That way, I can wear a suit or even a shirt that's not tucked in."

"Left or right?"

"Right handed."

He knelt at a table and began pulling out cardboard boxes.

"Here it is."

He brought the box to the counter where he rummaged around, pulling out first one, then another until he had a collection of about six holsters. "I think at least one of these will do. But, if you could spare the weapon for a few days, I could get one made."

Jack tried the pistol in first one, then another until he found one that had a good fit.

"With this one, you don't need a belt. See, it will clip on your trousers. The clip is very strong. See how you flip this lever and it locks. This one will not fall out if you're running."

"How much?"

"Nothing. I saw your ring. Semper Fi, buddy. Be careful out there."

The ring showed the eagle, globe and anchor of the Marine Corps emblem.

CHAPTER

3

H E ARRIVED at the United terminal at three, parking in a space that
said 'Police Only'. He looked around for a cop. He flashed his badge
and ID card to the one directing traffic and pointed to his car. "I'll be here
a half-hour or so. Any problem?"

"Not at all. That's what the spaces are for. Thanks for asking, though.
Sometimes I write a ticket and it turns out to be an officer. It helps
when I know."

He hung around the baggage carousel looking for his client. He immediately spotted her wearing a fur coat. It was difficult to imagine someone
wearing a fur coat in Miami. She was not alone. A beautiful woman about
his own age or younger was with her. The reddish color of her hair wasn't
real but everything else about her was. She wore a blue miniskirt with a
pink blouse. Both very tight and very revealing. She wasn't wearing a bra.
Over her arm, she carried a light blue jacket.

"Oh." Wilma squealed, waving her arm in the air, "There he is. Yoo-
hoo, Jackie! Here we are."

Jack was intending to shake her hand but she wrapped an arm around
his neck and kissed him on both cheeks.

"Oh, Jack, you're such a darling. Brenda, this is the one I was telling
you about. This is Jack Wexler. Jack, this is my friend, Brenda Mazzi."

"Oh, he is nice."

Jack took her hand in his with a firm grip.

"If you'll give me the luggage tags and identify your items when they
appear, I'll get them to the car."

After loading eight pieces of luggage in the huge trunk of the Lincoln,
they were on their way.

"Now, Jack, I've taken a lease on a four bedroom furnished condo for
six months. But it won't be ready for another few days. We will be at the
Coral Palms until then. I have a suite reserved."

Jack's mind was busy calculating what he could make in six months. If he skipped the summer semester he could be free for eight months. His fee depended on whether the job was part-time or live-in. Since she said there were four bedrooms in the condo, it could mean anything. The last time he worked for her, he got a thousand a week plus expenses. But that was based on an eight-hour day.

After the luggage was delivered to their suite, Jack started to leave. "I'll call on you later after you've settled in. Perhaps then we can discuss my contract. Will you be needing me or the car this evening?"

"No, I think we'll have dinner in the hotel tonight. But, if you would, try to find a housekeeper for us—you know, some cooking, keeping the place tidy, that sort of thing. She will be living in."

Jack left, wondering where he could find a cook. The thought about his aunt but rejected the idea. He knew she had trouble with her back and limped a little from time to time. Besides, she didn't need the grief of taking orders.

He stopped at the concierge desk to speak with Carl.

"Hey, Carl, how you doin'?"

"Not bad, not bad. I saw you when you came in. The red-head was really something."

"They're moving into a condo in a week. They need a housekeeper to keep things tidy and do a little cooking. Maybe breakfast and a few meals. I get the idea they'll be hitting all the four-star eating joints. By the way, what does a four bedroom furnished condo go for?"

"More money than we can ever make. I'd say twenty thousand a month and up. Depends on location and whether it's utility or lux."

"Oh, I'd definitely say lux. Now, how about a cook?"

"I'll ask Joanie, she's in personnel—maybe she knows someone. Will this be a live-in position?"

"I think so. Figure Sunday's off and a six-month contract. She'll need references and be bonded."

"I'll have news one way or another by tomorrow."

"Thanks pal. I owe you."

"Damn straight."

His aunt met him at the door. "How did it go? Are you working?"

"Looks like it. I think they'll want me to live in."

"They?"

"She brought a friend."

"Male or female?"

"Female and young."

"Hmm. Interesting."

The next morning, Jack packed a garment bag and a small suitcase with changes of clothing just to be prepared. On the way to the hotel, he filled up the car with gas, keeping the receipt.

As he entered the hotel, Carl waved him over. "Found a cook for your boss. Good references but she speaks little English."

"Spanish?"

"Same thing—Cuban."

"I speak a little Spanish. I can do okay if I choose the words and they reply with simple words and speak very slowly."

"Have Mrs. Ellman call hotel personnel and speak to Joanie. She's our personnel director."

He took the elevator to the floor and knocked. After a long wait, Brenda answered. She was wearing a tee shirt and little else. "Uh, could you come back in a couple of hours? We got pretty wasted last night in the club downstairs."

Jack smiled and stepped back from the door. He turned and headed to the elevator. As he passed the doorway to the next room across the hall, he noticed that the door was ajar. Through the crack in the door, he could see someone looking out. Quickly, the door closed. He made careful note of the room number.

He headed to the coffee shop, picking up the free newspaper in the lobby. He ordered coffee. Slowly, he read the paper, killing time. He was just getting to the business section when Carl approached his booth.

"Find anything new in the news?"

"Just killing time. You off duty?"

"Taking a break."

"Can you find out who is in room 923?"

"Sure. Now?"

"If you don't mind."

Carl slipped out of the booth and found a house phone. In a moment he returned."

"No one. The room is out of service for some reason or another."

"Nose around and see if anyone is camping out in that room. Someone is in there and they are very interested in my client."

Jack paid for his coffee and returned to the room. This time, it was

Mrs. Ellman answering the door. She looked a mess. When she had her makeup on she could appear in her early forties. But like this, Jack figured fifties at least.

"Come on in, Jack. Have some coffee. They just brought it up."

"Thank you, Mrs. Ellman. I just finished having coffee."

"Now we agreed that you would call me Wilma. Some juice, then?"

"Perhaps later."

"Please take a seat at the table while I have mine. We need to discuss your contract."

Jack took a seat at the small table. There was a thermos decanter of coffee, sugar and cream, plus a small pitcher of orange juice as well as a tray of pastries.

"First of all, let me tell you what kind of service I want from you. I need you to be on-call all the time. To that end, I have secured the room across the hall. I want you to move in today, if possible. Primarily, I need an escort and bodyguard. I do not expect trouble but I will gladly pay for the insurance of having you near. Do you still have a permit to carry a gun?"

"Yes. I am a reserve officer in the Sheriff's Department. It's the easiest way for me to be legally armed."

She indicated surprise. "Are you a police officer?"

"Not really. I have a friend who arranged it. I just have the ID and badge."

"Oh. So, can you start today?"

"Yes."

"As I recall, I paid a thousand a week last year. But that was for a regular day. How would two thousand a week plus expenses strike you?"

"That sounds more than fair. What would be the length of the contract?"

"About six months—say to the end of June."

"I would want to be paid in advance each week in cash if possible. Plus, I will need a few hours every week or so for personal business. I'll need to check on my Aunt Emily."

"Oh, you have an aunt. How nice. Did you find a cook?"

Jack paused a moment before answering. He really wanted to find out about the watchers next door. "Not yet, but I have a few feelers out."

She went to the small table near the door and brought back a magnetic key card. "Room 922, across the hall."

"What's the address of the condo you're renting?"

She rummaged in her purse for a note pad, tore off a sheet and wrote the address. Handing it to him, she asked, "Why do you need it?"

"I would like to check the place for security. Have you seen the condo?"

"No, but a friend of mine rented it last season for a month. She was delighted with it."

"Will you be going out later?"

"Yes. Dressed, of course. You do have a tux, don't you?"

"Yes. What time?"

"We have dinner reservations at nine."

Jack rose to leave.

"Aren't you forgetting something?"

He waited while Wilma went into another room. She returned stuffing a stack of bills into an envelope. "Turn in your expenses weekly. Just note them on a sheet of paper. You won't need receipts. I included an advance of a thousand to cover this week. Out of that, you will pay for dinner or any other costs involved with taking care of us. Fair enough?"

"More than fair, quite generous in fact."

When Jack opened the door, Brenda was standing in the hall with her key card poised in hand. "Oh, Jack. Leaving?"

"Afraid so. I'll be back before dinner, though."

He checked the door to 932 as he walked to the elevator. He left the hotel to walk across the street to a bank. He rented a deposit box and stowed his first week's pay. Back at the hotel, he rode with the valet parking attendant to the car where he retrieved his bag and suitcase.

After stowing his clothes in the closet and drawers, he called Colonel Reynolds.

"Colonel this is Jack Wexler. I thought this job would be straight forward but there are signs that something else is going on. First of all, this lady has a lot of money—all in cash. The hotel room next door is really occupied but the hotel records list the room as unoccupied and out of service. I really think the feds are sitting on her for some reason."

"I need the name of your client and the hotel and room numbers. I'll make a few calls to see who's active. Do you have any objection to working with these people?"

"Do they pay?"

"Think so, but it won't be much. I'll find out."

"Also, she's looking for a cook. Might mean another chance to get one of their people on the inside."

Jack gave the Colonel all the info he could think of, took a shower, set the alarm and went to bed.

Later, he woke when someone got in bed with him. There was a sliver of light entering from the partially closed drapes. The red tint of the hair told him it was Brenda. She was completely nude.

CHAPTER
4

THE ALARM WOKE THEM. Wordlessly, Jack went to the shower again. When he returned, Brenda was gone.

As Jack dressed, he felt hungry. He had not eaten since breakfast at his aunt's. He tried on the coat to his tuxedo for fit. As he stood sideways he looked in the mirror. He could see the bulge of the pistol holstered in the small of his back. When he unbuttoned the jacket the telltale bulge disappeared. He would have to get an under-the-arm holster for the 380 auto. He hung up the jacket neatly in the closet and finished dressing in slacks and a loose-fitting shirt.

The phone rang. It was the Colonel.

"I don't know how you do it, but you're in the middle of something big. I thought last year was a fluke but you have all the luck. All they told me is that it's an operation involving the FBI and mob connected. They want a meeting."

"When?"

"Tomorrow. They'll let you know."

He rose early the next morning, got breakfast in the coffee shop and charged it to his room. Counting the dinner the previous evening and his other expenses, he was into the thousand by four hundred and fifty dollars. At this rate, he figured he would be using his own money in another day or two.

He drove to the condo, parked the car and went inside the lobby. There was a man at the desk. He flashed his badge and asked for the manager.

"He ain't here. Be in this afternoon. Come back then."

"I need to get in to B4. I have to check on something."

"Here's the key, but they just left. Won't be anyone to talk to."

Jack picked up the key and entered the elevator. He pushed the fourth floor button. There were three suites. He entered B and began looking for signs of installation of audio or video equipment. He found two cameras and two or three microphones in each room including the two bathrooms. Only the closets were not monitored. He left the condo, wiping the doorknobs as he went.

He drove to the gun shop and bought an ankle holster and an underarm one. He was back at the hotel two hours after he left. When he entered his room, the message light on the phone was flashing. The voice mail was from Wilma.

"Come over when you hear this."

He knocked and Brenda opened the door with a smile. "Come on in, Jack. Wilma is in the sandbox." She pressed her body against him. "You want to fool around?"

Jack smiled back. "Can't, I'm on duty."

"Then do your duty."

Wilma returned. "What are you two doing? I told you to leave him alone." She didn't sound too angry.

Pouting, Brenda plopped down on the couch.

"Jack, dress in something less casual than jeans and tee shirt. We're going shopping. Be ready in ten or fifteen minutes."

He returned to his room. As he was closing the door, someone pushed in behind him.

"Just what the hell made you go to the condo?"

"And who are you? Show me some ID or get out."

He showed Jack his FBI card and badge. Special Agent W. T. Conover.

"What's the W. T. stand for?"

"Call me Will. Now answer my question."

"I wanted to check the place out."

"Yeah, we caught it on tape."

"I need to change clothes."

"Yeah, I know. Go ahead, I'll talk as you change. Talked to your Colonel. You're in an ideal position for us. He said you'd cooperate. I know this is a windfall job as far as the money is concerned. We want you to keep your job and the money. We may be able to find an informer's fee for you but it won't be much."

Jack had stripped down to his shorts and began dressing. He put on a light pink silk shirt, off-white slacks and a lime green blazer. He strapped on the ankle holster then slipped on his shoes. He looked at his image in the mirror. "Well, what do you think?"

"You look like a damn fairy. Are you in or not?"

"In. You can get another set of eyes and ears if you furnish a female agent to serve as cook and housekeeper when we move to the condo. Get someone who speaks Spanish, and then she can fake not speaking English. Fill me in later on what these people have done and the reason they're under investigation. But not now. I have to go. Now don't go messing around with my stuff."

"Too late, already did."

Back in the suite, Jack sat in a chair with Brenda seated on the couch. Wilma entered with a handful of cash. "Jack, put this in your pocket. You pay for anything we want. We'll try to keep it under ten thou." She looked closely at Jack. "Good choice in clothing. Very Miami. You armed?"

"Yes."

"Can't tell it from here."

She walked over and felt around his waist, under his arms, and then she felt around his crotch.

"Easy now."

"Don't be silly, I'm old enough to be your mother. Okay, where is it?"

He lifted his pant leg.

They spent the next four hours at several of the fashion designer stores, taking lunch at a tearoom with a snooty waiter. Since Jack was paying, he undertipped to send a message.

When they got back to the hotel with their packages, Jack counted his money. "Don't know where it all went, but I have only a little over two thousand left."

"Oh, poo! If it's too much trouble, don't bother to keep track. Just tell me when you need more."

"What are the plans for the evening?"

"I think dinner and dancing, don't you Brenda? So, Jack, do you have another tux?"

"Yes, I have another, but that's it."

"We should get you a couple more. We'll shop for you tomorrow. That would be a nice change of pace."

Jack left for his own room.

He took a shower, put on the hotel terry robe and called for valet service. He gathered his soiled clothing and stuffed the items in a plastic bag. He filled out the laundry check-off list tag of the included items and placed the tag in the bag. He took the bag to the door when he heard a knock. It was Brenda.

"I want you."

He opened the door wider. She entered at the same time that a young man in hotel uniform came to the door.

"Valet?"

"Yes sir."

"Like this by tomorrow."

"Can do."

He closed the door and flipped the latch.

It was an upscale supper club on Biscayne Boulevard with the dance band playing from ten to two. The seven-course dinner lasted two hours. The waiter was clearing away the remnants of their meal when the dance band began. They played a mixture of forties big band and Latin music. The dance floor filled before the first number had ended. Jack held out his hand to Wilma when the first few bars of a cha-cha were heard.

"I thought you would never ask."

They both shuffled to the beat of the music as they made their way to the floor. Jack glanced at the table to see Brenda heading toward the lady's room. After dancing three numbers, Wilma suggested a break.

Brenda was gone. Jack looked about. He finally caught a glimpse of her in heated argument with a rather large man—not obese, but built. Jack waved and got the attention of a bouncer. He pointed to Brenda. The bouncer nodded and spoke into a lapel mike. As if choreographed, two other bouncers zeroed in on Brenda and the man. Jack could see Brenda try to pull away but the man grabbed her by the arm and spun her around. He grabbed her by the shoulders and shook. He then let go with his right hand and slapped her hard.

The first two bouncers arrived. Each grabbed an arm, throwing him to the floor. The third snapped the handcuffs. They quickly moved the man to a side room through a door that said 'Private'. Jack followed, leaving Wilma to comfort Brenda.

Jack knocked on the door. The first bouncer answered. "Who's the giant?"

"Don't know yet. He was armed. Got a patrol car coming for him. All three of us are off duty Miami PD. You know what the beef was all about?"

Jack flashed his badge. "Off duty deputy. I was hired to be their escort and bodyguard. Appreciate you helping out. Is there any way we can be kept out of this? Can you just roust him on the weapon?" Jack handed him three hundred. "Split it with your crew, okay?"

On the way back to the hotel, Jack wanted to ask a lot of questions. But, he knew he would get lies instead of the truth so he kept quiet. In the elevator he looked at Brenda's eye. It would be black tomorrow.

After he showered and went to bed, he was in that in-between time of not yet sleeping, but not awake either. He was roused by the noise of the door latch. The lights came on. It was Will Conover.

"You sure got out of the supper club in a hurry."

"Don't you know how to knock?"

"It's against the law."

"Yeah, yeah, very funny."

"The big guy is Gus Montalvo. Although from New York, he has a Florida carry permit for the weapon. Arrested many times, never convicted."

"Don't tell me. He's mob connected, right?"

"You got it. Plus the fact that he's Brenda's brother."

"Brenda Montalvo?"

"Yeah, maiden name."

"Do you want to tell me how this all fits together or do you want to keep me in the dark a while longer?"

"Oh we always try to keep people working with us in the dark. But now you need to know a few things."

"Who is Wilma?"

"Wilma has no children of her own. She is a good-hearted lady who spends her life doing for others. She inherited over thirty million when her husband, Solomon, died. You're too young to remember Jackie Kennedy—you know, the presidents wife? Anyway, he copied all the designer fashions she wore and sold a line of clothing under the label Jackie Kay. He even hired models that looked like the presidents wife to advertise his clothing. He made millions. The sale of the business plus a wide range of investments made her very wealthy. Her wealth now is easily over one hundred million. But the interesting thing is she really doesn't have the lifestyle that kind of wealth would buy."

"Where does Brenda Mazzi come in?"

"A couple of years ago, Brenda was pregnant. She and her husband lived in the same building as Wilma—though their apartments were somewhat different. Wilma had an entire floor while Brenda and Umberto Mazzi had a one-bedroom unit. Well, Brenda had a difficult time so Wilma stepped forward in a motherly way. Eventually she miscarried."

"What about the husband?"

"It seems that Umberto was mobbed up. He is now awaiting trial. Brenda's brother Gus is also mobbed up. They're in the same crew. Brenda separated from Umberto about a year ago and just got divorced. We've been trying to get her to help us widen the case to include other crime figures."

"That's it?"

"So far, but we have hopes."

"Why wire her apartment for audio and video? This case can't be that important."

"Well, we have plenty in the budget and a sympathetic judge to sign the order."

Will looked at his watch. "Gotta go."

He picked up the phone and dialed a number.

"What are they doing now?"

He listened a moment and cradled the phone.

"Later."

He opened the door. Jack could see the door across the hall open. Will was in the other apartment in a split second.

CHAPTER
5

T HE PHONE RANG at seven-thirty. Jack was in the bathroom, shaving. He picked up the phone with lather still on his face.

"Hello."

"Good morning, Jackie. Hope you're ready for some shopping."

It was Wilma. She sounded in good spirits.

"I'll be ready in a half hour or so. How is Brenda this morning."

"Not too bad. Make-up can do wonders for a bruise, you know."

"I'm just sorry I wasn't in a position to keep her from harm."

"Oh, poo. Don't be silly. See you in a few minutes."

The three were at breakfast. This time, it was a little more elaborate with eggs, French toast and assorted Danish rolls. The phone rang. Wilma answered the call.

"Yes, this is Mrs. Ellman. It is? We'll be there later this morning."

She turned with a smile. "The condo is ready. We move in this morning. Oh, sorry Jack. We'll take you shopping tomorrow. Now we pack."

After finishing his coffee, Jack returned to his room to pack. A knock on the door brought his cleaning just in time. They had the car packed by ten.

When they drove away from the hotel, a gray Chevy followed. The Lincoln entered the traffic first with the Chevy entering after four cars had passed. The Chevy weaved through the traffic until the car was situated to the right of the Lincoln.

Brenda screamed. "Look out, Jack. They're after us."

Jack floored the Lincoln, running the red light. Shots rang out leaving the rear window shattered. Two more shots were fired. Jack felt the car fish-tail from a blown rear tire. He yelled, "Keep down."

The Chevy was now on the right. The driver steered the front of the Chevy into the rear of the Lincoln in such a way that the rear of the Lincoln went left and the front to the right. The Chevy continued to the left, hitting a parked car. Jack quickly set the emergency brake, opened the driver's door, pulled his pistol and rolled out on the pavement, being shielded by the car. Two more shots were fired. He heard the starter of the Chevy grinding. He rose and fired three shots at the shooter in the passenger's seat. The shooter slumped forward as the engine started. Since the shooter had his arm with the pistol hanging out the open window when Jack shot, he dropped the gun to the pavement. The driver put the Chevy in reverse, heading in the opposite direction.

Jack was sure he had hit the passenger. In the distance, he could hear a siren. Wilma and Brenda came to him, both were shaking with fear. Jack spread his arms and embraced both, holding them tightly. Brenda began sobbing.

When the police car arrived, Jack had his shield and ID out with his pistol out of sight in the ankle holster. They quickly transported the three to the nearest station. Jack called Captain Reynolds who called the FBI. Soon the station was awash with officers of the various agencies. The FBI took jurisdiction and released the three.

It was one in the morning when they finally arrived at the condo. It took two police cruisers to carry the trio and their luggage. The Lincoln as well as Jack's 380 automatic were kept for evidence. Several rounds had entered the trunk making holes in the luggage and clothing. When Wilma heard this she seemed really excited. After all, this was another excuse to go shopping. However, Brenda was uncharacteristically silent. It was obvious to all, though unspoken, that she was the target.

When six o'clock came, Jack hit the shower. No matter what time he went to bed, he couldn't stay in bed. Out of the shower, he got dressed and went into the living room when the phone rang. He picked up the receiver.

"Hello."

"Thought you would pick up. Saw you on the TV monitor. Tell Mrs. Ellman that a friend from the hotel called. What's his name? Oh, yeah—Carl. Tell her Carl called with a recommendation for cook. The cook will call in about an hour. Her name is Linda."

Wilma came in.

"Okay, thanks Carl. We'll be expecting her call."

"Who was that?"

"It was a friend from the hotel, the concierge, Carl. He has a line on a cook for you. She will call in about an hour. Anything in the fridge?"

"Let's look."

Jack opened the refrigerator. It was quite empty. Wilma searched the cabinets.

"Found some instant coffee, sugar and powered creamer."

"We're in business, then. I'll find the kettle and get the hot water going."

"No, I'll do that. You go looking for something to eat. There is surely a deli around here someplace."

Will got on the elevator at the third floor. He flipped the stop switch on the control panel.

"Got a present for you."

He gave Jack back his pistol with the extra clip.

"Thanks, you never know." Jack quickly checked the clips and found them fully loaded.

"Go out the door and take a right. Turn right again at the corner."

"Why?"

"The deli, of course." He turned the switch back on and got off at the second floor.

In a half-hour, Jack returned with a collection of bagels, cream cheese, a variety of Danish pastry, fruit, a container of scrambled eggs with mushrooms, as well as a quart thermos of coffee—real coffee and the morning newspaper. He figured they could reuse the thermos bottle.

He entered the elevator, pressed four and waited. The door opened on two. Will got in and stopped the elevator.

"Found the Chevy. The guy you hit was in the trunk, dead. No, you didn't kill him. It was a nine-millimeter that got him. They cut off his fingers so we won't be able to readily identify him. They left his teeth in, so maybe someday we can put a name to him."

"But, I did hit him, didn't I?"

"Yeah. Shattered the shoulder on his right side. Good shot. You kept him from doing any more shooting."

"How about prints on the pistol he dropped?"

"Nothing but smears on the weapon, clip and spent shells." He peeked into the bag. "Well, chow down." He started the elevator, again stopping on the third floor.

He opened the door with his key. Wilma had heard the key rattling in the lock and met him at the door. "Oh, food. Let me take care of this for you." She took the bag to the kitchen.

Jack grabbed the paper and sat at the table. He quickly scanned the front page and the metro section. There was no mention of the shooting.

Brenda entered the room. She positioned her chair to be near Jack. "You saved my life, you know, because they were truly after me." There were tears in her eyes.

Wilma entered bringing a tray with the china and silverware. "Jack, bring in the other tray, please."

Springing up, Brenda volunteered.

Surprisingly, all had a hearty appetite. The eggs and coffee were the first to go. All had second helpings.

The phone rang. It was the FBI housekeeper. Wilma quickly agreed on an interview. She was there in thirty minutes. She looked like a cook. No one would ever have figured her for anything else.

After showing her the kitchen and her room, they agreed on a salary. Two hours later she returned with her suitcase. They had a cook.

Jack and Brenda gravitated to the living room. Jack turned on the TV and sat in a large chair. Brenda sat first on the arm of the chair, she then slipped onto Jack's lap nestling her head against his shoulder. In the dining room, he could hear Wilma and Linda discussing a grocery order. With the John Wayne movie droning on, he soon heard the even breathing of Brenda. She was asleep. In a few minutes, he nodded off as well.

He woke with a start when Wilma turned off the TV. Brenda roused as well.

"Oh, I'm sorry. You two looked so sweet sleeping there so I thought I'd turn off the sound. If you really want to take a nap, just go to bed."

Brenda stood, smiling. "Well, I really didn't get much sleep last night."

Wilma turned to Jack. "I guess we'll have to get another car."

"We should at least tell them that the car is shot full of bullet holes. On second thought, if we told them that, they may not want to lease another."

"Well, Jack, I'll just buy a car. What does a car cost? I've never owned one."

"What was the cost of the lease on the Lincoln?"

"Oh poo, I don't remember. Something like a thousand a week, I think."

"Let's see, for six months that's twenty-four thousand. That's easily half the purchase price of a really nice car. You could have bought the Lincoln and sold it in six months. You would have been better off financially."

"Oh, Jack, you're so smart with numbers. My accountants try to tell me these things but the figures just go into one ear and out the other."

"You want me to call the rental agency with the bad news?"

"Yes, do that. We'll get a Cadillac. I've never really owned a car. I'll call my accountant. Do you remember the name of the bank on the first floor?"

"Merchant's Security Bank and Trust."

"I'll have him wire transfer a little something."

"Isn't it time you told me about Brenda?"

"Of course, you're right. I've kept you in the dark long enough. But, I'm sure you've figured a few things out by now."

"Yes, I know that it was her brother at the supper club."

"Oh, yes. I knew you could find out things like that since you're a constable or deputy or something."

"About Brenda."

"Well, three months ago her ex was arrested. They wanted Brenda to testify and name names. She was, and is for that matter, very frightened. And not without reason as you well know from the attack yesterday. She came to me for help. She has relied on me since her miscarriage and divorce. Truly, I think of her as the daughter I never had."

"About me and Brenda…."

"Oh, poo. Sex is healthy. I remember that Sol and I did the deed as often as we could, right up to the end. Oh, I miss him so."

She grabbed a Kleenex and daubed her eyes.

"Damn. I worked on this mascara for ten minutes this morning. I must look a mess."

"So, will she?"

"Will she what?"

"Testify."

"Maybe. She needs to know she'll be safe. That's why we came here. She wanted to leave the city so I offered to bring her along. You know me. A month of sunshine is all I want but I'll stay for six if it means that Brenda will be okay. I miss the city and my neighborhood and my building and my tenants. I know this sounds silly, but I think of all of them as my relatives. Not that I meddle in their business but I will always help those I can. I have enough money to do anything I want, at least that's what my business manager says."

"I'll make that call."

CHAPTER

6

J ACK TEST-DROVE the Caddy Escalade SUV.

"This is a very nice car," he said.

"Okay, but is this what you would want if you were buying the car?"

"A Chevy Blazer, Ford Bronco or the Jeep Cherokee would be my choice because of price. Of course, it's just this man's opinion."

"Since you're the one doing the driving, I'll buy whatever you prefer."

"Okay, we'll take the Caddy only if you pick the color."

She picked black.

Wilma spent fifteen minutes with the salesman before beckoning Jack to join them. "Jack, since you're the driver, they need your signature in a couple of places."

The salesman marked with a red X in on a couple of blank documents. Jack dutifully signed without reading the form.

"I must tell you, Mrs. Ellman, in all my years in the business, this is the first Cadillac I've sold by credit card."

"May I leave now? I have some shopping to do." She tossed her door key to Jack, "Here's my key. Get a copy made on the way back."

"It'll take an hour or so to finish. We want to vacuum and wash the car and fill it with gas. But, before you go, I want to personally thank you very much, Mrs. Ellman."

Jack walked across the street to a hardware store and had three copies of the door key made. After he returned to the Cadillac dealer, he still had to wait another fifteen minutes before he could drive back to the condo.

According to Wilma, they were supposed to have three parking spots assigned to the condo located in the basement. He found the driveway to the garage and then located the spaces. There was a scattering of kitty litter to absorb oil spills in the center of the three spaces as well as on several other vacant spaces. He straddled the litter with the car.

Sometimes, his attention to detail bothered him. Like the shine on his shoes or the crease in his trousers or the litter on the deck. He was in many ways still a squared-away Marine. It had been over three years since he left the Corps, but the training took a long time going. One of the few things he did skip was the weekly haircut. He now wore his hair in a more normal fashion. As he walked to the elevator, he noticed other things like the lack of metal polish on the brass fire hose nozzle hanging in the garage and crumpled-up papers near a trash can. He felt that someone should spend some time shining the brass but he was resigned to the fact that this wasn't the Marines.

When he took the elevator to the fourth floor, as usual, the elevator stopped at the second floor. Will, grinning, got on, stopping the elevator. "Lover boy. Way to go, making out with Brenda in the chair. She is really something."

Jack was not happy that he had been seen on the monitor. "You got anything to say to me?"

"Linda has some problems at home. Her husband is pissed that she's away from hearth and home, so to speak. We need to replace her. The cover story is that she has to leave to be with her sister who's having a baby. She'll send her cousin to replace her. We're working on finding a replacement now."

"Anything on the shooters?"

"We identified the one with no fingers and have a tentative name for his partner. We intervened in the case of Brenda's brother with Miami PD. We have him now. We're trying to flip him to testify in the OC investigation at hand."

"What is OC?"

"Organized crime. We're sitting on a multi-indictment of over a hundred people. It really hinges on Brenda and her ex-husband."

"You have a time frame?"

"We gotta nail this down in a month or so. The longer we take, the closer Brenda is to being killed. We can get her relocated with a new identity in the witness protection program as soon as she comes on board. So this can really be a win-win situation for her. Do what you can, okay?"

He started the elevator and pressed 3.

Jack entered the condo using one of the new keys. He looked at a pile of clothing on the couch. Brenda had been busy.

She quickly went to his side and kissed him. Pulling away she pointed to the clothing on the couch. "This is the pile with bullet holes. I separated my own earlier—I didn't have as much damage as you. Oh, the good items are in your closet. You know, you are a very neat person."

Jack whistled a low note. "I didn't think there were that many. Hey, just a second—these jeans and tee shirts are okay, a hole or two won't make a difference. And about my neatness, it's just that three months of boot camp and four years in a rifle platoon left me a very squared-away Marine."

Smiling, Brenda walked back to Jack, getting very close. "Now Jack", she purred, "You know you want to be rid of the messed up clothing and be a really gung-ho squared-away Marine, don't you?"

"Don't stand too close, I may take things in my own hands."

She rubbed against him. "Like this?"

"Your room or mine?"

There came a knock a the door. It was Wilma. The cab driver followed, loaded down with packages. "In that bedroom, there. Just put them on the bed." She fumbled in her purse, bringing out a hundred dollar bill. "This is for you. It should cover the fare as well as a gratuity."

He tipped his hat and replied with his thanks in Spanish.

"Here's your key back. I made copies. They're with your key. I kept one. Also, on the same ring is the extra key to the Caddy."

"You keep it. Jack, you know I can't drive." Turning her attention to the pile of clothes, "What's this?"

"It's Jack's things with bullet holes."

"Oh, goodie. We'll shop for him tomorrow. Now, 'though it's a little early, I want dinner. After all, I didn't have lunch."

Jack started disconnecting the spare Caddy key from the others.

Brenda spoke up. "Linda's gone."

"Gone? The cook's gone?"

"Yeah, she got a call from someone and left. She said that her sister had a baby and she was needed to help out."

"Was that all?"

"She said she would send her cousin, but didn't say when."

"Well, it's been years since I've had to cook. I'm sure if we all try, we can whip something up."

After broiled steaks, salad, green beans and corn, Jack volunteered to do the dishes. No one objected. Brenda found a cache of video disks so they all sat down for a couple of movies. When Wilma asked for a pause so she could go to the bathroom, Brenda put a bag of TV popcorn in the microwave.

At the end of the second movie, Wilma rose. "Well, children, I'm off to bed." Then brightly, "We'll need plenty of rest because we'll be busy shopping for Jack tomorrow."

Brenda rose as well. "I'll be sleeping with Jack tonight."

"Oh, why don't you use the bed in your room? You have a king and Jack's bed is a regular."

She smiled. "Oh, Wilma, I don't want him to have any trouble at all finding me."

Wilma winked at Jack. "I don't think he'll have any difficulty at all in that regard.

CHAPTER

7

J ACK WAS THE FIRST TO RISE. After he took his shower and dressed, he set about preparing breakfast. All he wanted was coffee, scrambled eggs with mushrooms, orange juice and toast. He prepared enough for three, except for the eggs.

He had just finished his second cup of coffee when Brenda staggered in. "Good morning, sunshine."

"Coffee." She growled, "Coffee now!"

He poured her a cupful. She took a sip. "Ugh, no sugar! What are you, a sadist? How can anyone drink coffee without sugar?"

He got the sugar and sat it before her. She took four spoonfuls.

"Four spoonfuls?"

"Yeah, four." She snapped, "But I don't stir it. I don't like it too sweet."

She was sitting on the chair with her knees folded under her chin, her feet on the front edge of the seat. She was wearing one of his tee shirts and a pair of his briefs. Both the tee shirt and briefs were from the pile that had bullet holes.

"Nice outfit."

"I'm going to keep these for myself."

Wilma breezed in, fully dressed and made-up. "Good morning. I'm so excited about today. I have so many ideas for Jack's wardrobe."

"Scrambled eggs with mushrooms in a couple of minutes. Okay?"

Picking up the thermos, Wilma raised her voice to speak to the retreating Jack. "Is this coffee?"

From the kitchen, Jack replied: "Brewed fresh a few minutes ago."

Then Wilma spoke in a whisper to Brenda. "Sex is wonderful for the complexion. You are absolutely glowing!"

Brenda smiled in reply.

Jack and Wilma did the dishes as Brenda readied herself. They all took the elevator to the garage.

As they approached the car, Jack grabbed Wilma and Brenda, pushing them back. "Go back to the condo and call the police. I think there's a bomb under the car."

"What? How do you know?"

"The kitty-litter had been scattered over there to soak up an oily area. When I parked yesterday, the litter was evenly distributed. Now, it's moved about like someone has crawled under the car. Tell them I'll be waiting by the entrance."

Brenda began crying and shaking with fear. Wilma put her arm around her, ushering her to the elevator.

It was almost twenty minutes before the first police car arrived. Jack flashed his badge and told them what he saw. Five minutes later, the bomb squad arrived.

They wouldn't let Jack take the elevator from the garage to the condo. "Look, its like this deputy, we're going to evacuate the building before we even look for a bomb. I'll need to have the key to the car in case we have to get inside or unlatch the hood."

Jack gave him the car key he had tried to give Wilma earlier. He left the garage, walked around to the front door of the building and entered. There was a policeman in the lobby.

"Sir, you can't go in. We're evacuating the building."

The elevator door opened, Will and two other FBI agents exited. Will grabbed Jack by the elbow and pulled him aside.

"What in the hell is going on?"

"Parked Wilma's car in the garage yesterday afternoon over a patch of kitty-litter used for soaking up an oil drip. This morning the litter is moved about and disturbed indicating that someone has been crawling under the car. I had Wilma call the police and bomb squad."

"Damn. That was us. We planted a tracking beacon last night. I don't know how we're going to get the police to back off and not blow our cover."

Jack started laughing.

"It's not funny."

The elevator opened, Brenda and Wilma exited. Brenda still looked upset. Unperturbed by it all, Wilma exclaimed, "Oh, there he is. Ready to do some shopping? We'll have to take a cab."

Wilma did not just buy individual items like shirts or trousers but bought entire outfits; ensembles, she called them. Items like suits, sports jackets and trousers that needed alteration, would be delivered over the next few days. By mid-afternoon, they were all weary but forged ahead. Their last stop was at Armani. She purchased three sets of formal wear including a dozen shirts and a white dinner jacket. The trunk of the cab was full of packages when they finally arrived at the condo. A policeman was waiting in the lobby.

"They told me to wait until you returned. We didn't realize it would take all afternoon. So, here's your keys. We didn't find anything. Some dogs or cats running around on the floor messed up the pattern of kitty-litter. So it wasn't anything at all. But, don't let this stop you if you have any future suspicions, we're here to serve."

He touched his fingers to his cap in a salute and left.

Wilma looked to Jack. "You know what this means?"

Both Jack and Brenda asked in unison, "What?"

"We're going dancing!" She said gleefully, "I've been told that there's a place called Pompano Bill's that serves great seafood and has an even greater band."

Their arms loaded down, the three took the elevator to the fourth floor. They dumped all the packages in Jack's room. With all the new things dumped on his bed, the Marine in him began stowing things away. When he got to unboxing the shoes, it finally hit him that he had seven new pairs of shoes. A lot of shoes to break in. He crushed all the boxes and stuffed the paper and cardboard in the largest of the plastic shopping bags. Having squared away his room, he quickly showered and dressed for the evening.

When he left his bedroom dressed for the evening, Wilma was busy interviewing the replacement cook. Jack introduced himself.

"Hi, I'm Jack Wexler."

"Jack, this is Gloria Diego. She has agreed to work for us and keep us comfortable here."

Gloria looked at Jack and smiled.

"She is ready to move in now, she brought her things. We'll even have breakfast in the morning."

Gloria smiled and spoke in halting English. "Yes, I cook morning."

Brenda came in from her room. She looked great.

Pompano Bill's place was huge. It was as large as a basketball arena. The partitioning of the dining area into clusters of booths reminded Jack of the stockyards in Chicago. The Latin band was good and loud. After placing their order for food, they gave up on holding a conversation across the table. Since Brenda was sitting on the same side of the booth as Jack, she could shout into his ear to be heard.

Just as they had finished their meal, the band took a break. Taking their place was a jazz combo playing forties ballads. Jack extended his hand to Wilma.

"I believe this is our kind of music."

"Oh, Jackie, you know me too well."

After dancing together for fifteen minutes, Wilma called a halt. Brenda met them as they returned to their booth.

"My turn. This is my kind of music too."

They danced for almost a half-hour. The band had come to the end of their set and the Latin band was taking their places. They were making their way back to the booth when Brenda stiffened.

"Jack, I know that man."

"Where?"

"Don't look. He's with that Italian looking guy over to my right. Oh, they've seen me looking."

"Well, it won't matter then if I look." Jack spotted the two. They were wearing clothing that no one in southern Florida would dare to wear. "Let's get Wilma and get out of here."

Jack quickly paid the check and they left. As they pulled out of the parking lot, Jack kept checking the rearview mirror for pursuit. He left the main street and made his way on a lightly traveled side street. He saw headlights that indicated they were being followed. He pulled to a stop at a green light and waited for it to turn amber before crossing the street. The pursuing car continued through the intersection on red. Jack repeated this at the next light. This time, when he looked back he could see a flashing blue light.

He continued on for another few minutes with his attention still on the rear mirror. "Wilma, we've got to ask how in the world they knew we would be at Pompano Bill's? There's no way it was a coincidence."

Brenda answered in a shrill voice indicating nervousness. "We've got to move."

Wilma agreed. "But where can we go, Jack?"

"From now on, we only communicate sensitive stuff in writing. For all I know, this car is bugged. As far as where we can go—just leave it to me."

When they arrived at their condo, police cars were everywhere with blue lights flashing. Jack drove on until he found an open convenience store. From there he called John Reynolds at his home.

"Colonel this is Jack Wexler."

"Are you in any trouble, Jack?"

"I really don't know. Brenda spotted some wiseguys she had seen in New York where we had dinner. When we left, they followed. Then when we got back to the condo, there were police everywhere."

"Give me your number. I'll find out for you."

"Can't do that. We're on the move. I'll call in twenty or thirty minutes."

They drove a few more miles south on US1. Jack spotted a service station. He soon had the car raised on the lift and inspecting the underside.

The mechanic asked, "If you would just tell me what you're looking for, I'll be glad to help."

"Anything that the factory didn't put on this car. Just anything at all."

Pulling a box with a dangling wire from under a fender well the mechanic asks, "Like this?"

"Yeah, now look some more."

"Here's some wires that look to be out of place. What do you make of this?"

Jack traced the wires to another plastic box attached to a magnet. There were other wires leading away. He kept pulling them away from the glue dots that kept them from flapping around. The wires went through the floor into the interior of the car. He gave the wires a strong yank. Out popped a small microphone.

"You got a water bucket?"

"Got that tank over yonder where I check tires for leaks."

Jack took the two boxes of electronics and dumped them in the tank.

"If you want to take them out, do it tomorrow, please."

Jack fished out two twenties for the mechanic. "This cover it?"

"Sure will."

"Got a phone?"

"No pay phone, but, you can use the one in the office if'n it's a local."

Jack called the Colonel again.

"This is me."

"I don't know how to put it but your cook has been shot."

"Shot?"

"Yeah, right in the head. She was at the door when they found her, half-in and half-out of the apartment. They want you for questioning."

"Me?"

"No, all of you."

"Is the FBI there?"

"Not as I could tell. Of course, I wasn't there."

"We're going to lay low for a few days until I can figure this out."

"Jack, keep in touch and let me know if I can do anything for you."

"Sure John. Bye."

Jack got back into the car. Wilma asked, "Well, what's the story? Why were all those police cars around our condo?"

"Jack, they were after me, those men that followed us."

"Afraid so. We were lucky to have ditched them."

Wilma again pressed for an answer.

"The police cars were there because our new cook has been shot and killed."

Brenda began crying. Through the sobs, she blurted out, "It's my fault. She was about my size and her hair color was similar. They just wanted to kill me!"

"Jack, surely that's not the case."

"Wilma, I believe she's right about this. You looked at her and saw a cook. As a man, I saw shape, color, size and facial features."

"Well, what do we do now?"

"We ditch this car and hide for a while. But more than that, I've been thinking—how did those two know where we were going this evening? Also, the FBI has been monitoring the condo. They've heard every word we've said. They have cameras installed as well. And the FBI probably put the electronic stuff I pulled from under the car there. So, my thinking is that someone with the FBI may be leaking info about our moment-to-moment plans."

The women became very quiet.

CHAPTER
8

As soon as they arrived at Jack's aunt's house, and introductions made, Jack backed her old Buick out of the driveway. He then pulled the Caddy back all the way to the tool shed. He retrieved an old tarp from the shed and covered the car. He moved Emily's Buick back to the driveway and left it in the usual place.

"Now, Aunt Emily, it's best that you don't know anything. If anyone comes by, don't volunteer any information, but don't lie either."

Jack started to get a couple of changes of clothing but thought better of it, after all, the women would have to do without. They got in Jack's Honda and started out. Jack drove to Key Largo and took first side-road, then another. Wilma and Brenda were soon hopelessly lost. He finally turned on a barely visible track at a sign that said simply: JOE'S.

The cabin was built over the water on pilings of old power poles. A rickety boardwalk led to the cabin a hundred and fifty feet from the parking area. A set of stairs led from the ocean side of the cabin to a skiff tethered to the small dock powered by an outboard engine. All boards were bleached white by the sun and sea. There were three old vehicles parked there, two pickups and an old school bus. All were so rust-covered the original paint color could only be guessed at. None of them had run for ten years or more. A dim yellow light could be seen at the door of the cabin.

They left the car and walked to the cabin. The walkway was shaky but secure enough with the handrail. The lantern at the doorway had been turned down so that it was barely glowing. Jack took the lantern and turned up the wick. He searched for the key to the padlock, finding it under a rock by the door. He opened the door and raised the lantern high. He found a lamp on a table with a box of matches nearby. He took off the globe and lit the lamp. He turned down the wick on the lantern before hanging it again by the door.

"Well, this is home for a few days. Doesn't look like much, does it?"

"Oh, I don't know, it'll do for a while. Brenda, how about you?"

"Where's the bathroom? I've got to pee."

"Over there in the corner, behind the curtain."

Brenda pulled back the curtain. There was no commode, only an outhouse type hole with a board covering it.

"Where does it go?"

"Into the water, of course. There's no other dwelling for miles. There are ocean critters that'll take care of anything that drops through."

"Eeoo, gross!"

Wilma walked over and glanced down the hole. "Don't be silly, Brenda. It'll do just fine."

The place was conveniently arranged with double-deck bunk beds against two of the walls. All three bunk beds were made up with corners tucked in neatly. The kitchen was in one corner with a propane gas stove and a small propane powered ammonia-cycle refrigerator. He opened the fridge—it felt warm inside. He checked the propane bottle noting that the valve had been closed.

"I'm ready for bed. We can all get an upper or lower. Brenda would you like to have first choice?"

"Jack, I still have to pee but I won't sit on that board!"

"You want to go outside and squat?"

"Will you go with me?"

"And hold your hand?"

"Oh, would you, Jack?"

"Wilma, hold down the fort. We're off to let Brenda pee."

"Now, I've seen everything," Wilma said laughing, "I'll remember this for a long time."

The pair returned laughing.

"Guess what Wilma? After I finished, Jack let me aim his thing." She fell on one of the beds giggling.

"She tried to write her name in the sand."

"Cute, but, listen Jack. I was just thinking, will Joe come back tonight?"

"Joe who?"

"You know, the guy who owns this place."

"Oh, the sign. No, I've been told that Joe sold this place over twenty years ago. The guy who owns it now is named Dennis. I expect he'll return sometime tonight since he left the lantern on. But, don't worry, he'll see my car and know we're here. Like as not he'll just curl up in his truck and wait 'till morning."

Brenda was sitting on the bunk with her legs crossed and a serious look on her face. "Jack, what's going to happen to me? I mean, all the problems we've been having are really my fault. That poor lady being shot and killed could have been me. In a way her death is on me. There are some very mean people that want to keep me from testifying and naming names. What should I do? If I really let the FBI protect me, how can I be sure they'll be able to keep me safe?"

"Brenda, I'm an ex-Marine and college student. I am also an unpaid deputy sheriff, not because I'm in law enforcement but just so I can carry a weapon. I have no vast organization like the FBI that can be brought to bear for your protection. I have been hired by my friend Wilma to be a bodyguard and companion. I gladly take on this responsibility as Wilma's friend. If it were otherwise, I would have left at the first sign of trouble. Right now, I would caution against going to the feds until I can figure out how the bad guys were able to find us so easily."

They heard the sound of a loud muffler. The engine died and a horn sounded. Jack went to the door and turned up the wick of the lantern. He held the lantern up so that Dennis could see his face.

"Hey Jack, what you doin' here? All the babes are in the clubs over on US1."

"I have two friends here. We want to hide a few days. Is that okay with you?"

"I'll just go over to Smitty's Camp and crash in the bunkhouse. You bring any food?"

"No, just ourselves."

"Got a little money? I'll bring back groceries in the morning."

"No booze, right?"

"Just beer. I've been cuttin' back."

Jack fished out two twenties. "This enough?"

"You been to the store lately?"

Jack gave him another twenty.

"Drive carefully Dennis, see you in the morning."

Nine o'clock came but no Dennis. Jack decided to venture out for food. Since Smitty's Fish Camp had the nearest store, he went there. He pulled up to the store, got out of his car and looked around for Dennis' pickup truck. He entered the store where he bought bread, oleo, bacon, eggs, milk, coffee, pop-tarts and a bag of chipped ice.

The guy behind the counter worked the cash register. "That be all?"

"Yeah. Oh, have you seen Dennis?'

"Haven't seen him in a week or so. Think he's guidin' over at the marina."

"Thanks."

Depending on his memory of years past, he drove the dirt lanes avoiding the main ones to the shack. He brought in the food, started the Coleman stove, lit the pilot on the fridge and put the milk and ice inside. Soon, Wilma and Brenda had a great breakfast prepared.

After they had eaten and washed the dishes, they gathered on the narrow porch.

"I think I should make a call. We're in the dark out here. Wilma, do you have your cell phone with you?"

"Yes, but it's turned off. I wanted to save the battery."

"I'm going to call the neighbor of my aunt to see if she can get her to her phone. They may have my aunt's phone tapped."

After calling for information and dialing the number, he waited on line for her neighbor to get his aunt to the phone.

"Aunt Emily, I'm okay and I'm not in any trouble. I'm going to ask you some questions you can answer with a simple yes or no. Do you understand?"

"Yes, of course, but why Jackie?'

"Yes or no, please. Has there been anyone asking for me?"

"Yes."

"Did they show any identification?"

"No."

"Did they have a New York type accent?"

"Yes, as a matter of fact, they did."

"Thick necks, Italian looking?"

"You know them?"

"I take that as a yes."

"Yes."

"I'll keep in touch. Bye."

"Bye Jackie. You take care of yourself."

Jack thought a few moments about whether he should call the Colonel. More than anything, he feared there was a leak in the FBI team. He didn't want Colonel Reynolds to inadvertently give information to the wrong people.

A shot rang out.

"Inside, now!"

They dove for the door as more shots were fired. The report sounded like pistol shots. Jack upended the table and piled mattresses against it.

"Keep behind the table. At this distance, there won't be any energy left after a bullet goes through the wall and mattresses. The table will stop anything they have. Now stay there."

He crawled to the open door and looked out. The shooting had stopped for the moment. He heard another shot and the whine of the ricochet. They were either poor shots or weren't trying to hit anyone. He decided to get some response.

"Hey, what do you want? You might just hit someone if you're not careful."

He heard an answer from behind the old bus. "Send out Brenda and we'll leave you alone."

He crawled back behind the table.

"I think they're concentrating on the door and boardwalk. I'm going down the stairs to the skiff to see if I can start the outboard. If I can get the motor running, I want both of you to jump in the water but be sure to go feet first. I don't know how deep it is so keep your knees slightly bent as you enter the water."

"Be careful, Jack. I wouldn't want anything to happen to you."

"Thanks, Wilma."

Since there was only one door, Jack left by the window facing the water. He descended the stairs backwards, hugging the stairway to keep his profile as small as possible. There were no warning shots. In the skiff, he checked the gas tank finding it about half full. He pushed the primer button a few times, set the choke and speed, then turned the spark to on. He gave the starter cord a sharp tug. Nothing. He pulled the cord again. He heard an encouraging pop-pop. It had fired. He pulled again and the motor began running. He adjusted the choke and speed, untied the painter and slowly pulled away from the small dock. He heard several shots. Above, he could see Wilma exiting the window followed by Brenda. Brenda jumped first. She went under the water and quickly bobbed to the surface. Jack pulled her aboard at the bow of the skiff. He looked up at Wilma.

"Jump, Wilma!" he shouted.

"I can't swim."

"Jump anyway. It's not very deep."

Holding her nose, Wilma stepped off the walkway and dropped to the water. In a moment, she came to the surface sputtering.

"Get me out of here!"

Jack took her hand, brought her around to the bow of the boat and wrestled her aboard.

They were still shooting from the beach. Jack could see three men walking toward the shack, shooting at them. He pulled his pistol and fired back. They quickly scurried to shelter.

Jack gunned the outboard, heading straight away from the shack.

After they had gone five hundred yards from shore, Jack turned the boat to the left, heading for the Bayside Marina where he knew there would be many people about.

Both Brenda and Wilma were shivering from their wet clothing and the cooling effect of the onshore breeze as well as the wind from the forward movement of the boat. The women were in a state of shock from the attack and their near-fatal brush with the criminals. However, as they neared the marina, Brenda started fluffing and combing her hair through her fingers letting the drying wind through. Wilma began doing the same.

As Jack was tying the boat up at the dock, a man with a badge yelled at them. "Hey, you can't tie up here, you're not a member."

Jack reached for his wallet and flashed his badge and ID card. "You got a phone nearby?"

"Got a pay phone over by the office you can use."

"Jack, give me some money. I left my purse at the shack."

The ladies headed for the store and the powder room while Jack made his call. The first call was to his Colonel, John Reynolds; the next call was to his aunt. He was just finishing up his call when he spotted Dennis.

As he opened the door to the phone booth, Dennis saw Jack and started to run away. It was a funny sort of run. His legs were moving rapidly, but he didn't cover much ground. He was headed for the parking lot. Jack was easily able to grab him by the collar and wrestle him to the ground.

As soon as he hit the ground, Dennis began complaining. "Ow. You're hurting me. Let go."

"Not until you tell me about the three gunmen you sent to kill me."

"Kill you? I didn't send any one to kill you. They just wanted to talk to you."

"Did they give you their names—show identification?"

"One of them said he was FBI but he didn't show a badge or anything."

"How much did they pay you?"

"Nothing."

"Nothing? Let's see what you have."

Jack fished in Dennis' pockets emptying the contents on the ground. He had two tens, three ones and two hundred dollar bills. "Nothing? What do you call this?"

"I earned that money as a fishin' guide for some folks."

"Get up."

Dennis sat up and fumbled around trying to recover the contents of his pockets. Jack grabbed the money and the truck keys.

"I'll just keep this. You can ride in the skiff back to your camp. I'll leave your money on the front seat of the truck."

"Where's it tied up?"

Jack pointed. Dennis left as the ladies walked up. They were wearing clothing they had bought at the store. Both looked a lot better than they did when they arrived. Jack followed Dennis to the dock, waiting for him to start the motor and leave.

The ladies had followed Jack. "Let's go." He motioned toward the parking lot. "I have us a ride."

When he opened the truck door, he found the floor covered with beer, wine and whisky bottles. He quickly tossed them to the bed of the truck. Brenda and Wilma got in as Jack started the motor. As they made their way out of the parking lot, Jack tapped the brake pedal—it went all the way to the floor.

"No brakes!" He yelled as he continued pumping the pedal. Finally, a little pressure built up.

He was able to slow the truck as they came to the main road. Still rolling, Jack checked left and right before entering. Luckily, there was no traffic as Jack had to use the gearbox to control the speed, gearing down to go slower. Feeling that the three shooters would have left when Jack and the ladies escaped, he decided to continue on to the parking area at Dennis' camp. He found no sign of the three as he parked.

"Wilma, you and Brenda hurry and get anything you left in the camp. I'm going to check out my car."

Jack crawled under the car, peering into every crevice for anything that looked out of place. He then lifted the hood, inspecting here and there. He knew the engine by heart since he had rebuilt it himself a year ago. He wiped his hands on a shop towel he kept stuffed behind the battery and closed the hood. He walked over to the pickup and began letting the air out of the right front tire. He then took Dennis' money and stuffed it into the top of a beer bottle and placed it on the front seat.

When the girls returned, they all got into Jack's car and left. Jack headed for the sheriff's sub-station.

CHAPTER
9

"COLONEL, I REALLY THINK the FBI has a spy in their group. Someone is on the take. It's the only reasonable answer to all of this. Brenda escaped a bullet only due to their incompetence."

"That's pretty harsh, Jack."

"Can you come up with any other reason?"

Ignoring his question, Colonel Reynolds continues. "I'm going out on a limb and call the US Attorney on this. I think he'll act on your suspicion and bring in another crew to investigate."

"I'm not going to recommend that Brenda cooperate until this is cleared up."

"I don't blame you in the least. Where is she now?"

"Here, sitting just outside. I couldn't take a chance on leaving them alone. Which brings me to asking a favor, a request, really."

"What's that?"

"Do you have a female officer you can trust, unmarried, with no children or family responsibilities, someone who could be away from home a couple of weeks?"

"Sure, I can name at least four. Why?"

"This job is a little more than I can handle. I can't cover enough territory by myself. Wilma can pay well for this, by the way. You could just put your officer on leave for a few weeks. Financially, it would be a very good deal for her."

"You going to be at the condo your boss rented?"

"No, it's still a crime scene. We're back at the Coral Palms. We've been told they'll need another few days—perhaps a week. Can you believe that? It's as though the FBI asked the police to keep the place locked up."

"I think Deputy Jenny McCaskey would be agreeable. She just broke up with her girlfriend—or so the rumor says."

"Girlfriend?"

"Gay."

"Oh."

"Either Jenny or someone else will call at your hotel this afternoon."

"Thanks Colonel.

Jack had loaded the rest of the clothing he had left at his aunt's place in the Caddie, since all their clothing was locked up at the condo. Jack had to take the ladies shopping for a few things on the way back to the hotel. He tried to keep account of the dollar amount but lost track at around six thousand. Every time Wilma went on a shopping trip, Jack mentally counted up how many months that money would keep him in school. But the thought didn't last long. She was paying him very well for what he was doing.

The bellboy carrying the clothing from the car led them to the twelfth floor. It was not the suite Wilma had used before. The mahogany sign with gold lettering said it was the Presidential Suite. It was quite plush with three bedrooms, three baths, dining alcove with a sitting room off at an angle, and a butler's pantry or small kitchen. Jack wondered how four of them would fit in the three rooms. He had visions of Brenda bunking with him when there was a knock on the door.

Virginia McCaskey was not what Jack expected. She didn't look butch; she was, in fact, quite attractive. She was dressed in jeans, tee shirt and a loose linen jacket. Jack guessed she was armed because of the jacket. When she introduced herself she used her proper first name, however, when she shook Jack's hand she corrected the name.

"Just call me Jenny, everybody else does."

"Your black hair and blue eyes are rare. Blue contacts?"

"No they're my natural color. I'm Irish, you know. You have black hair and blue eyes as well."

Her bright smile and warm attitude toward Jack did not go unnoticed by Brenda.

Wilma, noting the slight tension, spoke up. "Now, as to accommodations, I have asked housekeeping to take out the king size bed in the large bedroom and substitute two regular size ones. They balked at first; not wanting to upset the decor of the Presidential Suite but finally relented. It's funny what a little money will do. I'll take one of the rooms and Jack the other. When we get back to the condo, we can all take turns with meal preparation. We don't really need a cook. How does that sound? Okay, fine. That's what we will do. Jenny, darling, are you prepared to stay?"

"No, I'll have to go back to my place and pack a few things."

"Do bring something to wear this evening. We will dine out, I think."

"Umm, Mrs. Ellman, we didn't talk about my pay."

"Oh, poo. Call me Wilma. Is two thousand a week fair?"

"More than fair."

"I will want you to be armed, of course."

"Certainly."

Jack saw her to the door. He kept the door open as he watched her walk down the hall. After she had gone ten feet, she turned slightly and flashed Jack a smile. It was probably his imagination, but she seemed to walk with a pronounced hip-swinging gait as she headed for the elevator.

Back inside, Wilma was beside herself. She just realized that, except for the things that they bought that day, all her clothing was at the condo. "Jack, you simply must retrieve our clothes. I don't have anything. I could never go out dressed like this."

"I won't go until Jenny gets back. I can't leave you two unprotected."

"Oh, very well then. Did she say how long she would be?"

"No, but I'd guess a couple of hours. Where's Brenda?"

"She's asleep, poor dear. None of us got much sleep last night. Not to mention the excitement of the past few days."

Jack peeked into her room. Both beds were empty. He turned to Wilma.

"She went to your room. She didn't want to be disturbed by her new roommate when she returned."

"You want to watch the tube?"

"Sure, see what you can find."

They agreed on a tennis tournament and watched a few elimination sets. Jack kept the sound turned down for Brenda's sake. In a half-hour or so, Wilma melted onto the couch and started snoring.

When the doorbell chimed, Jack quickly let Jenny in and helped her with two large suitcases and a stuffed garment bag. The bellboy was kept outside as Jack put his finger to his lips to keep both of them quiet.

In a quiet voice, Jenny whispered: "I've got more in the car, but I can bring it in later."

Jack wrestled the two heavy suitcases to the room.

"Where's Brenda?"

"She's taking a nap in my room."

Jenny shot him a quick glance. Jack could tell that her mind was racing ahead of the facts.

"She didn't want to be disturbed when you returned. We've been through a trying few days."

"Oh."

Wilma roused. "Jenny, dear. I'm so glad to have you back. We were waiting for your return so that Jack could retrieve some of our clothing. So, unpack your things. I think you and Brenda have worked out some sharing of closet and drawer space. And Jack, see what you can get for us, will you?"

Wilma followed Jenny into her room talking as she went. After picking up Wilma's cell phone, Jack left for the Condo.

Jack stopped by the hotel security office to speak with the director, Glenn Massey, retired Army Military Police.

"Glenn, you may not remember me. We met last year when I was working for one of your guests."

"Yeah, I remember you. Wexler, right? Ex-gyrene, right?"

"Yes, sir, Jack Wexler. I'm working security for Mrs. Ellman who is in the Presidential Suite. I have an off-duty deputy sheriff, Virginia McCaskey, working with me. I want to have your people tell anyone who asks for Mrs. Ellman or Brenda Mazzi to be told that she is not a guest. That goes for Deputy McCaskey and myself as well. There have been several attempts at doing them harm."

"We have a set routine for situations such as this. I will take care of this immediately."

"Also, if the FBI, Miami PD or anyone in law enforcement asks, I want to be told. I will share this with you: There is a leak from some official source. I really don't trust anybody."

"I hope you're wrong."

"So do I."

Jack left looking for his friend Carl.

"Hey, Jack, see you're back."

"Yeah, but keep it quiet. We don't want anyone to know we're here."

"Okay, I can do that."

"Can I borrow one of your crew and your airport shuttle bus for a couple of hours. I need to bring a bunch of things from the condo back to the hotel. It's for the ladies."

"Sure, if we have to take someone to the airport, the hotel will just spring for a taxi. For a guest like Mrs. Ellman it's not too much to ask. Juan just got back from a run, you can leave now."

When they got to the condo, Jack directed Juan to the parking garage. They took the elevator.

Jack broke the police seal on the door of the condo and entered. Jack tossed the things from the drawers into the luggage; the hanging items were carried in their arms. Five trips for both of them had all the clothing stripped, including Jack's.

As they exited the parking garage, a nondescript Ford cut them off.

Drawing his pistol, Jack yelled for Juan to get to the floor. The passenger side door opened. FBI agent Will Conover strode out. He looked pissed.

"Just what the hell have you been doing?"

"Getting our clothing, what do you think?"

"You broke the damn seal, you know."

"So what? It wasn't your seal—it belonged to Miami PD. Now get your car out of the way."

"Where's Brenda Mazzi?"

"Safe and alive, which is a lot better than you could do for your own agent. What were you guys doing, taking a vacation?"

Will calmed down a bit. "Yeah, we're still getting an ass chewing hourly on this. The US Attorney's office has stepped in. Damn, they're investigating us now."

"So, are you going to move your car?"

"You going to tell me where Brenda is?"

"If you even try to approach her, I will shoot you. Is that clear?"

"Are you threatening a Federal Officer?"

"Damn straight! Now move it or we will ram. You can then try to explain your actions when the cops come."

Will got into the car and sped away.

When Jack got back into the minibus, Juan was visibly shaken.

"You okay? Do you want me to drive?"

"No, I'll be okay. It's just that I haven't been this scared since I left Cuba."

CHAPTER
10

THEY WERE ELATED with the delivery of their wardrobe. Although they should have complained about the rough-handed way Jack had stuffed the small items into the luggage and the fact that he had emptied the dressing room cosmetics into a plastic bag, they were too busy putting it all away again to say anything.

It only took Jack a few minutes to stow away his things. Being a squared away ex-Marine, the sox were segregated according to color, aligned in a row, shorts and t-shirts folded neatly. In the closet, jackets, shirts then trousers according to color with hangers equally spaced on the rod. Shoes lined up on the floor according to color.

As Jack stepped back, looking at the closet, Jenny appeared at the door. "Very neat."

"Yeah, Marine Corps training will do that to you every time."

"You can straighten up my things anytime you want."

Jack looked in her direction. There was a sly smile on her face.

The door opened. "Oh, there you are. Brenda suggested dancing. They have a great band playing at the Starlight."

"Starlight?"

"The supper club located on the roof. It's a great place."

"We'll dress up, of course. I haven't had a chance to wear my Armani tux yet."

"Jenny, dear. Did you pack anything suitable for an evening out?"

"I'll have to go to my car. Shouldn't take but a few minutes."

"Do that then. I'll tell Brenda. We'll have dinner at nine. Jack, would you please call for a nice table. I think you know the concierge, don't you?"

Jenny wore black. It wrapped tightly around her all the way to the floor. The front plunged almost to her navel, the back to a couple of inches below her waist. She wore no bra.

Before they left, Jack got a loose hair from Brenda's hairbrush and a spot of mousse on the tip of his finger. When all had exited the suite, Jack fastened the two ends of the hair from the doorjamb to the door with the mousse as glue and placed the 'Do Not Disturb' sign on the door knob. He wanted to make sure no one entered the suite while they were gone.

On their way to the elevator, Jack whispered to Jenny. "How does the dress stay on?"

"It's a secret, but I'll tell you. I use rubber contact cement. It's a bitch to get it off my skin later but the dress stays on."

"Are you armed?"

"Of course."

He paused, glancing from head to toe. "I'm not even going to ask where."

Brenda and Wilma were dressed well, even attractively, but Jenny was outstanding. Jack could tell that Brenda was slightly piqued. Seated at the restaurant, Jack was placed between Brenda and Wilma. Soon Brenda and Jenny were whispering and joking with each other.

After the meal, Jack and Wilma left the table to dance. Jack bent over to whisper to Jenny. He then saw the outline of the pistol holster on the calf of her crossed leg.

"Look, any place Brenda goes, you go too. Don't let her out of your sight for any reason."

"Don't worry, I'll do my job."

As they approached the dance floor, Jack scanned the crowd to see if their table was being watched. The only ones that stood out were a pair in business suits. Could be that the attraction was the pretty girls. As they danced, Jack kept his eyes on the men.

An hour later, the two suits left. A few moments later, Will Conover and another agent came in and walked up to the table. Jack left Wilma to intercept.

As Jack arrived, he could hear Agent Conover speaking. "Brenda Mazzi, you're coming with us."

Jack moved between Brenda and the men. "Show me the arrest warrant."

"I don't need to show you any warrant."

"Then you don't take her. I suggest you both leave. If you put one hand on her, either Officer McCaskey or myself as sheriff deputies charged with her protection will shoot you. Do you understand?"

Jenny grabbed the sides of her dress, pulled up her skirt and lifted her leg in order to remove her weapon. She spoke in a firm voice. "Show the warrant or leave. Otherwise, I will put you under arrest, have you tossed into jail and loose the paperwork for a few days."

Jack interjected, "You don't have a warrant, do you?"

Will looked to the other agent, nodded toward the door and left.

"Jenny, I think we should go back to our room."

"Good idea. Otherwise, they may try something else."

Jack got to the door first. The hair was gone. Jenny started to speak but Jack put his finger to his lips for silence. Jack escorted them to a door labeled 'Custodian", took out a plastic credit card and fiddled with the lock a moment. He shoved Wilma and Brenda in.

"Keep quiet and don't open the door unless you hear my voice."

Jack opened the door with his weapon drawn. The sitting room was empty. Jack motioned for Jenny to take Wilma's room. He took Brenda's room. He pushed the door open and turned on the lights. He quickly checked the closet, bathroom and under the bed. He heard a scream and two shots in rapid succession.

Jack ran toward the sound. As he was about to enter Wilma's bedroom, he saw a blur off to his side running from his bedroom toward the door then heard a slam as the door shut. He hesitated a moment, then ran to aid Jenny.

Jenny was sitting astride a man laying on his belly. She had her pistol pointing to his head. She was speaking in a low forceful voice.

"You son of a bitch, just twitch and you're dead."

Seeing Jack, she said, "Both of us shot, both missed. But at this range I'll not miss. You hear me, ass-hole? Jack, get my handcuffs, they're in the top drawer of the chest on the right side."

After cuffing him, Jack retrieved Wilma and Brenda.

"My God, Jack! When we heard the shots, I just knew both of you were dead."

They went to the bedroom where Jenny kept the intruder on the floor. The man struggled to sit up.

"I told you not to move, you ass-hole. I'll shoot you where you are, take off the cuffs and put your pistol in your hand." Turning to Wilma and Brenda, Jenny asked, "You recognize him?"

"Can you have him move his face toward us?"

"Okay, you prick, roll over. But do it slowly."

"The cuffs are biting my wrists."

"Ohh, poor baby. Now turn over." She stepped over and put her stiletto heel into his back. He moved over.

Brenda gasped. "I know him. He's one of the criminals who worked with my ex-husband."

Jack stepped forward. "He's also one of the two men I spotted at the Starlight."

Jack stepped into the sitting room and dialed the operator. "This is Jack Wexler, get me security."

Two detectives and three uniformed cops responded. They retrieved the two bullets. One from a doorjamb the other from the headboard of the bed.

One of the detectives pointed to Jack. "What is your connection here?"

"Deputy Sheriff, Special Investigator on temporary assignment."

Pointing to Jenny, "And you?"

"Deputy Sheriff, temporary assignment. Now, when will I get my weapon back?"

"Soon as we can get a test round. I'll have it sent over within an hour. I'll contact your colonel. What's his name?"

"Reynolds, John Reynolds."

"I don't know the Sheriff's Department procedure for an officer in-volved shooting but you may have to do some paperwork."

"Look, try to pile on enough charges so that this ass-hole will at least have a high bail. This isn't the first time."

"I know who you are now. That shoot-out on Drake street a few days ago—that was you, right?"

"Yeah, and those shooters were from the same outfit."

After the police left, they were all too excited to go to bed. They stayed up until after one o'clock re-hashing the whole event. Wilma even found coffee in the small butler's kitchen and brewed up a pot. When the patrol-man came back with Jenny's weapon, they sent him off with a fresh cup of coffee.

Jack left the shower wearing only his boxer shorts. Jenny was sitting on the bed in her pj's.

"Jack, would you please help me get the cement from my shoulders. This fluid is supposed to get it off."

"Excuse me, I'll get something on."

"Don't bother, I have five brothers at home. I'm used to it." She turned her back to him, undid the top two buttons of her pjs. "Just start on the top."

Jack took the bottle and one of the cotton balls and began removing the rubber cement. She turned around, dropping the shirt lower. "Now please help me with the front." He began rubbing gently with each pass getting closer to her bare breasts.

He drew back. "I think that gets it all."

She stood, shed her top, then hooked her hands in the band of her pj bottom and let it fall. "I think there's something both of us wants." As she turned down the covers, she asked, "Please get the light."

CHAPTER
11

A CREATURE OF HABIT, Jack was the first to rise. He quickly ordered room service before taking his shower. He was just finishing dressing when the doorbell chimed. After looking through the peephole, he let the girl in with the food.

He was reading the paper, finishing the last of his scrambled eggs, bacon and dry whole-wheat toast when Brenda entered. Her dressing robe was fastened loosely so that when she walked, the front would flash open revealing all.

She sat next to Jack and gently put her hand in his lap. "Were you surprised with your visitor last night?"

"What do you know about that?"

"Oh, Jack, Jenny and I are roomies now. You should know that girls talk about these things."

"You've been talking about me?"

"Now, don't get all angry. She just asked if we were a number. You know, romantic and all that. I replied that I only used you for sex. I told her that I would be tied down for almost a year for the trial and after that I would go into the witness program. So, there would be no future for us."

"But...."

"Don't interrupt, there's more. It seems she's had little experience except for one time with a boy while in High School and a Lesbian affair that lasted about a year. She realized that you would be perfect for her as she was only interested in sex as well."

"So, you decided to share me. Is that right?"

"You got it. For me, tonight's the night."

Wilma entered the room. "Coffee, there must be coffee in that carafe."

"There's more coffee warming in the butler's pantry."

Brenda jumped up, her gown flaring open. She quickly cinched the sash. "I'll get it." She took the carafe away and returned moments later.

"Thank you, dear. Where's Jenny?"

"Didn't sleep well last night. She's sleeping in."

"It's just as well. I don't feel like doing anything today. It's not that I'm afraid. I mean, with Jack here and with Jenny on hand as well, I feel we're quite safe. But, you must admit, we've had some close calls."

Brenda got serious. "Jack, is there any way we can bypass the FBI? I do want to eventually testify, but I feel someone in their camp is responsible for all the attempts on my life."

"I've worried about those same suspicions and told my friend in the Sheriff's Department about it. He's at work now finding a way for you to be safe. I'll call him later this morning."

Both Brenda and Wilma concentrated on their breakfast. Jack shared the front sections of the paper with Wilma. Brenda grabbed the comic's section.

Jenny shuffled in, still in her pj's. She sat between Wilma and Jack. With her hand she brushed the lock of hair from his face and smiled as she purred, "Good morning, Jack."

Jack smiled, "You sleep well?"

"Well enough."

"Hungry?"

"Famished. What have we got?"

Jack started lifting the lids covering several plates on the teacart. "Let's see, plenty of eggs and bacon, toast from the butler's pantry. Now, here are Danish, bear claws, and jelly donuts. Oh, cereal, fruit and milk. Orange juice, coffee and, if you want, tea. So, what'll it be?"

"Toast and coffee, I guess."

"Is that all?"

"Well, maybe some fruit later."

Jack stood up. "I'll just put the bread in the toaster for you. Are you sure you don't want any cereal?"

"No, toast is okay. Uh, is there any jelly?"

"I'll look."

After Jack disappeared behind the partition, he called out to her. "No jelly, but there may be a jelly donut on the cart. You still want the toast."

"No, I'll just eat a donut. Where are they?"

Jack returned from the butler's pantry in time to find the donut for her. He rolled the cart closer to Jenny's chair and uncovered the pastry.

She rolled her eyes up and smiled. "You are too kind, you know that?"

Brenda had been watching all this with interest. "Jack is truly a rare person, so willing to share his talent with others."

Wilma lifted her eyes from the paper. "What's going on here?"

"Oh, we're just complimenting Jack for his kindness and talent."

The phone rang.

"I'll get it."

Jack walked over to the writing desk and picked up.

"Hello."

"Jack, this is Colonel Reynolds."

"I guess you heard what happened last night."

"Yeah, but I'll get your slant on the events later. How's Jenny?"

"She's doing great. She was the one that subdued the intruder, you know."

"Yeah, that's what I heard."

"You have any news concerning the leak?"

"No but I think the US Attorney is going to bring in the US Marshals and take the FBI off the case."

"I'll tell you this: Brenda doesn't trust anyone except myself and Jenny. Plus, of course, her friend Wilma. She will not go with anyone unless we accompany her as personal bodyguards. So, pass that along to the US Attorney, will you?"

"We discussed that very thing. I'll bring the US Attorney to your hotel for a meeting this afternoon. We'll meet in your room. Is two o'clock okay?"

"That'll be fine. See you then."

Jack cradled the phone.

"Wilma, I need to borrow your cell phone for a minute. I need to make a call and I don't want it to go through the switchboard."

Jack picked up the phone book and searched for a number. He dialed the number on the cell phone and waited for an answer.

"US Attorney."

"Yes, hello. My name is Joe Winston. I'm a reporter for the *Miami Herald.* Would you please give me the full names of the US Attorney and the Deputy Attorneys and spell the names for me. My editor really gets upset when I have a name misspelled."

"What is the article about?"

"No article, just background information for the computer. I'm a college student working part-time. It'll be a while before he trusts me with anything like writing an article."

Jack wrote down all the information, thanked the lady, and turned the phone off.

"What's happening, Jack?"

"The call was from my friend, Colonel John Reynolds of the Sheriff's Department—Jenny's boss. I've been keeping him up-to-date on everything. He has contacted the US Attorney about pulling the FBI off this case and bringing in the US Marshals instead. They'll be here at two."

"Well, Brenda and Jenny, you know what that means, don't you?"

"What?"

"We play dress-up for the attorney!"

"Me too?"

"No, not you, Jack. Just the three of us. I'll call the beauty salon and see if they can send someone to give us a quick cut, shampoo and set. In the meanwhile, let's pick out our outfits."

Jack settled into a comfortable chair to watch the show. He had a good view of the girl's room. They kept the door open as they traveled from their room to Wilma's in various stages of undress. Since Jack had seen both in the nude, they showed no embarrassment. They settled on a micro-mini skirt for Brenda and an Armani suit of Brenda's for Jenny. The slacks fit perfectly, but the jacket was a size too large. But the advantage with the roomy top was that Jenny could hide her weapon.

When the ladies from the salon showed up with a portable sink and hair dryer as well as a case with all sorts of appliances and hair chemicals, Jack inspected everything including their hotel employee ID cards. All seemed in order. They set up their gear in the dining alcove. Jack found a movie on the television.

Lunchtime came and went. Jack was feeling a bit hungry. "You ladies want a sandwich or something?"

Jenny was still under the dryer. Wilma and Brenda were being attended with comb and spray. "I'll have a turkey club on whole wheat."

"How about you, Wilma?"

"The same, I guess."

Jack walked over and tapped on the hair dryer hood. "Lunch, what do you want for lunch?"

"I don't care. Whatever you're having."

"How does a turkey club sound?"

"Fine."

After ordering the sandwiches and an assortment of canned soft drinks, he went back to the movie on TV. Just as the food arrived, the salon people finished with Jenny and left.

At one-forty, the ladies were ready for their dress-up show. Wilma asked, "Jack, aren't you dressing up as well?"

"You said I wouldn't be playing. But, what's wrong with this?"

"Well, nothing, I guess. It's just that you look so casual. We want you to match us. Would you, please?"

Jack quickly took a shower and donned his dark gray pinstripe Armani with an Italian silk tie. The shoes were new and a little stiff, but no one except him would know. The door had been kept open so Brenda and Jenny could make comments.

He stepped into the sitting room as the doorbell rang. Jack looked through the peephole. Only one person was at the door.

Jack stepped back and whispered to Jenny. "Get armed and ready. Colonel Reynolds isn't with him."

Keeping the chain attached, Jack opened the door. "Who are you and what do you want?"

"I'm Rupert Whatley, US Attorney. I have an appointment."

"Where is Colonel Reynolds?"

"He had an emergency at the last minute."

"Do you have any identification?"

Rupert Whatley produced an official looking ID card and passed it through the opening. Jack checked the photo against the man, undid the chain and invited him in.

"I see your name is Rupert K. Whatley. What does the K stand for?"

"Uh, Kevin, Rupert Kevin Whatley."

Jack dropped the ID card, diverting the man's attention. Jack pulled his weapon. "Now, please put your arms over your head."

The man kept his arms at his side and blustered, "How dare you pull a pistol on me. You are in a great deal of trouble."

"Jenny?"

"I'm here."

"If he moves in any direction other than slowly raising his hands, put a hole in him. I will do the same."

He raised his hands.

"Now, intertwine your fingers together. You should know the drill."

Jack holstered his weapon, stepped behind him, grabbed his fingers and held them tight as he frisked the man. "Gun!"

Jack reached around and removed the pistol. It was a .357 magnum with silencer. He was serious about hurting someone. "Now, slowly, drop to your knees. Jenny, put a hole in him if he even twitches."

Jack let loose of the man's entwined fingers after he was on his knees. "Now, face down on the floor, arms straight out."

Jack tucked the man's pistol into his waistband, pulled his own weapon. "Cuff him, Jenny."

Jenny placed her knee on the small of the man's back and deftly snapped the cuffs.

"How in the hell did you know he wasn't the real thing?"

"Knowledge is power. I called the US Attorney's office. His middle name is Kelly." Stepping back, he announced, "Now we call Colonel Reynolds and the real Rupert Whatley."

CHAPTER
12

$\mathbf{J}$ACK CALLED REYNOLDS' OFFICE. The clerk told him that the Colonel was out. Jack asked for the clerk to page him on the radio with the message to call Jack's number.

The ladies had heard Jack's side of the phone call. So, Jack explained. "He'll call here as soon as he answers his page."

Jenny went over to the supine intruder, straddled his back facing his legs, reached between his legs and started squeezing. "Who are you and who sent you?" She squeezed again. He yelled and moaned with his legs thrashing. "Jack, sit on his legs." She started twisting again. Again he screamed. "Stop, oh God, please stop. I'll tell you what you want to know."

The doorbell rang. Jack got up and walked to the peep-hole. "It's the Colonel and he has someone with him."

Jack opened the door and invited them in.

Reynolds pointed to the man on the floor. "Jack, who is this?"

"He said his name is Rupert Whatley. But I didn't believe him. He didn't know his middle name, but I did." He extended his hand to the real Rupert Whatley. "I'm Jack Wexler."

"How in the world did you know my middle name?"

"I asked. Knowledge is power, you know. It's just that I had a hunch, that's all. Someone out there has knowledge about what we do. I have not been able to find out how. So, I take precautions. I called your office and got the full names of all the attorneys."

Reynolds stepped over to the handcuffed man on the floor. "You read him his rights?"

"Not yet."

Jenny recited the memorized list of rights. "Now, do you understand your rights? Speak up."

"Yeah, I understand. Now can you loosen the cuffs?"

"Not yet. What is your name?"

"I do not care to answer. How's that?"

Whatley stepped forward. "You are under arrest for impersonating a federal officer, possession of a weapon equipped with a silencer and attempted murder of a federal witness. I can stack up enough charges to keep you in federal prison for over twenty years."

Jenny left for a moment and returned pulling on latex gloves. She began searching through his pockets, placing every item on the floor. She removed scraps of paper, half a pack of cigarettes, a Bic, his wallet, small change and a set of keys.

Jack was thinking ahead. "Colonel, where are you going to lock this guy up? If I'm right, and there is someone with official connections involved in this, he could be dead before morning."

"Jack, the usual procedure would be to call the FBI so they can take him into custody."

Whatley interjected, "But we aren't going to do that, are we? What I am going to do is authorize you, Colonel Reynolds, to take this man into custody as a John Doe, take his prints and get them to me. I will forward them to Washington. We'll find out who he is."

Reynolds stepped to one side to make a call on his cell phone. "Two cars, six deputies and no lights or siren. Service entrance in thirty minutes." He looked at the hit man. "Help him up."

Rupert and Jack each grabbed an elbow and raised the man to his feet.

Colonel Reynolds grabbed his lapels. "You are a very lucky man. Lucky, in that, you weren't able to carry out the murder. And lucky that you will be hidden from the people who will do anything to keep you from talking. Now, you have the chance of a lifetime to tell what you know and let the Marshals hide you somewhere so you can start a new life. You think about it."

Reynolds, Whatley and Jack escorted the man to the basement. They had to wait for ten minutes for the cars to arrive.

After they left, Reynolds explained the situation to Jack. "We'll hold him at our satellite lock-up until the Marshals can move him to a safe house. I'm certain he'll cooperate. Freedom and a new life is better than twenty in a federal pen."

"Do what you can about allowing us to move back to the condo, will you?"

"I'll try to get you in by tomorrow."

Jack accompanied them to the lobby, shook hands and returned to the suite.

Jenny met him at the door with her weapon drawn. "Sorry, I heard the door open and just reacted. I should have known it was you."

"I only wish that there had been a few minutes more of you working on that guy. He was ready to spill it all."

"Yeah, that'll bring it out all right. Being raised with a house full of brothers, you learn their vulnerabilities."

"So, you've done that before."

"Let's just say that the rape attempt was not successful."

Jack left the foyer and entered the sitting room. "Where's Wilma?"

"Sandbox. She'll be out in a minute."

Wilma returned. Jack could hear the sound of the commode tank filling up.

"Tell me, Jack, who was he?"

"Don't know yet. He kept pretty quiet but I think they'll be able to get him to do whatever he needs to do in order to stay out of prison."

"Are we safe now, Jack?"

"No, we only caught a soldier. Brenda, there are plenty others where he came from, I think."

"What I'd like to know is how you knew he was dirty."

"Just a hunch, really. I've learned to obey my hunches. It's a matter of not being able to go back and redo anything once it's done. Regret means that I didn't act when I knew I should. Oh, by the way, Reynolds said we could go back to the condo tomorrow."

"Then we'll leave just after breakfast. Now, girls, I need to talk to Jack alone for a few minutes. You will excuse us, won't you?"

Brenda and Jenny traded quizzical looks and went to their room.

Smiling, she asked, "Jack, I really don't know how you do it."

"What do you mean?"

"Musical beds night-after-night. And from what I've seen, you have not been the aggressor, so to speak."

"Wilma, I have tried to be professional, but they come to me at night. Sometimes even after I'm asleep. Do you want me to put a stop to it?"

"Of course not. But, please, just keep it on a recreational level if you can."

Seeing an opportunity to tease, Jack retorted, "I have noticed that you haven't visited me yet."

"Please, I'm old enough to by your moth… your aunt."

They could hear laughing from the girl's bedroom. Knowing that they had heard it all, Wilma and Jack began laughing as well.

Three hours later, Colonel Reynolds called. "I thought I would fill you in on the latest."

"Stop, don't say anything else. Give me your number. I'll call you."

Reynolds recited his number. Jack got Wilma's cell phone and called. "John, I don't trust the hotel's phone system. I may be paranoid but I think someone is listening."

"Okay, we've got him named but he's not talking yet. He is a former FBI agent. He did time for removing evidence in a case involving OC."

"OC? Oh, yeah organized crime. Go on."

"He got out two years ago. He didn't flip then so there's a good chance he won't now. So that makes you right about the feds being involved."

"Cap, how come I don't feel better about that?"

"Oh, yeah, the condo is released now. You can move in this afternoon."

"You got anything else?"

"Nope, I'll keep in touch."

He turned off the cell phone and handed it to Wilma. "Wilma, let's leave for the condo as soon as we can. This very evening if possible. I don't trust the security here."

On their way to the condo, they stopped at the drive-through at Burger King. They had all their things moved in by eight that evening. Jack set about disconnecting all the cameras and microphones.

By ten each retired to their own room. Jack took a shower and hit the sack. As he waited for sleep to come, he was glad in a way that he was alone. He was really bushed. However, he woke a few hours later with Brenda whispering in his ear.

"Jack, can I stay with you tonight? I need to snuggle with you. I feel so alone and frightened."

CHAPTER
13

AFTER BREAKFAST, Jack turned his attention to security. The door to the apartment was made of steel with a steel jamb and frame. However, there was only a single lock with no dead-bolt. He felt that a keyless deadbolt, which could only be locked and unlocked from the inside, would make the door a little safer. He stepped into the hall and closed the door. In a few moments he had pushed the latch back and opened the door with only a small pocketknife. He inspected the bolt. It was made of one piece. He decided that a better lock was needed there too—one with a two-piece bolt.

He also wondered whether the FBI would again inhabit their monitoring station. He called Rupert Whatley on Wilma's cell phone. After he identified himself to the receptionist, he was quickly connected.

"Rupert, we're back at the condo without incident. I've disconnected the video and audio that the Bureau installed earlier but the monitoring station still exists on the floor just below us."

"I didn't know they were that closely involved in monitoring our witness."

"If you don't mind a suggestion, could you get the US Marshals to take over the monitoring operation? I would be willing to reconnect some of the audio and video for them."

"Jack, politically it's a hot potato situation. It's obvious there is some leak in the Bureau locally, but we still don't know where. I've talked to the director and suggested an entire swap-out of personnel. But he didn't want to jeopardize investigations in other cities by an exchange of agents."

"This brings us back to having the US Marshal's office undertake protection of Brenda Mazzi. Believe me, she will not go with anybody unless we agree that it's safe."

"In spite of blackening the reputation of many fine agents, I agree. I'll send a supervisor to the condo early this afternoon. When he gets there, keep him outside until you call me for a password. God, you've got me paranoid now!"

Alerting Jenny about his plans, Jack left for a builder's supply store. He returned in an hour with all he would need to change the main lock and add a deadbolt. With eighty-five dollars worth of locks and a hundred and thirty-five dollars worth of tools, Jack was able to install the locks in short order with Jenny standing guard.

Wilma prepared a lunch of canned soup and toasted cheese sandwiches. Brenda looked a mess but had a good appetite. When the doorbell finally rang, Brenda scurried to her room taking Wilma with her.

Jack and Jenny pulled their weapons as Jack looked through the peephole. Jack raised his voice and asked, "Who are you?"

"Steve Barnes but most call me Skip. I'm a supervisor with the US Marshal Service."

Jack called Rupert. "He's here."

"What name did he give?"

"Steve Barnes, aka Skip."

"You say 'Paducah New' and he should answer 'Canoe Canal'."

"Thanks."

Jack closed up the cell phone and walked back to the door. "Paducah New."

"Canoe Canal. Now let me in."

Jack released the latch and opened the door. "It's like a James Bond movie, right?"

"You must be Jack Wexler and you are Virginia McCaskey."

Jack shook his hand. "I'm sure Rupert got you up to date on all that has happened."

"Pretty much. Could I meet the witness?"

"Sure. Jenny would you please?"

"Have you seen the monitoring equipment on the floor below us?"

"No, have you?"

"Not yet. Maybe we can inspect the place in a few minutes. Oh, here she is. Marshal Steve Barnes, this is Brenda Mazzi."

Jack noticed that she was wearing makeup and had changed to a different outfit.

"Mrs. Mazzi, I want to assure you that it will be my personal responsibility to see that you are kept safe. Safe now and in the future. Do you have any questions?"

"Call me Brenda. I'm sure we'll be seeing a lot of each other so let's just use first names. Okay?"

"Call me Skip. Anything else?"

"Most important thing I want is to have Wilma, Jack and Jenny with me, no matter what. Next is no FBI, no matter what."

"Anything else?"

Brenda flashed a sweet, flirtatious smile. "Are you married or seeing someone? If you're married, are you happily married and if you're seeing someone, is it serious?"

"Not at the present. No more personal questions, please."

Jack looked around. "Where's Wilma?"

Brenda answered, "In her bedroom arranging some clothing in the closet. I'll get her."

When Wilma entered it was as if the Grand Duchess herself had made an appearance. It was dress-up all over again. She extended her hand with the palm down. Jack stifled a laugh as Skip took her hand and started to kiss it. Wilma retrieved her hand just in time.

"This is Mrs. Ellman."

"Pleased to meet you, Mrs. Ellman. Now, could you tell me how are you connected to Brenda?"

"Call me Wilma. As far as my connection with Brenda, I am an old friend. I love her as the daughter I never had. I would do anything for her."

"We're going to inspect the building for a while. Jenny will keep guard."

In the hall, Skip removed a bundle of keys from his pocket. As he walked down the hall to the neighboring condo. "There are two condo's on each floor with shops and other business on the first floor and the parking garage in the basement. We are on the top floor. This building shares the block with three others. None of the other buildings are as tall. So we can rule out entry from the roof."

He pointed down the hall. "Stairway is there, and at the other end is the elevator. Access to the roof is from the stairway. You need a ladder to get there. The apartment across the hall is a mirror image of yours. The rooms on the left in yours are on the right in this one. This condo is up for sale and is unfurnished. We have it for a few months. That means we will take over the entire floor."

Skip opened the door. Jack walked in and looked around. Other than wallpaper and the layout being a mirror reversal, they were the same. They stepped back into the hall. Skip locked the door.

"Now we go to the third floor. There should be nobody from the Bureau there. They have leased both condos. The one on the left is empty just as the left one is empty on the fourth floor."

Since they were nearer the stairs, Skip led the way down. They stood before the door a few moments while he fiddled with the keys looking for the proper one. "Ah, yes. Here it is."

As Skip attempted to put the key in the lock, the door opened violently inward. A man hit the two with his lowered shoulder and body, pushing both Jack and Skip backwards to the floor. Jack quickly rolled over so that he was on his hands and knees. He pulled his weapon as he started running toward the fleeing man. In a moment, the man reached the stairs. As he opened the door the man turned, firing two shots wildly. Jack shot twice. The door to the stairs closed behind him.

"Did you get him?"

"Probably not. Let's go after him."

Fearing an ambush they cautiously opened the door and descended the stairs. Half way down, Skip pointed to the steps.

"Blood. You hit him, Jack. See there? And there. Look, the drops are getting bigger and more of them. Let's go."

They ran down the stairs keeping watch for the man while they followed the trail. When they got to the basement garage, Skip pointed to the bloody handprint on the door and doorknob. Avoiding the prints, Skip opened the door in time to see a black Ford exit quickly to the street.

Skip quickly dialed a number on his cell phone. He told the story to someone, answered a few questions and put the phone away.

"Okay, Jack, we get the Miami PD crime lab in here in a few minutes, there will be no FBI and no paperwork. They will come in, do their thing and leave. The US Attorney will get all the evidence, unfiltered by the Bureau. With a little luck, they'll put a name to the prints and blood."

They waited in the basement for the crime lab people. They quickly lifted all the prints, shot pictures, retrieved blood samples and the bullet fragments. Jack was able to keep his weapon after he reminded them of the shootout the previous week when they test fired his pistol. Skip allowed them to lift prints from the third floor apartment door knob but wouldn't let them in. They were there for about an hour.

As soon as the crew left, Jack and Skip entered the third floor monitor station. The place was a mess with fast food wrappers, soft drink cans and cups, paper coffee cups and a large assortment of nudie magazines scattered all over the place. There were multiple video monitors and a large computer with two dvd write drives and a crate half-full of blank dvd disks.

There were wires exiting from various walls that lined up with identical walls in the unit above.

"Look where the cables exit from the walls. When you look upstairs, the cameras are very well hidden. These men really knew what they were doing. Even after I knew they were there, I had a hard time finding them."

"No video tape machines like in the old days. They record the video on the hard drive of a computer and transfer it to video disks. You can put a lot of stuff on one of those disks."

"Yeah, if you can get an entire movie on one disk, you can surely put a couple of hours of monitoring on one as well."

"Okay, let's turn this baby on."

Skip started flipping switches on the ten monitors. Each monitor in turn came on to a blue screen. The last one came on with a view of the hallway in front of the condo.

"That checks out, Skip. That's one I didn't disconnect."

"Hey, I saw a camera in the parking garage."

"Maybe the building has a security monitor someplace"

"Maybe they have a video tape of our guy!"

They quickly turned off the equipment and locked the door behind them. They took the elevator to the first floor lobby. The attendant was slouched in his chair behind a small desk, hardly noticing their arrival as he read a magazine.

Jack showed him his badge. "Where is the recorder for the security tapes of the garage?"

"I don't know. I just stay here in the lobby. The night shift guy opens the front door at night for residents and watches the video."

"Who would know?"

"My boss, I guess."

"Well?"

"You want me to call him?"

"Well?"

"I'll call but he won't like it. He gets all pissed if I call."

He opened a desk drawer and removed a phone. He looked at a piece of paper taped to the desk and called.

"Hello, this is Walter. There's some cops that want to look at the security tape."

"Yeah, okay, the one that says 'Video Closet', right?"

He cradled the phone and fished around in the drawer for the key.

"Here's the key, but you gotta bring it back. Okay?"

Skip grabbed the key. "Where's the door?"

He pointed across the lobby.

When they opened the door, the room was lit by the glow of a video screen and a video tape recorder. The image on the screen changed every second to another camera. As they watched the progression of images, it was evident that only four cameras were involved. The images changed from lobby to garage elevator door to garage stairway door to elevator interior and back to the lobby again.

"Damn, Skip, you know anything about this stuff?"

"Lets get the tape out of the machine and put in one of these new ones since it's still in the plastic. That way, we won't be taping over anything of value." Skip took the tape and left to meet with the Miami PD.

Back at the condo on the fourth floor, Jack opened the door to three women gathered at the doorway. They were all talking at once.

14

"OKAY, JACK, where have you been? We heard shots, then nothing."
"Yeah, Jack. What's going on?"

"Skip and I opened the door to the apartment just below this one. You know, the one that the Bureau had some audio-visual equipment in it. Well, as soon as the door was unlocked, this guy jumps out and rams in to us, knocking us to the deck. He takes off and I run after him. At the door to the stairway, he turns and fires off two shots. I returned fire and hit him. There was a blood trail down to the parking garage. Miami PD worked the scene. They'll turn over all the evidence to the US Attorney. No FBI will be involved."

"That's good news."

Brenda inquired, "That cute guy Skip didn't get hurt, did he?"

"No, just a bruised tush, that's all."

Grinning, Jenny remarked, "He does have a cute tush. Huh, Brenda?"

Brenda got a mock hurt look on her face then both she and Jenny broke into peals of laughter.

It took Wilma to bring them back to reality. "So, what's next?"

"The Marshals Service is going to take over the entire floor and control access to this floor and the one below. In a few days, they'll have things very secure."

Jack reached behind him and locked the deatbolt.

The next few days saw a flurry of activity on their floor. A heavy chain-link fence cage was built at each end of the hall. A desk for a watchman was installed at the elevator end to intercept any visitor. Furniture was delivered to the condo across the hall. Men came from the phone company to install the phones and new lines. Jack visited Skip from time-to-time but felt in the way. Finally, he had to get out for a while.

"I need to see my aunt sometime in the next day or two. And maybe shop for a Christmas present for her."

"Well, it's ten more days 'till Christmas so today is as good as any other."

"Thanks, Wilma. Jenny, can you hold down the fort? I'll be back before five."

Wilma answered for her. "Go ahead, Jack. We'll be fine."

Jack drove three blocks west to Biscayne Boulevard, turned left and finally merged into US1. From time to time he would check out the cars following. He kept his speed right at the limit. Most all of the traffic seemed to go at a speed slightly above that. So, he kept to the right lane, giving all the others a chance to pass. However, there was a blue Dodge behind him keeping several car-lengths space. At times, a truck or car wanting to exit the highway would fill in the space, but the blue Dodge was ever there.

He stopped at a shopping center. He bought his aunt a present and waited for it to be wrapped. He looked around for the Dodge but didn't spot it.

After he arrived at Homestead and left US1, he kept looking for the Dodge. He drove to his aunt's house by a circuitous route just in case. He parked in front. His aunt came to the front door, wiping her hands on her apron.

"Well, Jackie. I didn't know you were coming. Are you hungry? I'll cook you some pork chops. I have some fresh green beans and left-over potato salad I can fix too. It'll just take a few minutes."

"You know I'm always ready to eat."

Aunt Emily quickly turned and went back into the house. The blue Dodge pulled up behind Jack's car. Will Conover got out. Jack tried to make out who the person was in the passenger's seat.

"You're a long way away from Miami, Will."

"I'd like to know what in the hell you've been telling the US Attorney about us?"

"Not me, buddy. I've just been keeping my Colonel informed, that's all."

"We've been catching all kinds of heat because of you. And it isn't fair."

"Will, it's obvious that someone is feeding information about us to the bad guys. If it isn't you, it's someone close to you. You better start looking. It would be a good thing if all of you were hooked up to the machine and tested. Then you might stand a chance to find the truth."

"Aw, hell, Jack. You know, with a little training and Vallium, most anyone can beat the thing."

"Okay, your message has been delivered. By the way, who's the passenger?"

"None of your damn business."

Jack had a flash of an idea. "How's his injury? Is he in much pain?"

"He's okay. Hey, how did you know?"

"I'm psychic, of course. I'm going in and eat some of my aunt's fine cooking."

When Jack reached the porch, he turned to see the Dodge go past. The passenger really did look like the shooter he was able to wing. He was disappointed with the notion that Will could be involved. He really seemed to be a nice guy.

When he passed through the living room, Jack noticed that his aunt had put up her artificial Christmas tree. He remembered the tree from years past. He slipped her present under the tree and joined her in the kitchen.

After lunch, Jack did a few odd jobs around the house. He repaired two window screens and the lock on the back door. Finally he had to go.

As he walked out to his car, he looked at his old Honda with the 'For Sale' sign. "Any bites on the car?"

"No, Jackie. But I did put a notice on the bulletin board at the senior center. This old geezer—I really can't stand him—said he might be interested. He wanted to come by to look at it. But I knew better. He only wanted to pester me with his offers of a movie and whatever."

"What is the whatever?"

"Oh, Jackie, you should know."

"You should get out more, you know?"

"Oh, I almost forgot. A letter from the motor vehicle people came today. Just wait a sec, I'll get it for you."

She brought out the letter. Jack opened it up and found the title to the Cadillac. He was surprised to find his name entered as owner.

On his way to the hotel, he stopped by the bank to put the title in his lock box. He started counting his money but quit. He knew how much he had to the last dollar.

Jack tried his key but the deadbolt had been turned. He knocked and was let in by Jenny. She kissed him and molded her body to his.

She whispered, "Hey, don't I know you?"

"Very funny. I was only gone a little over four hours."

"Wilma wants to talk to you."

"Is she here?"

"Yeah, I'll get her."

Jack flopped down on the couch. Wilma breezed in from her bedroom.

Jenny followed her out and went directly to her room.

"You'll never believe what has happened while you were gone."

Jack straightened up from his slouch. "Tell me."

"Brenda has decided she can trust Skip and the US Marshal's Service to protect her. They have several weeks of planning for the upcoming court cases. As for myself, I've been away from New York far too long. I miss the food, my friends and most of all, the New York papers."

"You've only been away for a little over a week. Are you leaving soon?"

"We have reservations for tomorrow."

"We?"

"Yes, dear Jenny has agreed to come with me. I have come to regard her as the daughter I never had."

"The car title came. You really shouldn't have done that."

"Oh, poo. I'm a rich old Jewish broad who can do anything she wants to. My accountant tells me that I haven't been able to spend even a part of the earnings on my investments, let alone the principal."

"Well, I do thank you very much."

"Just a moment, Jack." She went to her bedroom and returned with her check book and started writing "Now then, this should cover the amount promised for the entire six month contract plus a little extra."

"But, you gave me the car . . ."

"Nonsense. I will give you what I wish to. Don't say another word. You've put your life on the line for me several times and have given me memories to last a lifetime. I'm the one indebted to you."

"Where's Brenda?"

"Across the hall. She's quite taken with Skip, you know."

"Yeah, I expected as much. Oh, by the way, when does your flight leave?"

"A very convenient three-oh-five in the afternoon. I guess we should be there by two or so."

"You will never be able to get all your clothing in your luggage. I'll get some wardrobe boxes from Allied Van Lines. I'll have them sent by Fed-X to your apartment." Jack looked at his watch. "I'll go over now so you'll have plenty of time."

Jenny came in from her bedroom. She had been crying. "Could you follow me as I drive my car to my cousin's place? I need to leave my car. I can't just park it on the street, can I?"

"Sure, you ready to go now?"

As they left, Jack made sure that Skip would be there to guard Brenda.

On the way down in the elevator, Jenny briefly gave directions to her cousin's house. Jenny led the way in her five-year-old Mustang.

At her cousin's house, Jenny picked up an armload of clothing on hangers as well as three grocery bags full of other items. Jack helped load her things as she said her good-byes.

When they pulled away, she kept looking back. "I hope I'm doing the right thing. I've hardly been out of the state my whole life. New York will be a great adventure for me."

"I'll miss you too."

"I know, Jack. We just were getting to know each other."

She was quiet for a while. "Jack, can I be with you tonight?"

Jack smiled. "It'll be my pleasure."

When they got to the condo, Jack wrestled with the six flattened wardrobe boxes. Jenny carried the metal rails that attached to the boxes for clothes hangers. They both made another trip to get Jenny's things out of the car.

After taping the boxes together, Jack got out of the way to let the ladies do the actual packing. Aside from the items reserved for their luggage, they filled all six of the boxes.

Jenny brought her service weapon to Jack. "Turn this in to the Colonel, will you? I'm keeping my badge and ID card until I can get a carry permit in New York. I'm also taking my personal weapon and handcuffs packed in my suitcase. Maybe the badge and ID plus packing my pistol away in the luggage will keep me from having trouble at the airport."

"I'll go with you and Wilma to the gate. I don't think you'll have a problem."

The next morning, excited about the trip, Jenny got up first. She left Jack still in bed to make the coffee. When she returned, she whispered, "Jack, guess who's in the bed with Brenda."

"Oh, I'll take a stab and guess Skip."

"Was it that obvious? I really had no idea romance was brewing between the two."

He started to kiss her on the neck. She responded. "Jack, after running a marathon last night, can you really go again?"

"Maybe not a marathon but surely I can run a hundred yard dash."

Jack was up, showered and dressed by nine. After breakfast of bagel, cream cheese and coffee, he checked on the work across the hall. He was surprised to be met at the door by Brenda dressed only in a man's tee shirt.

"Come on in. I've made coffee. Skip is up and taking a shower. He'll be out in a minute. When Wilma moves out, we'll move over there and leave this side for the US Attorney and the steno staff. They plan to issue over a hundred indictments from this. Oh, there he is."

"Hey, chief, what's up?"

"Looks like after today, I'll be on vacation for a while."

"Give me a little time and I'm sure I can get you into the Marshal's Service."

"No, I'll just wait for something temporary to turn up. You know, a couple of weeks here, and another there. Before long it'll be the eighteenth of May and time to return to summer semester at Auburn."

"Are you coming here after you put them on their flight?"

"Yeah, I need to ship some of their clothing. Plus, I have to get my stuff loaded in my car."

"If there's another marshal here, I'll give you a hand."

"Thanks, it'll save me a few trips."

A knock came at the door. It was Jenny. "Jack, can you please come over, Wilma has some questions."

"Duty calls. See you later this afternoon."

Back in the condo, Wilma was seated in the midst of a stack of luggage and boxes.

"How could I accumulate so much?"

"Don't worry, we'll get it all to the airport and have the rest delivered tomorrow. I've called Fed-X for a pickup at five this evening for overnight delivery. I've charged it to your credit card number. Oh, yes, here is your card."

"You can take the luggage now."

Jack took two of the suitcases to the elevator and placed one of the items in the doorway to keep the elevator open and stopped at their floor. Jenny arrived with two more as he started back. Another trip for both had it all in the elevator.

They stopped at a burger place and went through the drive-thru line on the way. At the airport, Jack unloaded the luggage, parking as usual in the police-only space.

When he caught up with Jenny and Wilma, the luggage had been checked through to JFK. He flashed his badge and ID when they came to security. Jack bypassed the metal detector, meeting Jenny and Wilma on the other side.

They waited at the gate until their flight was called hardly speaking at all. Boarding started with the rear seats first. First class would be the last ones boarding. Wilma hugged Jack and held him close.

"If you ever need anything Jack, anything at all, you call me. You understand?"

"Yes."

Then it was Jenny's turn. She placed her arms on his shoulders and gave him a very passionate kiss.

"Jack, if you want me, you know where to find me."

He cupped her face in his hands and gently kissed her. "I'm truly sorry. My future for the next two years is engineering school. A lot can happen to you and to me in that time. Live your life. Will you do that?"

"I'll never forget you, Jack."

As they entered the jetway ramp, both turned and waved. Jack waved back. He waited until the plane backed away from the gate before leaving.

CHAPTER
15

CLIENT: Robert Fossgrave, Jr.

J ACK HAD TAKEN on the task of removing all of his Uncle Joe's ham radio
equipment. He drove around the town looking for the telltale antenna
system. When he spotted one, he knocked on the door.

"Hi, my name is Jack Wexler. I spotted your antennas. Are you a ham
radio operator?"

"Sure am. My name is Ephram Zendt. Folks call me Zennie. You're not
picking me up on your stereo, are you?"

"No, nothing like that. My late Uncle Joe Noonan was a ham too. I
need to find a sale for his equipment so my aunt can use the space. You
know of anybody that deals in used ham gear?"

"You know, son, I might be interested. I go back to Detroit every summer to visit my son. I would like to have another set of equipment there to
keep in touch with my buddies. You know the names and model numbers
of the gear?"

"No, but if you want, you can ride with me to the house and check for
yourself."

"I'll bring along a copy of the Ham Trader so we can figure on a price."

Zennie turned on the gear and made a few contacts with other hams.
He then showed Jack the range of prices in the magazine and offered slightly
less than the smallest price listed.

Jack looked to Aunt Emily. She nodded.

"Now, for that price, we would expect you to remove all the wire antennas, cable and the two telephone poles."

"It'll take me a few days to get a crew together. We'll get all of it down
for you."

He wrote the check.

Next, Jack tackled the shrubbery. Since many of the ornamentals were fast becoming trees, he took the drastic approach. He figured that if they lived or died, it would be okay either way.

Aunt Emily viewed the carnage from the street. "Jackie, it don't look like the same place." She thought a moment, "But that's a good thing. At least it's not like a jungle anymore."

A phone could be heard ringing through the open front door. Emily quickly ran to answer it. In a moment, she came to the door. "Jackie, it's for you."

It was Carl from the hotel. "Hey, buddy. How's it goin'?"

"Taking my ease, helping my aunt around the house. How about you?"

"Same ol', same ol'. You know how it goes."

"What's on your mind?"

"Jack, are you free to take a job?"

"Well, the last job left me pretty well off money-wise. What's up?"

"I've got this ex Marine Colonel who's in a wheelchair due to an auto accident. It's like this, he wants to go on a cruise but none of the lines will let him on unless he has someone to go with him. He's a really personable guy. I like being around him, myself. You want to talk to him and check it out?"

"Yeah, sounds like a hoot. What's his name?"

"Let's see, oh yeah, here it is: Robert Fossgrave, Jr., Colonel USMC, retired."

Jack looked at his watch. "I can be there about two this afternoon."

"Go to the bar, he'll be the only one there in a wheelchair."

Jack showered and dressed. He arrived at the hotel fifteen minutes early. He parked at a loading zone and flashed his badge to the attendant rushing out to tell him to move his car. "Watch my car, please. Don't let anyone ticket or tow it. If anything happens to it, you won't be my buddy." Jack put a five in his palm.

Looking at the tip, the attendant smiled, "I'll keep it safe."

Jack found him in the bar, yelling at the game on the huge television screen.

"Colonel Fossgrave?"

"That's me, son. Pull up a chair and take the load off."

"I'm Jack Wexler."

"Yeah, figured you were. What are you drinking?"

"Usually club soda, rocks."

"No booze? That's okay, leaves more for me."

Jack sat down. He ordered a Diet Pepsi when the waiter came by.

"That stuff'll kill you, you know. Rot out your pipes." He rolled the chair around from facing the TV to face Jack. "Car accident. My car was t-boned by a cement truck. I had the right-of-way. Little satisfaction, you know, being right. Took both legs at the knees. I'm still alive, though. The award was twenty million, the lawyers got a third. At least I don't have to depend on my military pension. You been in the service, son?"

"Yes sir. Four years in the Corps. Rifle Company, made Gunnery Sergeant. I'm in engineering school now. I'll finish in a year and a half. I'm working now to pay my tuition and expenses."

"Okay, here's the deal. Two week cruise. We hit all the islands—get plenty of good chow and booze. We'll feel up a few broads. You may get lucky. Unfortunately, the accident left me with little to attract the opposite sex. Have to pay for my nookie now. But, what the hell, I wasn't getting much before anyway. Been married three times, all of them dumped me. I'll bet any of them would be glad to be back now that I have all this money."

"What will be my duties?"

"You won't have to wipe my ass or give me a bath or anything. I have plenty of upper body strength. I can do everything for myself. The cruise line insists that I have a person to tend my special needs. Hell, they won't tell me just what my special needs are."

"Will we be sharing a room?"

"Hell no! Each of us will be in separate first-class births with balcony. The rooms have a connecting doorway. This way, I can fart out loud and snore all I want. You, of course, can con as many babes as you can for a little mattress thrashing."

"If you need any references, Colonel, I can supply whatever you require. Also, I am a special Deputy Sheriff, presently off duty and I'm bonded to one hundred thousand."

"I don't need any of that documentation crap. But, I'm interested in the bodyguard aspect. What kind of salary do you require?"

"Since it'll be a vacation for me, a thousand a week plus expenses."

"Done. But, please call me Bob and I'll call you Jack."

"What makes you think you need a bodyguard?"

"Well, my oldest son by my first wife looked me up about a week ago and hit me for a loan. Yeah loan. He was just looking for money to feed his heroin habit. Anyways, I told him to hit the road and he became all pissed. He let slip that he knew I hit it big on the accident and that I owed him and all that crap. The last thing he spoke to me had a hint of a threat. I saw him again before I left for Miami with a couple of hard cases driving past my house really slow. I wouldn't put it past him to try something. I don't have a will or anything now, but I have plans to set things up when I get back home."

"When do we leave?"

"Friday. That's five days from now. You're going to need a passport or birth certificate. Can you handle that?"

"I have a passport."

"Okay, plan to spend the night here on Thursday so we can get an early start. We need to be dockside at nine. I'll see to getting a room for you."

Jack felt that he was being dismissed. He stood and shook his hand. "See you Thursday, Colonel."

"The name is Bob. Try to remember."

"I'll try. It's the Marine Corps training, you know."

He stopped at a discount brokerage company where he opened an account with the check for fifty thousand that Wilma had given him. He hated to have his Social Security number tied to his money but since it was in a bank check, he had no choice. Besides, inflation would eventually erode its value if left as cash. He felt that the market was about as low as it could possibly go. After an interview with a broker, Jack decided to let the money sit for a few weeks while he studied various opportunities for investment. The remaining two thousand in cash was left in the bank box. He still felt uneasy about taking Wilma's money, but years ago, his father told him to receive a gift with thanks and not question the giver.

The date for the cruise was near. Jack set about getting his clothing in order. Since there were several pair of shoes that were still new and stiff, he changed shoes several times each day to break them in. He even filled a couple of inches of water in the bathtub, put on the shoes and stood in the water for a while. That way, in a few hours of wear the wet new shoes became as comfortable as shoes worn for weeks. He still had the "squared away" mindset, so he spit-shined them so they were ready for inspection.

When he tried his luggage for fit, he came to the conclusion that he needed at least two expanding garment bags in addition to a larger suitcase. He hated to spend his school money but he headed for the department store at the mall to get what he needed. While there, he stopped by the Key Kiosk and had luggage tags made with his photograph laminated in plastic. After two days of preparation, he was ready.

Thursday afternoon, he took the 'For Sale' sign off his Honda and loaded his luggage. He couldn't chance parking his Caddy for two weeks at the hotel.

The next morning the bellboy led the way, taking their luggage down to the lobby. Jack positioned himself behind the wheelchair.

"Hey, what the hell are you doing?"

"Just trying to help."

"Look, son, sorry I yelled at you. I need to row my own boat. If I slack off, my strength will suffer. My independence depends on my upper body strength. If I need anything I'll ask. I'm certainly not bashful in that regard. Okay?"

They entered the elevator to the lobby. They were a few minutes early.

"Had breakfast, kid?"

"Yeah, a bagel and a cup of coffee. You?"

"Orange juice from the minibar."

"That's not much."

"I could stand to loose a little."

The bellboy beckoned. "The minibus is here."

The bellboy removed the ramp from the rear and positioned it at the side door. The entire second seat had been removed for the wheelchair.

"Okay, son. You can now help me push."

They tied the chair down with bungee cords, loaded the ramp and the luggage. The driver, Juan, arrived in a hurry.

"Hey, Juan. How's it going?"

"Damn, Jack. I never thought I'd see you again. We ain't goin' to have trouble with the FBI again, are we?"

"What's this about the FBI, Jack?"

"A client I had a month ago was being harassed by the Bureau."

"Bunch of damn bullies, if you ask me. By the way, Jack, did you bring your piece?"

Jack remembered the drill instructor in boot camp when someone called his piece a gun: Touching the rifle, he said, "This is my piece." And grabbing his crotch, "This is my gun." Pointing to his rifle, "This is for business." Crotch again. "This is for fun."

He answered, "Yeah, in the suitcase wrapped in a lead foil bag."

"Where did you get something like that?"

"Photo shop. Low intensity x-rays won't show the weapon."

"Nice."

They checked their luggage and lined up for passport check. Since the ramp was a little steep at times, Jack gave a hand when the going got tough.

The first task they had to endure was the lifeboat instructions. Jack was assigned to fit the life preserver on Bob first and then himself second. Afterward, they went on deck to view the ship leaving the pier and watched as the skyline of Miami slipped away.

"I don't know about you, Jack, but I'm getting hungry and ready for a drink."

They stopped by one of the bars for Bob to get a highball before hitting the casual self-service restaurant. Bob got his own tray and pushed it along while Jack assisted by loading up Bob's plate.

When they returned to their rooms, their luggage was sitting in the hall. After Jack tossed his bags on his bed, he helped Bob put his stuff away. He placed the empty luggage in the hallway for storage below.

Jack had opened the sliding pocket door between the two rooms. Bob rolled over. "Let's shut the damn door. I want to take a nap. I'll call you if I need you."

"I'm leaving for an hour or so. Want me to lock your door?"

"Yeah, do that."

CHAPTER
16

HE FOUND THE INFORMATION DESK, "I'd like to speak to the person in charge of security."

"What's the matter? Is there anything I can do?"

"No this is a private matter. Where do I find the security person?"

She brought out a map from behind the counter. With a felt pen, she traced the way to the security office.

He found the door and knocked. An older woman answered.

"I'm looking for the person in charge of security."

"You found me. I'm Lieutenant Monica Chalmers, what seems to be the problem?"

Jack reached for his badge and identification. "I'm Deputy Sheriff Jack Wexler. I'm on released duty serving as a bodyguard for Robert Fossgrave. We have adjoining rooms."

She made a few keystrokes on the computer keyboard and gazed at the screen. "Yes, I see. He's in a wheelchair, isn't he?"

"Yes. There has been a threat on his life. I was called in at the last minute. I didn't get a chance to determine your policy on armed officers."

"Are you armed?"

"Yes and no. I have my weapon locked in the safe in my room."

"I'm afraid it's the policy of the cruise line that firearms are not permitted. For now, just keep it locked up. Now, let me see your identification so I can make a copy for my log."

She took his card and left for a few moments. "There, I made a copy. I'll notify my people to be on the alert for anything suspicious concerning Mister Fossgrave."

"It's Colonel."

"Beg your pardon."

"It's Colonel Fossgrave."

"Okay, whatever."

On the way back to the room, Jack picked up the ship's daily newspaper. As he looked for the events of the evening he noted a single's mixer starting at nine-thirty.

He rounded the corner leading to his room and spotted two men loitering near Bob's door. They started moving toward him as he advanced. As they passed him, he noticed extensive prison tattoos on both of them. Most people can recognize that kind. The ones that look amateurish, dim and not well defined with a light blue color.

As he unlocked his door, the situation hit him. Bob was right about someone doing him in. He silently slid the connecting door open and peered in. Bob was stretched out on the bed snoring. He closed the door again.

During their evening meal in the formal dining room, Jack told Bob of the pair he found at his door. He passed it off as a coincidence, but Jack noticed a change. Bob looked shaken.

They went to the casino where Bob ordered a drink and played the slot machines. When they opened the blackjack table, Bob wheeled his chair over. However, the table was too elevated for him to comfortably play so they returned to the slots.

Jack wandered around the room watching the players. He was too much the engineer and mathematician to play anyone's gambling game. He knew that if you gamble long enough you lose everything. He was especially interested in the action at the craps table. Try as he might, he couldn't figure out the logic in the maneuvers the players made. Now, roulette was simple enough. The house got the edge on zero and double zero so playing red or black was slightly off as an even bet. He walked past a couple of tables set up for poker, as yet empty. He returned to the slots.

"How you doing, Bob."

"Oh, you know. Win a little—lose a lot. It's the story of my life. I want another drink but the waiter can't seem to get around to me."

"You want to go to one of the bars? The slots can't be very much fun. Personally, I like to watch the people."

"Damn, Jack, I do too. Lets go where the people are."

"Yeah, there's a singles mixer later on. Maybe you can find some babe just looking for a sugar daddy."

Laughing he replied, "Oh, I've been there before, that's for sure."

As they sat at the table with Bob sipping on his highball and Jack on his club soda, Jack noticed the passing parade of ladies and girls giving the pair more than casual looks. The wheelchair aside, Bob looked younger than his forty and more years. With the smattering of gray hair at the temples and the roguish smile, he could really attract the ladies.

Jack saw the men he had seen by Bob's door start to enter the club. They stopped short when they saw Bob, quickly turned and left.

"Bob, did you see that?"

"Was that them?"

"Yeah. You recognize anything about them?"

"Not at all."

"Look Bob, don't open the door for anybody and see if you can get a weapon of some kind."

"Where would I get a weapon?"

"Oh, I don't know. How about a wine bottle or a sharp knife."

"How about your piece?"

"Security had me lock it up."

"Not much damn good it'll do locked up."

A young lady in uniform approached the table. "The lounge is reserved for a singles mixer. Will you be attending?"

"Yes, we're both single. I'm Jack Wexler and this is Bob…."

"Not me, I'm going to bed."

"I'll be back in a few minutes. Save this table for me."

She wrote his name on an adhesive-backed tag that said 'HELLO, MY NAME IS' and placed it on the table. "It'll be here when you get back."

At each turn in the hallway to their rooms, Jack would pause a moment after the turn and quickly look back. They weren't being followed.

Jack took a quick shower and changed clothes. When he stepped into the hall he checked Bob's door. It was locked. He checked his own door—it was locked as well.

When he arrived at the lounge, there was a small table set up at the entrance. The same lady in uniform was seated handing out nametags. He bypassed the line and entered. There were three ladies seated at his table.

He picked up the nametag. "I believe this is mine."

"Oh, is this your table?"

"It was. Do you mind if I join you?"

"We would be upset if you didn't. After all, this is a mixer."

Pointing to his tag, "Let's see, I'm Jack Wexler." He studied the other tags. "Karen, Allison and Jo Ellen. And all single, right?"

Jo Ellen giggled. "Now we are." The others laughed as well.

"Explain."

Karen put her hand on Jacks arm. "We're all in the same divorce support group."

"So, all three of you are recently divorced?"

"Well, really four. Betsy is still in our room. Poor thing, she's a little unsteady from the boat rocking."

"She should be okay in another hour or so. Our first stop is Bermuda. The ship newspaper has us dropping anchor a little later."

The Latin band started playing.

"Anyone want to dance? How about you, Karen?"

"I don't think I can dance that style."

"But it would be fun trying, right?"

Jack and Karen were the first couple dancing. It only took a few steps before Karen was matching everything Jack did. When the music ended, she came into his arms, kissing him on the neck.

They returned to the table. "We didn't know what you were drinking so we ordered you a lite beer."

"Thank you, but I don't drink."

Jo Ellen exclaimed, "I think I'm in love."

Allison explained, "Her ex was a boozer. When he was sober he was a decent man but when he was drinking, he was pure evil."

"Yeah, I've known people like that." He waved his hand to get the attention of the waiter. He ordered a diet 7up.

There were other single men at the mixer who came by their table to ask one of the girls to dance, but they all received the same polite refusal. It seemed they were more than satisfied dancing every third number with Jack. As the evening continued, the girls became bolder in their attention to Jack. In response to their complaint that their two rooms were painfully small, Jack offhandedly told them that he was alone in his first class room.

The evening ended with Jack worn out. After all, he had danced almost every number. Each of the girls gave Jack a passionate kiss. Karen's kiss lasted longer than anyone's. They made a date for breakfast and went to their own rooms.

When Jack returned to his room, he quietly slid the connecting door open and peered in. Bob was sitting in his chair reading a book.

"Well, did you get any?"

"All I could handle. Any excitement here?"

"Yeah, I got rid of the babes right before you came in."

"No, I meant, did anyone come knocking at the door?"

"The room steward came by to turn down the bed. He let himself in with his card key."

"You need to flip the privacy latch so no one can come in."

"Yeah, yeah. I'll try to remember."

"No, I'm serious. I really believe those two are out to get you."

"Okay, I'll keep the damned latch flipped."

"We're stopped, you know. This is Bermuda. You going ashore tomorrow?"

"Not unless they make me. How about you?"

"Don't think so."

Jack was up at six, jogging around the ship twelve times. The sign said that six laps equaled a mile. He showered and dressed in time to go with Bob to breakfast. It was still almost an hour before he was to meet the girls so he got a bagel, cream cheese and coffee. Bob got the works.

"Damn, Bob, I thought you were wanting to shed a few."

"I'm not going to eat it all, just a taste of everything."

"That sounds like a philosophy of life."

"Yeah, I guess it could be."

Jack accompanied Bob to the deck. "Is that true? Six laps make a mile? That's just what I need. See you later, Jack."

With that, Bob joined a group doing a power walk and kept up. Jack returned to the cafeteria to wait for the girls. To his surprise they were there waiting for him.

"There he is Betsy, isn't he the most beautiful man you've ever seen?"

"Come on, Karen, you can stop that right now. Betsy, I'm Jack Wexler. Don't believe anything these three tell you."

"I didn't before, but now I do."

He picked up his coffee cup and made to leave. "This is too much for me."

"Oh, sit down, Jack, we'll stop."

Jo Ellen piped up, "Yeah, for now."

"What do you do for a living?"

"You want the short history of my life? Okay, here it is. After High School I joined the Marine Corps for four years. Then, I entered Auburn University to study Mechanical Engineering. I go to school a couple of semesters and work for a like time to pay my way through. Right now, I have a job as companion for a handicapped man. So, that's it, book, chapter and verse.

"That would put you in your late twenties, right?"

"Yeah, I'll be twenty-nine in two months."

"Are you gay?"

"No, not me. I have a very healthy interest in girls. Why did you ask?"

Allison answered, "It's been my experience that someone as drop-dead good looking as you has to have a flaw of some kind."

"When are you planning to graduate?"

"In a little over a year and a half if all goes well."

Karen lovingly put her hand on his cheek. "I'll wait for you, Jack."

Both Jo Ellen and Allison agreed in unison. "I will too."

Karen changed to a more serious tone. "Jack, we asked you to meet with us for a reason. We are all recently divorced and as a result, each of us has more or less suffered a loss of self-esteem. We came on this cruise to seek out a little shipboard romance. You know, the kind of romance that'll have a definite ending with no strings attached. We have further decided that you are it, although Betsy has reserved her decision until later. Now don't get me wrong, we are more than willing to share with each other. In other words, you get lucky any time you want as long as you provide us with attention and romance, attend to only one of us at a time, and have each affair last at least three days. You can either draw straws or just pick one of us. What do you say?"

17

J ACK WAS CLEARLY EMBARRASSED and red-faced. He felt like a prize bull at a cattle auction.

"Are you sure this is what you want to do?"

Betsy spoke up, "Oh, this is so embarrassing."

"Now, Betsy, we decided we should be bold in this. The first thing in getting what you want is to ask for it, you know."

"Now you're sounding just like the support group leader."

Not wanting to press him for an answer, Jo Ellen gave Jack a temporary reprieve. "You don't have to answer now, just let us know by this evening. You can do that, can't you?"

Jack got up. "I'll be back in a moment."

He returned with four straws. He took out his ballpoint pen and wrote numbers one through four on the straws. After wrapping the straws in his napkin he offered them to the girls.

"Take one. Now, I want you to understand that I will not be offended if any of you decide not to do this either now or later."

Each of the girls took a straw.

"Don't tell me your number now. I'll meet each one of you the same way. I'll be in front of the formal dining room at eight-thirty. Dress to impress and I'll do the same."

Before leaving, he circled the table, paused at each girl, and lightly kissed them.

He took the elevator to the security office. Lt. Chalmers was there as before.

"Good morning, Lieutenant."

"Good morning to you Deputy Wexler, any news?"

"Yes, I think I've spotted the ones that are after my man."

"How so?"

"First, I saw two men with obvious prison tattoos loitering in front of

Colonel Fossgrave's door. They quickly moved away when they saw me coming. And again, we were in the lounge when I saw them enter. When they spotted us, they quickly turned around and left. Now, I know that's not much but it bears consideration."

"I'll ask all the room stewards to report a pair of men with prison tattoos. The stewards notice everything. Check back this afternoon."

"Thanks, that'll help."

Jack left the office and started looking for Bob. He found him in the library.

"Hey, Jack, I see you found me. This is a great library. The shelves are full of titles I've wanted to read for years. I could spend the entire cruise here."

"But you won't, right?"

"Jack, let me tell you something. There is no good reason for me to be on this cruise. The only way I can explain it is this way: Did you ever get things so fouled up that you felt that the only way out was to pick up and leave? Well, that's me. My life is a total mess. All my kids hate me. My oldest son is screwed up more than me. He hates me so much that he wants me dead. Now the accident has left me in this chair. I really have nothing to live for, but I don't want to die either. I was looking out the door to the little balcony and thought how easy it would be to just hoist myself over the damn rail. I could do it, you know."

"Bob, there are many things in life worth pursuing. Like knowledge or art or dedicating your talent and ability to a good cause. Also, have you looked into getting prostheses for your legs? They're doing wonders, you know."

"Yeah, I'm scheduled to get fitted in a few months. Let's get a drink. You know, Jack, you're much wiser than your years."

"I have a couple of errands to run. I think you know the way."

Jack went to the formal dining room. The sign indicated that the room was closed, but Jack entered anyway. There was a man behind a stand-up desk.

"We're closed, sir."

"I know seating at a given table is according to room number but is it possible to reserve a table for two?"

"I don't know. It'll be difficult handling it all."

Jack reached into his pocket and pulled out a pair of twenties. "Let's look around and find a small table that's out of the way, shall we?"

Jack walked into the room.

"How about that table over there. You can remove two of the chairs, couldn't you?"

"Of course, your name, sir?"

"Jack Wexler. I would like that table several more times on this cruise. I will be just as thankful each time. Do we understand each other?"

"Consider it your table, Mister Wexler. Just ask for Carlos. I'm the headwaiter. What time shall I expect you?"

"Eight thirty."

Jack then went to the gift shop. He hesitated for a moment before asking the girl, "Condoms, please."

"You'll have to get those at the pharmacy." She pointed to a layout map of the ship on the wall. "You are here and you want to go here. It's two decks down right next to the doctor's office."

The pharmacist brought out a pack of four and a box of twelve. Jack pointed to the box of twelve, signed his name and room number and turned to leave.

"Uh, don't you want a bag for that?"

"Oh, yeah, plain brown wrapper, right?"

He dropped the package off at his room, changed into his sweats and went looking for Bob. As he passed the throng of people headed for shore, he saw the quartet of girls just descending the gangway to the launch. He stopped and waited for them to get aboard. When he caught their attention, he waved and blew them a kiss. He could swear that Betsy blushed.

Bob was alone in the lounge.

"Well, kid, you going to work out or just appear that way?"

"Thought I would give the machines an hour or so."

"I've got a bunch of exercise stuff at my house. Let's see, I've got a treadmill, Stairmaster and a stationary bike. Not a lot of use since the accident."

"Bob, there's not much hope for your long-term happiness with all this negative thought."

"Son, believe me I've given my situation more than a casual thought. I've done everything but see a shrink. The only thing keeping me from doing that is the fact that I've never known a shrink that wasn't a bit crazy and had more problems than I could ever have."

"Seriously Bob, there must be something that gives you happiness."

"If there is, I don't know what it could be."

"Think about what you can do for others."

"See you later, Jack."

Jack returned to his room, took a shower and rested up after his workout for a few minutes watching the ship's closed-circuit television. He noticed his laundry bag and decided to take care of that chore. He had found the coin laundry on the way to the pharmacy. He was back in his room again in a little less than an hour.

After lunch with Bob, he accompanied him to the library. While Bob was reading, Jack found a book of his own and settled down. From time to time, he thought about his date that evening. He wondered who had straw number one.

It was twenty past eight when he fastened the cummerbund and put on his jacket. The full-length mirror showed his James Bond appearance. He was ready.

He arrived promptly at eight-thirty but his date had yet to arrive. He slowly paced in front of the dining room, glancing at his watch every few minutes.

"Mister Wexler."

He turned around—it was the headwaiter. "Yes, oh Carlos, how are you this evening?"

"Mister Wexler, your lady friend arrived a few minutes ago. I took the liberty of seating her at your table. Please follow me."

As he approached the table, he could tell that it was Allison. She didn't see him approach because she was facing away from him.

He smiled as he sat down, "Allison, you look lovely this evening. I'm sorry I'm late. I was waiting outside for you for a few minutes before Carlos noticed. Please forgive me for not arriving early enough to meet you at the door."

"God, Jack, you look so pretty."

"Hey, pretty is not a word to describe a man."

"If your hair were blonde, you would look just like Ken. You know, Barbie's beau?"

"I'll have to remember that and put it in my resumé."

They both laughed.

"I must confess that I didn't draw straw number one. Actually, someone else drew that one. She didn't want to be first so two of us tossed a coin."

"What was it, heads or tails?" Jack said grinning.

"You can have both, a little head and a little tail."

"How's that?" Jack couldn't believe what he heard. He recovered by confessing, "I'm a bit nervous."

"All of us are. Several times we discussed dropping the whole thing."

"So, why didn't you?"

"Later, here's the waiter."

"Good evening, I am Jules. Have you considered the menu?

"We'll need another few minutes."

"Something from the bar perhaps?"

Jack looked at Allison—she shook her head. "No. Water, please, with a twist of lemon."

"Mineral water, sir? With or without gas."

"Yes, mineral water with the bubbles, please."

When the waiter left they studied their menus. The choice was between vegetarian, lamb, veal or duck. There was a pen clipped to each menu to mark your choice. Jack finished marking his, but Allison was still undecided.

"I don't know. What did you pick, Jack?"

"I picked the lamb because of the sauce. See, it says á lá Greco. I think it will have olives, tomatoes and cucumbers with vinegar and olive oil. The duck would be good. They probably remove all the bones so you won't have all that fuss. Or the veal would be good. I'd pass on the duck—duck is usually too oily for my taste. It's your choice."

"I'll pick the same dish as you did. After all, it's only a meal."

"You were going to tell me why you didn't back out."

"It was because you were so drop-dead good looking and absolutely perfect in the way you treated us. You showed no favoritism where the normal guy would try to separate one of us from the group in order to try to get… well you know what I mean."

A man arrived with their mineral water wearing a white coat. He silently filled their glasses and left. The waiter appeared soon afterward.

"You have finished with your order, yes?"

They handed him their completed menus. Soon the pasta course was served, followed by a series of dishes and finally dessert. For each course, a wine was offered. Both declined.

They stood to leave. Jack spotted Jules and beckoned him over. He placed two twenties in his palm. "Thank you, Jules for a pleasant meal."

"Oh, sir. It is not permitted."

Jack winked. "It will be our secret, then."

They left the dining room and took the elevator to the ballroom. A twelve-piece orchestra was playing. They were shown to a table near the dance floor.

Jack had not yet taken his seat when the orchestra started a waltz. "Do you waltz?"

"I'd be delighted."

They hardly left the dance floor, waiting after each number for the start of another. The orchestra did take one break lasting thirty minutes.

At midnight when the orchestra paused for another break, Jack took her hand and stared intently into her eyes. "Shall we leave now?"

"Yes. I've got to stop at my room and get a tote bag. It's something for me to wear tomorrow morning. I can't be seen walking down the halls wearing this."

When she entered her room, the other girls crowded the doorway checking him out.

As they left her room she said, "I told them not to wait up for me, but I sort of expected they would be."

When they entered Jack's room, Allison was amazed. "Wow! You could play a tennis match in here. We have to go out in the hall to change our minds."

"The bathroom is in there. And over here is the balcony and this, of course, is the bed."

For some reason, Allison blushed.

"I realize this is an awkward situation. Would you prefer the lights out?"

"No not at all. It would be a good start if you kissed me."

CHAPTER
18

JACK WAS AWAKE at first light. Even though the curtains were closed, there was enough light for him to see everything. He located the bedding wadded up at the foot of the bed. He found the sheet and covered her nude body. When the coolness of the sheet touched her, she stirred.

"I've got to pee."

When she returned, she snuggled against Jack and whispered, "Jack do it again."

Jack moved to get out of bed. "Where are you going?"

"Condom."

"Oh, okay, but hurry back."

Hunger drove them out of the room at two that afternoon. They would walk a few feet then stop and cling to each other in a sensual embrace.

After eating, they returned to Jack's room.

"Jack, I need rest and sleep."

"So do I. I'll just look in on Bob."

Jack opened the connecting door. Bob was next to the balcony reading.

"Where the hell have you been?"

"I got lucky."

"Oh, that's all right, then. She there now?"

"Yeah."

He saluted. "Carry on, sergeant."

He returned the salute. "Aye, aye, sir." Then closed the connecting door.

"Jack, I need to tell you something."

"Okay."

"I was married for a little over five years. In all my married life, I was never treated with the kindness you've given me. I have never attained such sexual gratification, either. I just thought you would want to know."

He kissed her gently, she responded.

He said, "Again?"

"I don't think so. I'm a little sore. Maybe in the morning."

She showered and went to bed wearing one of Jack's tee shirts. Since the shower was small, they had to bathe separately. After drying off, Jack turned off the light and joined her. Soon her even breathing indicated that she was asleep. Jack dropped off soon afterward.

Jack was awake when the sun could be seen around the curtains. The ship had stopped and all was quiet. He rose and went to the bathroom to brush is teeth and relieve himself. As he came out, Allison was waiting to enter.

"Pee, I've got to pee."

Jack went to the window and drew the curtains slightly. They were in port. He tried to figure out which one. No matter, he wouldn't be going ashore.

She came up behind him and placed her arms around his naked body. She drew close and placed her cheek against his shoulder. "Jack, I am enjoying being with you very much."

He thought a moment before answering.

"It is my pleasure, I assure you."

He turned with her arms still around his waist, although not holding him as tightly. He put his arms around her. She had tilted her head up so that she was facing him. There was the beginning of a tear in her eyes.

Jack cupped her face gently in his hands and tenderly kissed her.

"Jack, I'm scared. You know what they say about shipboard romances."

They made love, separated and slept again. Jack was roused by a bump on the connecting door as it closed. He heard Bob's muffled voice.

"Jack, I've talked to the people at the desk. They say I can go ashore since we're tied up at the pier. I'd appreciate it if you would come along. Oh, yeah, if you want to, bring your friend with you."

Jack was sure Bob had looked in and had seen them naked on the bed.

He looked at his watch, and then propped up on one elbow. "Sure, when."

"One. Meet you at the gangway."

"Are we going ashore?"

"You heard him. Do you need to go by your room to get a change of clothing?"

"I need something to eat too. Come by my room in a half-hour or so. We'll have enough time to grab a bite at the cafeteria."

"Sounds like a plan."

Jack took a quick shower as Allison dressed. He was drying off when Allison opened the door. "Kiss me, I'm leaving."

They briefly kissed. When they parted, Allison pointed to his penis. "That's the first time I've seen it so, uh, relaxed."

Jack was still grinning when she closed the door behind her.

It was thirty-five minutes later when Jack got to her room. She was wearing shorts, sleeveless top and deck shoes. Jack was wearing jeans and tee with jogging shoes.

"You get your passport?"

She slapped her hip pocket. "Right here. And I brought my own money too. I'll not have you buying for me."

Both had ravenous appetites, after all, they had missed dinner last night and breakfast that morning. They raced to the gangway so they could meet Bob on time.

Bob was there, waiting. "About time you got here. Who's the lady?"

"Bob, this is Allison. Allison this is Bob."

"Does the lady have a last name?"

Jack was startled. He really didn't know her full name. Allison took charge. "Allison Womack. When I got my divorce I had my maiden name restored."

"Where is your home?"

"Norfolk, Virginia."

"Originally from?"

"How did you know?"

"I detect Kansas, Nebraska or Iowa in you voice."

"Almost right. St. Joseph, Missouri to be exact."

The line moved forward. A young lady in the ship's uniform stepped up. "Passport and room number, please."

With that done they were ushered to the gangway. "Now Jack, since it's quite steep, I'll need some safety from you to keep me from rolling ahead too quickly. Just grab the handles and pull back to keep me going at a reasonable pace."

When they got to the pier, they were ushered to the local immigration officials who stamped their passports. It was a production line affair with hardly a glance at the passengers.

On the street, individual merchants accosted them trying to sell various poorly made jewelry and brightly colored clothing. Jack forced his way through this gauntlet to reach the street beyond.

"Well Bob, where to now?"

"Book store, of course. Just leave me there while you two go off by yourselves. At four, come back for me. Okay?"

They found a cluster of three bookstores. Bob was in heaven. He hardly paid attention to the pair as they left.

As they left, Allison asked, "Where are we going? Or do you even know?"

"We're going to visit an Obeah Priestess."

"A what?"

"It's the local native religion. Some call it Voodoo, but it's a real thing to the African descendents who inhabit these islands."

Jack pulled out a hand-drawn map and looked at the street names. "It's down here."

They walked a few more blocks and turned to an alley. He knocked on the door. An old woman answered. "Ah, the seekers are here. Come in, I've been expecting you. Please be seated. Jacques, you sit there and Allizon will sit here."

"We have come to find the future."

"My name is Naomi. I know why you have come to me and that is not it. You are here because you fear the future."

Allison leaned forward. "Then tell us the truth about our future."

"Ten dollars."

Jack gave her the ten.

She took a Bic lighter and lit a large candle. From a red bowl she took a pinch of powder and sprinkled it on the flame. The flame flashed red. The lingering smoke filled the small room. She began to sway from side-to-side, her eyes rolled back until only the whites were visible. She uttered a low moan and began a chant in an unknown language. She shook her head, her eyes focused and she reached over to turn on a fan. Soon the smoke cleared.

"Jacques, you will have long life and many children. Allizon, Your future is clouded and uncertain but all I see is happiness."

"Please tell me more."

"I see no more for you Allizon. The person's name is hidden but Jacques will marry soon, perhaps a year or less."

Jack asked, "Do you have any other visions."

"I see some danger for you soon but no lasting harm will come. Visit again another day. Perhaps then I can see something more for you. Goodbye and tell your friends. There is the door, you may leave now."

Out in the alley, Jack remarked, "It was strange about the reading for you. I received the most attention even though I asked specifically for you."

"To whom did you ask?"

He hugged her. "When I found out that this was the home island of our room steward, I asked if he knew of something different for us to do. He went ashore for a few minutes to place a call and set it up."

With his arm around her waist, his hand resting on her hip and with her hand in Jack's hip pocket, they continued in a grand circle around the streets lined with shop after shop. They paused at each one but bought nothing.

Jack was alerted by a voice he recognized. It was Bob and it was coming from the alley just ahead of them.

"You sons-a-bitches get your hands off of me."

Jack ran ahead. Two men of the island were wrestling with Bob. Bob had one in a headlock; the other was hitting Bob in the face. Jack quickly pulled the one hitting Bob away and hit him once in the stomach, doubling him over. Jack then pulled the arm of the other one around his back into a hammerlock. Bob got in a good punch to the man's jaw before he released him. The man on the ground ran away.

"Let me get at that bastard."

Bob rolled his chair to the remaining man and hit him in his groin. The man writhed in agony. Jack then released him, allowing him to stumble away.

"Jack, those bastards were going to kill me."

"Well, they're gone now."

Allison approached and bent down to inspect the bruises on Bob's face. "What on earth were they after?"

"Damned if I know. Jack, give me that bag of books over there. Just put them in my lap."

"Do you think it would do any good if we report this to the local police?"

"No, let's just go back to the ship." Turning to Allison, "Is that okay with you, honey?"

"Fine with me."

Jack began pushing the wheelchair, Bob didn't object.

CHAPTER

19

THEY ATE IN THE CAFETERIA their last night together. There was little
conversation. Allison would pause from time-to-time and gaze at Jack's
face intently. Neither had much of an appetite. They left more than half of
their meal untouched.

They went to the country bar where a five-piece band was playing
with a girl singer belting out current hits. A few of the more daring souls
were line dancing.

"You want to get a table?"

She shook her head no.

"What would you like?"

She mouthed, "You."

They took the elevator to their deck. Between floors, Allison was in
Jack's arms kissing. In the room, Jack opened the door to Bob's room.

"How are you doing?"

"A little bruised up but that'll go away. You in for the night?"

"Yeah."

"Alone?"

Jack winked and closed the door.

Allison exited the bathroom wearing only one of Jack's tee shirts. "I
took it from the clothes bag. I think you wore it yesterday. I like to have
the smell of you near. Can I take it with me tomorrow?"

Jack smiled. "Sure, take anything you want."

"I'd like to take you."

Jack started to remove his clothing. "You want me to take a shower?"

"No, I want you just as you are."

Again at daybreak, they made love again. They slept 'till ten.

Allison dressed first. After they kissed a lingering kiss at the door, she
pressed a slip of paper into his hand.

"Don't ever lose this."

HEADS OR TAILS   103

After she left, he looked at the paper. It was her home and email addresses in Norfolk with her home, cell and business phone numbers. He found his address book and transcribed the data. He folded the paper and placed it in his wallet.

He showered and dressed before taking care of the errands he needed to do before the evening. He checked with Carlos about their special table for two. He stopped by security to report on the events of the preceding afternoon's run-in with the local tuffs.

As he went about, he couldn't get Allison off his mind.

As he prepared for his evening, he took a damp cloth and renewed the crease in his trousers. Luckily, the formal shirt had returned from the laundry. No matter, though, he had and extra just in case. Before he took his shower, he polished his shoes. He left for the dining room fifteen minutes early. He didn't want to repeat being late again.

It was eight forty-five when Betsy arrived. She wore a frown as well as a formal black pantsuit with sequins sparkling the top.

Jack greeted her with a kiss. At the last moment she averted her mouth so the kiss landed on her cheek. She was stiff and unyielding as he attempted the embrace.

"I thought about not showing up."

"Well, I'm happy you're here. Shall we?"

She took his arm as Carlos led them to their table. Jules arrived soon afterward with the menu. They both ordered lobster.

Time and again, Jack attempted conversation but failed. Betsy really didn't want to be there.

Later, after an hour of dancing, Betsy asked, "Would you please take me to my room? I think I'll call it a night. You have been a gentleman in every way but the truth is I'm still married though legally divorced. I guess for some people it takes far longer to really be over your husband. Even though he was the worse man ever created and I am well rid of him, I'm not ready right now for romance of any kind."

"Whatever you say."

"By the way, I think Allison is in love with you. She cried all afternoon."

"This is somewhat upsetting to me. I have feelings for her. I wouldn't want to hurt her in any way."

When they got to the door of her room, Jack noticed it was not the room shared with Allison.

"Please tell the ladies to meet with me tomorrow morning for breakfast at eight. We need to discuss our situation again."

She opened her door. "I'm sorry I feel the way I do."

However at breakfast the next day, only Karen and Jo Ellen appeared. "Will the others be joining us?"

Karen and Jo Ellen exchanged glances before Karen answered. "Yeah, it's like this. Betsy backed out and Allison is upset with the original plan."

Jo Ellen continued. "If you haven't suspected it by now, Allison is in love and she doesn't know what to do about it. She suspects that one of us will come between what you two have."

"I do have strong feelings for Allison. Call me a jerk, but you must understand that the kind of love that leads to commitment takes a lot of time to develop for some people."

Karen summed it all up. "Anyway, I guess the date deal is off. You want me to tell Allison anything?"

"Tell her that I called off the arrangement because of my feelings for her. It's true, you know."

"Well, Jack, you did call this meeting."

Within an hour, Allison was knocking at Jack's door. Her eyes were puffy from crying.

"Hey, Jack, I guess we have some talking to do."

"Yeah, I was hoping you would be at breakfast. I had something to say."

"They told me."

"So, what do we do now?"

Smiling, "First of all, I don't need to stand in the doorway, do I?"

"Come in, please."

When the door closed, she was in his arms. "Oh, Jack, I never thought it would lead to this."

"Neither did I. If you remember, it really wasn't my idea to begin with."

"After my three days with you, I couldn't stand the thought of you being in the arms of another, even though they are my best friends."

"So, it's now only us."

"I certainly hope so!"

"I need to tell you about my only other love."

"Should I be sitting down?"

Laughing, "You are sitting down."

"Silly, you know what I mean."

"I fell in love when I was a junior in High School. We made detailed plans for a life together. When I graduated, there were no jobs that would pay enough and truly, I wasn't mature enough either. So, we decided we would wait until I finished my enlistment in the Marines to get married. But, as they say, the best of plans often go wrong. I got a letter from her after only six months telling me that she had met some guy and married him. It took me three years before I would even consider dating. I tell you this to show that I am slow to come to a commitment but after I do, I am hooked for life."

"What does that mean for me?"

"I have deep feelings of love toward you, but give me a little time before you start picking out a china pattern. In other words, for now, there is no one else for me and I don't expect that to change."

"Now it's up to me to confess my secret. My ex-husband had a sweet disposition. He was kind, courteous and considerate. We weren't intimate until our marriage night. After that, we made love infrequently, and then only after I insisted. One day, I caught him dressing in my bra and panties. He confessed he was gay and had a boyfriend. I was devastated. I cried for several days. I finally booted him out and got a divorce. Because he wanted to keep it quiet, I leveraged a nice settlement including alimony. I would gladly give all that up to be with you."

Day and night they shared their personal life experiences and background. At each telling, they began to remove the masks that hid who they truly were. With familiarity came trust. Their lovemaking became more comfortable as each instructed the other. The frequency of their lovemaking was reduced by half, settling down to once at mid-day, again at bedtime and again early in the morning.

They often met with Betsy, Karen and Jo Ellen for breakfast. At first, there was a polite nervousness, but later the girls started a little good-natured kidding.

The pair took long walks around the deck when they were underway and in port. On the days when stage shows were held, they would attend the matinee, leaving their evenings together in Jack's room.

However, one subject was never broached: What would happen when the ship reached Miami? Several times Jack tried to discuss the future, but Allison quickly changed the subject. Their last night came and Jack pushed for a discussion when Allison joined him in his room.

"Well, I've packed all my things except for the one tote bag. I hope you have a tee shirt for me to wear tonight. I saw your luggage in the hall. Did Bob get his stuff packed?"

"Yes, all that has been taken care of. We've got to talk, you know."

"Jack, I'm frightened."

"Why?"

"I'm afraid we'll separate and it'll be over."

"Again, why?"

Her chin started quivering. He knew tears would soon come.

"You've never once told me that you love me. Oh, you've told me that you have love feelings but that's not the same. I've told you many times about my love for you."

Smiling, he took her in his arms. "Okay. I love you completely, calmly, passionately, tenderly and fully. I want to spend my life with you. There, is that enough or did I miss something?"

She reached for a tissue and blew her nose and dabbed at the corner of her eyes. "Okay, tell me what's next."

"How does this sound? We'll load our luggage in my old Honda, drive to my aunt's place, transfer the luggage to my other car, run a few errands and drive to Norfolk to meet your parents."

"They don't live in Norfolk, they're in St. Joe."

"Okay, we'll drive to Norfolk, move your things to storage, take a plane to Kansas City, rent a car, meet your folks and get married. Is that a plan?"

"Do you mean it? Really? Married? God, you do mean it. I'll have to call my parents as soon as possible. Knowing my mom, she'll take charge and make all the preparations."

"After the wedding, we will get an apartment at Auburn."

"How soon will you have to report for classes?"

"Third week in May for the summer term. Plenty of time to do all that must be done."

"Yeah, I've got to sell my house too."

"I didn't know you owned a house."

"It's still in both my and my ex's name. The deal is, he pays the mortgage while I live there. If the house is sold, he gets half the equity as of the date of the divorce. With five hundred dollars a month alimony and the house and car, I got a good deal. My lawyer thought I should get a lot more. Oh, yeah, I own all the furniture as well."

"We'll figure out the logistics later."

"Are there plenty of apartments?"

"Sure, either in Auburn or Opelika. We'll rent a place that's unfurnished."

"Where I can plant flowers?"

"Why not?"

"Oh, Jack, I'm so happy."

Later that night Jack woke. He could hear the hum of the ship's engines. They were still underway. He slipped out of bed quietly as he didn't want to wake Allison. It was then he heard voices coming from Bob's room. There were angry shouts from at least three people. He turned on a light, pushed the four-digit code on the in-room safe and removed his pistol. As quietly as possible he pulled back the slide in order to chamber a cartridge from the clip. He was ready.

Allison roused up. "What is it, Jack?"

"Shh. Bob's in trouble. Stay here."

Turning off the light, he slid open the door in time to see two men dragging Bob toward the open door to the balcony. Bob was bleeding from cuts to his hands. He was unconscious. The sweet smell of chloroform filled the room.

"Put him down or I'll put a hole in you. Gently now. That's right, on the bed. You with the knife, drop it to the floor. Now both assume the position on the floor, you know the drill."

"I don't think he'll shoot, Eddie."

Jack shot him in the thigh.

"Damn, you shot him. You shot my brother."

"Now, Eddie, your brother's on the floor with a hole in his leg. Do you want me to put one in you too?"

Allison came to the door. "Jack, are you all right?"

"Get on the phone. We have a medical emergency so get a doctor and security people here quickly. Tell them shots have been fired." Seeing Allison tugging at one of his tee shirts in an attempt to cover her bottom, he advised, "Then get dressed. This is going to be a long night."

Security arrived in five minutes. To Jack, it seemed like hours. The wounded attacker was bleeding heavily. When the doctor entered, she went first to the bleeder."

"The hell with him, see to Bob there on the bed."

"The guy on the bed is breathing, he'll come around in a few minutes. This guy is loosing a lot of blood."

Security handcuffed both men. The doctor went to work to stop the bleeding. After slitting the pant leg, she applied a compression bandage. She then turned her attention to the knife wounds to Bob's hands and arms.

"He really put up a fight."

"Yeah, after they drugged him they were attempting to toss him overboard."

"What I'd like to know is how did you get that weapon aboard?"

"I'm a deputy sheriff guarding Colonel Fossgrave. Lieutenant Chalmers knows about my presence."

Chalmers entered still in her pjs and robe. "Jack, are these the ones?"

"Yeah, they finally acted."

"What's that smell?"

"Chloroform."

Bob started rousing up. He heaved and vomited. Jack got a bath towel and cleaned him up. The doctor took over and broke an ammonia stick under his nose. Bob started cursing.

Jack remarked, "That's a good sign."

"Jack, did you get the sons-a-bitches?"

"Yeah, shot one, both are in custody. You okay now?"

"The bastards got in the room somehow. I fought them off but one of them kept cutting me. I passed out when they drugged me."

The doctor spoke to Chalmers, "I need to stitch him up and give him a tetanus shot." Turning to Bob, she said, "I need to treat you in the clinic. Are you up to sitting in your chair?"

"Sure, my head is clearing now."

Jack helped Bob to his chair.

"Jack, let Doctor Schwartz take him down."

"Oh, yeah. I need to get dressed."

She laughed, "I was wondering when you would notice."

Jack was wearing only his boxer shorts.

He entered his room. Allison hugged him tightly. "Are you okay?"

"Yeah. I was the one doing the shooting. I have to put on some clothes and go with security for a while. Will you be okay here?"

"Hurry back."

After Jack had dressed, he looked around for Chalmers, then made his way to the security office. She wasn't there but the unwounded bad guy was locked up in a jail of sorts. He sat and waited.

Finally, she breezed in. "Found out how they got in the Colonel's room. They left the orderly tied up in their room. They took his master key."

"You get anything from asshole there?"

"Not yet. We'll let the FBI do all the follow-up. We entered Florida waters some time ago so it's their baby. I'll need your weapon, though. It'll take some time before they release it back to you, if ever."

"That's okay, it's department issue. Just give me a receipt noting the circumstances and serial number."

Jack removed the pistol from his hip pocket, cleared the weapon and removed the clip. Chalmers got a plastic bag from the desk drawer.

"Drop it in here. I don't want to touch it. The ammo and clip go in the bag too. It's all evidence."

Jack called out the serial number, make and model of the pistol for Chalmer's records.

"Okay, Jack. You can go back to your room now. But, please don't go into Bob's room. They'll want to go over it later."

Jack knocked on his door. "Allison, it's me. I left my key in the room."

She opened the door and covered him with kisses. "Oh, Jack, when you went into Bob's room with the pistol, I just knew you would get hurt. Tell me you won't make this a career."

"This is it. From now on I'm a student, husband and father to our kids."

20

THEY DISEMBARKED according to room number. Jack and Bob waited for Allison on the pier until she appeared. They gathered their luggage and got in line to go through customs together. Jack had taken a moment to call the hotel from a nearby phone booth so they would have the minivan waiting for them. He also called his aunt to tell her she would have company for a few days.

When the FBI tried to get a statement, Jack was able to put off the interview until the next day since he had to escort Bob safely to his hotel.

They loaded up the minivan and settled down for the short trip to the hotel. Bob started the conversation.

"Jack, as soon as we get to the hotel, I'm getting a lawyer and cut that damn worthless son of mine out. No doubt in my mind that he hired those bastards."

"Not a bad idea, Bob. The next step would be to let him know what you've done. That should put a stop to the attempts on your life."

"Yeah, that's what I figured."

Turning to Allison, "Aunt Emily was really excited when I told her that my fiancé would be visiting for a while."

"Fiancé…" She said, "I like the sound of it. Hey world, I have a great fee-an-say."

When she stretched out fiancé for emphasis, Bob chuckled for the first time since the attack.

The driver swung the minivan under the covered area in front of the hotel. Jack helped him with the ramp getting Bob down to the driveway. They waited for the bellboy to load their luggage on a large cart before crossing the drive to the entrance.

Allison noticed a piece of her luggage was trying to slip off the pile so she walked along side the cart with her hand resting on the suitcase to steady it.

As Bob led the way with Jack close behind, an old Ford Escort accelerated toward them. Jack quickly pushed Bob's wheelchair between two parked cars and turned to get Allison out of the way when the Ford hit them scattering bodies and luggage across the driveway.

When Jack woke, his Aunt Emily was at his bedside.

"Lord be praised. You're finally awake."

"How long have I been here?"

"Since yesterday."

"What happened?"

"Don't you remember?"

"The last thing I remember was being on a ship."

"You were hit by a car."

"Oh. Uh, where is Allison?"

Emily started to weep. "Poor thing. She died at the scene."

"No. No. It can't be." He turned his head away as his tears started to flow. "And Bob, is he okay?"

"He's fine. You were able to push him out of danger."

"Aunt Em, could you please let me be alone for a while."

"Sure, Jackie. I need to return home anyways. My neighbor, Gladys, will be concerned about me. I'll be back real soon."

Tears were continuing to flow. He reached for a tissue on the stand beside the bed. As he lifted his head the throbbing pain was almost more than he could stand. He figured he had suffered a concussion. A nurse came in.

"Well, nice to see that you're awake now. I'll tell the doctor."

Soon, a woman in a white coat and a stethoscope dangling around her neck came in.

"Hey, I remember you. You sewed me up. You're Doctor Simms. Uh... Janet, right?"

"I remember you too. You never called. Your loss, you know."

"But you were working in the emergency room."

"Rotation. It's been a hard four years. I'll finish my internship in a little over a month from now."

"What happened to me?"

"You were struck by a car. You have a concussion and your urine had a little blood. The scans showed you probably don't have a lasting injury so we're waiting until the brain swelling goes down before releasing you."

"Is the tube in my Johnson really necessary?"

She laughs. "Yes, for two reasons. First, we want to monitor for any blood and secondly, you need to keep still for a while longer. It'll be removed tomorrow morning. You probably noticed that any sudden movement is painful because of the concussion."

"How about food?"

"I'll get something for you now and put you down for regular service. The nurse will bring a form for your choices. Anything else?"

"When will I be able to leave, I don't have insurance."

"I would think that in your line of work, insurance would be the first thing to buy. I suspect you'll be up and around by tomorrow and released the next day."

That evening Bob came to visit. Pedro, a bellboy from the hotel, pushed the wheelchair into the room and stood back. Bob's hands were still bandaged from the knife wounds.

"Hey, Jack. You think you'll live?"

"Allison died, Bob."

"Yeah, her parents are here to claim the body. She didn't die right away, you know. She told me to tell you that she loved you. I heard later that she died on the way to the hospital. Your Colonel Reynolds spent several hours here yesterday. He may have been here today. Your aunt was here too."

"Yeah, I saw her when I woke up."

"Oh, by the way, I'm taking care of all your hospital bills. Damn, son, you saved my life when you pushed my chair out of the way."

"Bob, the last thing I am able to remember is getting on the minivan at the pier."

"Well, the best I can figure is that my oldest son Herbert, after failing to have me killed on the ship, decided to handle the killing himself. He was the driver of the Ford that ran down the four of us."

"Four?"

"Yeah. The bellboy, Juan, has a broken leg."

"Has your son been arrested?"

"Yes. The murder of Allison and the attempt on me as well as other charges will be filed after the investigation is complete."

"How about the two from the ship?"

"Now that Herbert is in jail, they're telling everything."

A knock was followed by John Reynolds sticking his head around the door.

"Hey, Jack. How's it going?"

"Got a headache and they put a tube in my dong. But other than that, I'm glad to be alive. You heard that my fiancé was killed?"

"Yeah."

After a long moment, Bob rolled his chair back.

"Well, gotta go. They're holding the minibus for me. Talked them into shuttling me over here. I'm staying at the hotel until they convict my son. Then I'm going to try to mend some fences with the rest of my kids. And sometime I'll try to find a good woman. I really miss getting regular nookie."

"I'm going too. I know how tiring visitors can be. I'll check in on you tomorrow."

Relieved to be alone, Jack closed his eyes and tried to sleep.

"Ahem. Mister Wexler?"

Jack opened his eyes. There was a man and a woman in their fifties standing near his bed.

"Yes."

"I'm Jason Womack, this is my wife Patsy. Allison is my daughter. I understand that you two were engaged?"

"Yes. We had made plans to be married. We fell in love on the ship."

Patsy spoke up. "Her friends told us how happy she was that she found you."

"I feel the same way."

"We're flying back tomorrow with her. Do you have any idea when you will be released from the hospital?"

"Maybe in two days. At least that's what they told me."

"Then, the funeral in five days wouldn't be a problem for you?"

"Please leave your phone number and address. I'll fly into KC in three days. I'll let you know the flight number. Also, I'll give you the number of my aunt, she can always get a message to me."

As they were leaving, Patsy kissed Jack as tears were flowing all around.

When he saw Allison lying peacefully in the casket, Jack broke down and wept bitterly. Never had he felt such loss, even when his parents died. Later, he would remember little of the services that followed.

CHAPTER

21

Red Dog Camera

"I DON'T KNOW, John. I've got enough money to see me through to graduation if I'm very careful. I'm thinking about getting out of this business and finding a regular eight-to-five job until it's time to go back to Auburn."

The colonel leaned back in his swivel chair and looked out the window. "Did the last job get to you that much?"

"You don't know the half of it."

"Well, just listen to this and then decide, okay?"

"Shoot."

"Vermilion Importing Company is looking for an inside loss investigator. They can't figure how they are losing so much of their inventory. When they balance invoices against inventory they are seeing over a hundred-thousand dollars a month in losses."

"Colonel, I've never heard of them. What do they do?"

"They import photography equipment for their retail stores. Have you heard of Red Dog Camera?"

"Yeah, they're in most of the malls."

"Well, they have over eight hundred stores with about half of them owned by the company and the rest franchised to private individuals."

"So, basically import and wholesale, right?"

"Yes."

"Okay, when do I start?"

"As soon as possible."

"Do you have a background bio for me or should I just make one up?"

"Just be yourself except for the deputy part."

"Did the subject of my pay come up?"

"Yeah. I said your rate was two thousand a week plus expenses. Is that right?"

"I would do it for less but thanks for the boost."

"The contact is Gordon Clemmons. He's expecting you at nine tonight. His home address is in the folder. Hope you don't have a hot date or anything."

"No, I won't be dating any women for a while."

John reached into his desk and pulled out a pistol. "The FBI kept your weapon. I used department money to buy another of the same make and model. Did they keep your extra clip?"

"No, I didn't have it with me on the cruise."

"Just keep this one for now. I doubt they'll ever return it. They keep everything for evidence. It could be years."

He got to Clemmons' house a few minutes early. After the introductions were made, Jack and Gordon went to the kitchen where the smell of freshly brewed coffee filled the air. They sat at the kitchen table.

"I read the folder they gave me on you. Never saw a Marine that didn't like coffee. How do you want it?"

"Black."

"The Colonel tells me that you're quite good at what you do."

"I appreciate the confidence."

"You ever do security loss investigative work before?"

"Yes, but I usually work as a personal security bodyguard."

"Okay, here's the setup. The orders come to the office by fax and phone. There are five girls that enter the orders into the computer and generate a pick ticket. A pick ticket is like an invoice; it contains the order number and item numbers. The pickers use that sheet to get the items and scan them using a barcode wand as they are picked. Finally, the pick ticket scan results are used to generate the shipping invoice and alerts the order generation department to back-order any out of stock items. Okay, so far?"

"Go on."

"Now, at all stages, we use a barcode wand to verify the items. When the tray with the picked items reaches shipping, all items are scanned again before a shipping invoice is printed. A copy is placed in the shipping box along with the original pick sheet and another copy is mailed to the customer's store."

"Seems fairly fool-proof. If the software is reliable, you ought to reduce your loss to an occasional item taken out in a lunch-box or purse. With as much as twenty-five thousand dollars worth of stock missing each week, your loss is far from trivial."

"That's what I figured. It ought to be obvious how the theft is done but it escapes me."

"Put me in the pick crew for a few days. This has to be a cooperative effort between office, picking and shipping. In other words, I don't think one guy acting alone could pull this off."

"You're right. I think I knew that all along. It's hard to believe, though. We only have twenty-eight employees so friendships have developed to the point where we're really like a family."

"So I start tomorrow then?"

"Yes, I've filled out the employment form for you with the exception of signature and your social security number."

"I would like to be paid in cash, please."

"The auditors will be upset, but I can handle it. I will need your signed receipt for my personal use if I get jammed up. I'll clear it with the principal owner though. What I will do is have checks issued for five hundred each to several aliases and I'll cash them with my own endorsement at my personal bank. I sure hope you can find the problem within a week. If it lasts longer than that, I'll have to put you on the books."

"I'll try my best."

The Vermillion building was typical of most warehouse construction. It looked to be about twenty thousand square feet in size. Not large but large enough. The brick front contrasted with the steel covered exterior walls of the rear. Blooming plants and neatly trimmed grassy areas next to the paved parking lot spoke of pride and care.

After parking in a space marked for visitors, Jack put his badge and weapon in the trunk. He entered the door marked Office. The pretty girl at the desk fired off a pleasant smile.

"Hi, you must be Jack Wexler. I'm Wanda. Please have a seat, Mister Clemmons will be with you in a few minutes."

Jack matched her smile with his own. "Thanks."

"Say, you're not married are you?"

Jack paused before sitting. "No."

She wrote quickly on a note pad, "Here, call me. I'm free most any night. If I'm not, call me anyway and I'll dump my date."

Grinning, Jack took the paper and put it in his pocket. Gordon came into the lobby.

"Hi Jack, I see you've found the place. Follow me and I'll show you around."

The first stop was an office with six desks loaded with computers. Only four were occupied. All of the girls looked up and smiled when they came into the room.

"We have overlapping hours. The first four operators start at eight with the fifth at eleven and the sixth at one. We do this because of the three hour differential to west coast time."

"How about shipping?"

"We have a late pickup from Fed-Ex. The truck gets here at six and is loaded out by six-thirty. The truck is usually full."

"Where do we go next?"

"The pick line where we put you to work."

Gordon led the way into the warehouse. There, a long conveyor was setup from one end of the warehouse to the other. The employees were gathered in groups of three or four, laughing and talking.

Gordon walked up to one group. "Spence, this is Jack Wexler. He'll be working on the pick line for the next couple of weeks to fill in for Bob and Gloria."

"Yeah, I forgot they were on vacation. Thanks, we'll need the help."

"I'll leave him with you. Tell him what's expected, will you?"

"Sure." Turning to Jack, he held out his hand. "I'm Joe Spencer, but everyone calls me Spence."

Jack shook his hand. "I appreciate this opportunity for a little work before I go back to school."

Spence took Jack to his station and explained the job. When the line started moving, Jack had a chance to see how the people ahead of him on the line were quickly looking at the pick list, getting the items and scanning the barcode with a wand.

At the end of the day, Jack had learned nothing about the nature of the losses. It was all he could do to keep up with the moving belt of containers. He was charged with picking from seven different stock items. Sometimes several pick sheets in a row would not call for any of his stuff so he was able to take a rest. Other times, he would have to delay the line. This brought a roar from the other pickers.

"Hey, keep up the pace." One of them yelled, "You're in my pocket now."

He knew that. With the piece-rate bonus, any delay would cost them all.

On the second day, the picking chore became more instinctive so he didn't have to delay the line even once. Still, even with the extra time, he could detect no way for the huge loss to occur on the pick line. However, on the third day, he detected a curious thing. The order numbers were mostly serial with only a few exceptions of one or two numbers in sequence. But the odd thing was that occasionally, instead of ten-digit order numbers beginning with several zeros, he spotted numbers starting in double nines.

That night he met with Gordon. "Well, I think I know how the theft is done."

"Damn! So soon?"

"Is that fresh coffee I smell?"

"Grace is fixing it now."

"Okay on the coffee. Now, as to the theft, it appears that your software has a backdoor."

"What the hell is that?"

"The software engineer created a method so he could check one portion of the process without changing the bookkeeping bottom line. He either did it to steal from you or, perhaps he planned on deleting the code after he checked out the operation but either forgot or was transferred or laid-off before he could complete the job."

The coffee arrived on a tray with a plate of cookies.

"I still don't understand."

Jack pointed to his mouth full of cookie and held up his hand to signal. He downed a sip of coffee.

"Good cookies. Okay, here's how it's done. Someone in the department that receives the orders takes an order from one of the thieving stores, but does not allow the computer generated order number. She manually alters the number by adding a double nine as the first two digits. The store name and address are legitimate. The pick sheet is generated and items scanned against it. The items are verified by shipping and out the door they go. But, since this is a test mode, nothing is deleted from the record of the computer inventory and no real invoice is issued to the customer."

"Damn! And you found this out in just three days?"

"Well, I think I know the how part but I don't know who. The next step is to identify the person generating the double nine orders. Then we scare the shit out of her and get her to name her partners."

"Hey, Jack, the pick sheet carries the initials of the person taking the order. The computer tabulates this data for bonus payment."

"I also noticed all orders are being shipped by either regular Fed-Ex or Fed-Ex ground."

"That's right. Local orders go by Fed-Ex ground."

"Get the cooperation of the Fed-Ex people first thing tomorrow. See if they will divert the special pick-up and have all packages delivered to your garage. We will open the boxes and pull all the pick sheets with the double-nine order number and seal up the legitimate boxes for shipment. Oh, yeah, have it all video taped."

"When do we get the police involved?"

"I'll call Colonel Reynolds tonight."

Jack didn't go to work at Vermilion the next day. Instead, he filled in the FBI and Miami PD on how the theft was done. Each promised to have an officer at Gordon's garage to witness the opening of the packages. After double-checking with Fed-Ex about the package pick-up, he stopped by the Sheriff's sub-station and his Colonel, John Reynolds.

"Come on in, Jack. Thanks for the heads-up call last night. Way to go, man. Gordon Clemmons called and absolutely gushed, he was so pleased. He was most delighted with the quick work. He still can't figure how you spotted what they were doing so soon."

"Pure luck, John."

"I know better. If you ever need a permanent job, you know where to look."

"My part is over now. The real work is proving who was involved in the theft and who got the money. I'll bet the software developer had something to do with it. With a ten digit order number and a thousand orders a day, it would take a little less than thirty-thousand years to use up the range of numbers. I suspect the software guy because ten is way too many digits."

John reached for a calculator, pushed buttons and exclaimed: "Let's see, figuring they work seven days a week and a thousand orders a day—damn, twenty-seven thousand years and change. How did you do that so fast?"

"All engineers are accustomed to estimating. It's a matter of rounding off and keeping account of the decimal point."

Jack arrived just in time to help unloaded the Fed-Ex truck. Gordon had a couple of eight-foot folding tables set up in his garage.

"Jack, this is Special Agent Turnbull from the FBI and Sergeant Flores from Miami PD. Jack is a Special Deputy Investigator on released duty from the Sheriff's Department. I believe you all have met my wife. She'll be taking a video of this."

After shaking hands all round, Jack took a box cutter and started opening the boxes. Gordon and the officers pulled the invoices and resealed the proper shipments. Out of two hundred and sixty boxes, fifteen were with double nine invoices.

Gordon leafed through the stack of invoices. "Hey guys, it's just as I expected, all of these are bound for franchise stores."

Jack answered. "You'll be opening up shipments for some days in order to find how many stores are involved."

Turnbull cautioned, "Look, we must keep this quiet until we get the US Attorney to hit all the thieving stores with search warrants. Since interstate commerce is involved, it'll probably be a federal matter."

Jack interrupted, "Agent Turnbull, the real culprit is the software developer. There is no way the office people, especially the girls in the order-taking department, could find the back door by themselves. As soon as you've named the stores, you must nail the people who developed the software. It's my bet there are other similar companies in the same fix."

"Damn! You may be right."

"Gordon, it looks like you don't need me anymore. I'll come by here and pick up my fee tomorrow evening."

"No, I'll meet you for lunch at the Domino Steak House at noon if that meets with your plans."

"That'll be fine but expect to buy me the best steak in the house."

chapter 22

HE GOT TO DOMINO'S at twelve fifteen. Gordon was already seated at a booth. Jack slid in on the opposite side.

Jack nodded at the bag resting next to Gordon. "Is that for me?"

"Yeah. I included a digital camera as a bonus. Three point one megapixels and shirt-pocket size. You got a computer?"

"A laptop. No engineering student would be without one."

"You can load your pictures directly to the computer and copy them to a CD. It's really handy."

"Thanks, I'll give it a try."

The waiter came over to take their order. After he left, Gordon grinned, "Hey, I thought you were going to hit me with the biggest steak on the menu and here you order a sandwich."

"Man, you don't know my aunt's cooking. With three-egg omelets, waffles or pancakes, and several kinds of meats for breakfast followed by piles of food for lunch and dinner, the lady simply does not know how to stop cooking. So, when I eat out, I try to go light."

After they had finished lunch, Gordon passed the bag over to Jack. "Here's the money we agreed on. But I would appreciate it if you could do me a favor for the next couple of days. I'll pick up the expenses."

"Sure, you've got another four days on the week contract."

"My wife Rose's sister Martha lives in Venezuela. She and her husband, Reverend Mark Daggett are missionaries there. They have this twenty-year-old daughter who was getting too romantic with a local boy so they sent her to live with us. She needs someone to take her dancing instead of moping around the house feeling sad."

"I'd be honored, Gordon. Just tell her to dress to impress and I'll do the same. I'll pick her up at eight for dinner and dancing."

After a very good meal of barbecued chicken at Mama Anita's, Lucy kept silent seated next to Jack in the car. When they arrived at Swan's Inn,

Jack got out and opened the door for her. They waited for the valet parking attendant to give him a claim check before entering the club.

They could hear a soft *bossa* as they were shown to their table. Soon a waiter came over to take their drink order.

"Miss?"

"Rum, please, make it a double. And a diet Pepsi on the side."

"And you, sir?"

"Ginger ale, rocks, with a twist over shaved ice."

After the waiter left, Jack rose and extended his hand.

"Dance?"

They made their way to the dance floor. The bossa ended and a cha-cha began. Lucy did not even pause but continued with the different tempo and dance. It soon became quite clear that Lucy could really dance. When they finally returned to their table, the ice had melted in Jack's ginger ale.

Lucy downed half of the rum and followed it with the Pepsi. "Damn, it's too cold. Pepsi should be served warm."

"Mine's warm too but plenty wet."

Lucy finished the rum as the band started a slow forties ballad. Jack asked, "Again?"

"Sure, we either dance or stay here and be put to sleep by the music."

Jack was not sure whether it was the rum or the music. Lucy was definitely mellow as she molded her body to his. As the number continued, she started kissing him on the neck. When the band started a rumba, Lucy came alive again. After two hours of non-stop dancing, Jack was ready to call it a night. When the latest number finished, he escorted her to their table.

"Jack, I don't know about you, but I'm tired and a little hungry. Let's go find a donut shop. I want donuts and coffee. Can you find such a place?"

Jack paid the tab with his credit card. Valet parking got his Cadillac for him. He continued down Biscayne until he saw the neon sign advertising, Krispy Kreme.

"Eat in or drive through?"

"In, of course."

Jack ordered a cup of coffee and a donut. Lucy, however, ordered a pint of milk and a dozen jelly-filled. At their booth, Lucy opened up for the first time.

Pointing at Jack, "Ha, ha, look, on your nose. You've got some of the sugar from the donut there and around your mouth. Messy, messy!"

"Well, you've got a milk mustache and jelly on your mouth."

She got a paper napkin, dipped it in her glass of water and wiped Jack's mouth.

"Here, let me have that. I'll return the favor now and clean you up."

Lucy pursed her lips and thrust her chin forward. She closed her eyes and allowed her tongue to protrude and follow the damp cloth.

Back in the car, Jack asked, "Shall we call it a night?"

"Maybe. Do you have anything else in mind?"

Jack didn't answer to her suggestive question. Lucy turned on the radio and found one of the Cuban music stations. It was a song she knew. She sang along but not well. The next three songs were familiar to her also.

She remarked, "Jack, how do I set the button for this station. I like their music, you know?"

Jack reached over to the radio. "I'll set you up on button six. So, remember, your station is on number six." He pushed button one. "Now get your station back."

She pushed six and was delighted that a new song was being played. It was pure salsa. "I do not know this one, but it's really good. Listen to the beat. Don't you want to dance when you hear music like this?"

Jack glanced over, her feet weren't moving but her body was. First chance he got he would take her to La Fiesta where every number is hot, hot, hot.

"Jack, where is the Disney World? Is it near Miami?"

"Two hundred and thirty miles. It's not too far. It would take four hours or so depending on how many stops we make."

"I want to go there. I will tell Grace, she will permit this if I insist. We will go tomorrow. We can leave before lunch and be back in three or four days. This is true, yes?"

Jack noticed that in her excitement she was speaking English but her phrasing was Spanish. "Yes, we could leave on one day, spend two days in Orlando attending the attractions and return the fourth day with three nights in a hotel there."

"I will wake her up when we get back to the house."

"Give me a call, I'll give you the number at my Aunt's house."

There was an awkward moment at her door when he vacillated on whether to kiss her or not. He waited too long.

In his room at his aunt's, Jack removed his tux and carefully hung both the jacket and trousers. He stripped down in preparation for his shower and stowed his shirt, undershirt, shorts and socks in the laundry bag. He placed his shoes in the closet in a row with the others. He stowed his tie, suspenders and cummerbund and placed his shirt studs and cuff links in a small box in the top drawer.

The phone rang. Jack quickly grabbed the extension in his room before it rang again.

"Hello. This is Jack."

"We go to Disney World tomorrow, spend three nights and return. And, best of all, Aunt Grace isn't going with us."

"Great, be packed and ready, we'll leave right after lunch."

"Aunt Grace said she would get us hotel reservations."

There was a sameness of the scenery on the Florida Turnpike. Every hour or so they stopped to use the restroom or get gas or a soft drink.

Lucy couldn't keep her hands off the radio. Finally, Jack switched to the CD player. The six-disk changer filled the car with some of the finest jazz in the world. Lucy pouted for a while. During some of the lighter guitar trio passages by Ronny Escheté, Lucy nodded off. How could she, he thought, here is one of the finest seven-string jazz guitar players in the world and she sleeps.

As he left Kissimmee, he pulled out the slip of paper with the directions to their hotel. The Beverly Crest name had a ring of luxury. Watch it be a dump, he thought.

Lucy roused when he slowed on the off-ramp. "Where are we?"

"We're here. This is Orlando, the city of magic, Disney, Epcot and Universal. The vacation spot for the entire world. And there is our hotel."

"Where?"

"Ahead, on the right."

Jack parked the Caddy under a canopy. Both got out, Jack to check in and Lucy to stretch.

The girl at the desk was all smiles. "Help you, sir?"

"Yes, Jack Wexler. I have a reservation for two."

"Wexler. Now let me see. Oh, here it is. Two double beds, balcony facing south."

"No, the reservation was for two singles with adjoining door."

"Sorry, Mr. Wexler, I can only go by what's in the computer."

"Then move us to the kind of rooms we want."

"You heard the news? UAW has gone on strike at some plant that makes transmissions. That shut down the whole company. Just drive down the street, they all have Michigan tags. I guarantee there's not a room left in town or even within a hundred miles."

Lucy walked up. "Did you get the rooms?"

"We've got a problem. We have only one room with two beds."

The counter girl interrupted, "They're both queen size."

"Can we go somewhere else?"

"Tell her."

The desk clerk retold the entire story.

"I guess we'll have to take it. It'll be like camping out. Oh, you will be a good boy, won't you Jack?"

The clerk pushed a form for Jack to fill out. After making an imprint of his credit card, they were issued key cards.

"You can go up to the room while I get the luggage and park the car."

Jack went to the Caddy and started putting their luggage on the sidewalk. The bellboy rushed over with his polished brass carrier.

"Is there valet parking?"

"No sir, park anywhere there's an empty space."

"Is there a shuttle to Disney, Universal or Epcot?"

"Sure, every half-hour. Just speak to the bell captain."

After parking, Jack followed the bellboy to the room. He could hear the sound of the shower. He tipped the bellboy and started unpacking his clothing. He picked the top drawer and the left side of the closet. As he finished, he heard the shower stop. He kicked off his shoes, turned on the TV and flopped on the bed.

"Jack. Jack!"

He turned off the TV and walked over to the bathroom door. "Yes."

"Get my robe, please. The towels are much too small to wrap around."

Jack opened first one, then the other. He found her terry robe."

"I found it. Open the door."

"Promise you'll turn your head away."

"Okay, promise."

She timidly opened the door to see Jack; his head turned away with his arm extended holding the robe. As she reached for it, she could see his face in a full-length mirror.

She quickly snatched the robe and slammed the door. "Oh, Jack, how could you?"

"Hey, I didn't know until I saw you in the mirror."

"Well, did you get a good look?"

"Not really. I'd like to see more."

"Another time. Well, anyway, we got that out of the way."

"What?"

"The nude thing. Now, let me see you."

He smiled, "Another time."

Jack grabbed his own robe and took a shower. When he exited the bathroom, Lucy was curled up on one of the beds asleep.

Jack got out his new camera and instruction book. As he read, he fiddled with the buttons. Finally, he took a flash shot of Lucy. He walked over to the window and took a picture of the parking lot. Satisfied he could handle the camera, he put the battery on charge, curled up on his bed and went to sleep.

He stirred and woke when he heard the toilet flush. He looked up in time to see Lucy, fully dressed, leaving the bathroom. "Sorry I woke you but I had to pee."

Jack looked at his watch. "I'm hungry, how about you?"

"Famished."

"Want to call room service or go to the dining room?"

"Dining room. Hurry and get dressed."

The menu was limited but the food was good. It was the sort of food that office workers chose in the serving line at the company cafeteria.

Lucy didn't talk much at dinner. Jack made several efforts but Lucy was subdued. Oh, she listened to Jack's stories and even laughed at the right places, but she didn't share anything of her own.

On the elevator ride to their room, Jack asked, "You've been very quiet."

"I've been thinking of doing the sex with you later."

"That's nice."

"I'm serious, Jack. I have not had the sex for five years."

"Let's see, you're twenty now. That means you were fifteen."

"Okay, it was three years or maybe two. But it seems like a long time ago. Tell me, do you know how is it possible to do the sex and not get pregnant?"

Before he could answer, the elevator door opened at their floor.

CHAPTER
23

A S SOON AS THEY ENTERED their room, Jack took Lucy by the shoulders and spoke forcefully.

"Look, we're both in this room as a result of a mistake. I have a trust to keep to both Grace and Gordon. You are a beautiful and desirable woman, however, we will not be doing anything intimate. Do you understand?"

Her lower lip started quivering. A tear formed and dropped to her cheek.

"I'm sorry, Jack. I just thought we.... I'm sorry. I'll be good. I promise."

"Okay, we're still friends. Now, the shuttle bus leaves at eight-twenty. So, if we're to have enough time in the morning to get dressed and have breakfast, we'll need to get to bed early. We can watch television for a while or if you want, we can hit the club across the street for some dancing. It's up to you."

"How about swimming? The hotel has a pool just outside. I saw it when we came in."

"Okay, you can change in the bathroom and I'll change here."

Lucy rummaged in her suitcase for her bathing suit while Jack found his. When she had finished dressing she held open her robe for Jack to see.

"How do you like my swimsuit?"

"Very nice. You'll draw a crowd with that."

In an hour they were back in their room, a little tired and ready for bed.

Jack hit the shower to get the chlorine from the pool washed off. He removed his swimsuit while in the shower, rinsed it out and draped it over the shower curtain rail. After toweling off, he put on his boxer shorts and left the bathroom.

Lucy was wearing her robe with the wet suit wadded up in her hand. She quickly entered the bathroom. Jack could hear the door lock snap followed by the sound of the shower.

Jack turned on the television to a sports channel. He really wasn't paying attention—his mind was elsewhere. He was vaguely aware of the jai alai scores as he thought about the mess he was in with Lucy. He heard the whine of the hair dryer. Lucy would be out soon. Reaching for the remote, he turned the television off.

She left the bathroom and struck a pose for Jack. Her arms were out-stretched with palms up. One leg was slightly bent at the knee. She had left her robe in the bathroom.

"Ta-da! I just wanted you to see what you will be missing."

She slowly turned around with her arms still outstretched.

"You can always change your mind, you know."

"Please, just get your clothes on. You promised you'd be good."

Without comment she began dressing. First, she put on a short skirt, then a thin blouse. No bra and no panties. She slipped into her high heel shoes.

"Now, do you have any of the rubber thingies that go on your thingie?"

"Do you mean a condom?"

"Yes. Do you have such a condom?"

"Of course."

"I would like one, please. No, I would like two, if you don't mind."

"Why? Where are you going?"

"I am going to the club across the street to find someone who will give me the sex."

"With no bra or panties?"

"Yes, I want to be ready."

This really put Jack in a bind. He knew the kind of characters that were out there. She, however, was totally naïve. So, he decided to take the avenue that kept control with him.

"Hold on, I'll go with you. Just introduce me as your cousin. I'll be there in case you need me. Okay?"

She thought for a minute. She really didn't want to leave. Her action was a ploy designed to get Jack to relent. So now her bluff was called.

"Sure, I'll wait. Maybe I'll put my underwear on. Don't want to cause a riot."

In a few minutes both were ready to go.

They crossed the highway at the traffic light and walked the half block back to the club. When they entered, Jack knew this was not a place they should be. The country music band was backing up a girl singer wailing out a nondescript song about a man who had done her wrong.

They found an empty table. The waitress came over, dumped the ashtray on the floor and took a swipe at the surface of the table with a dirty rag.

"Gitcha anythin'?"

"Seven-Up over ice. She'll have rum and cola. No ice with the cola warm."

She turned to Lucy.

"Is that right, no ice and warm?"

"Yes."

The waitress left. Jack waved his hand in a sweeping motion across the room.

"Well, Lucy, of all the men here, do you see anyone you want?"

"Let's just finish our drink and leave. This place scares me."

"You mean none of these guys measure up? How about the one at the end of the bar?"

"Oh Jack. Stop teasing!"

The man at the microphone announced the end of the set with the band returning in fifteen minutes.

"Uh oh!"

"What?"

Jack scooted his chair back about six inches. "Trouble coming. See the three guys walking our way?"

The lead badass sported a wide grin. He looked back to assure himself that he had company with him. The guy behind prodded him in the ribs, urging him on. Each was carrying a long-necked bottle of Bud.

"Hey, y'all down here from up north or sumpin?"

Jack grinned and answered. "No, we're from Homestead. Just up here to see the sights."

The second one giggled. "See the sights. Did'ja hear that?"

The grin disappeared from badass number one. "Air we some of the sights you were lookin' t' see? We don't like being made fun of."

Calmly, Jack replied. "Look, friend, we were sitting here minding our own business. So just back off."

Badass number two chimed in. "We don't take no orders from some sissy from Miami."

Jack moved his arm so a quarter coin, left on the table by the waitress making change, fell to the floor. He bent over to retrieve it but pulled his pistol from the ankle holster instead. Hiding his pistol at his side, he stood with his chair between him and the first badass.

"Now, it seems you folks find it fun to bait visitors. But we don't think it's fun at all. Since you are armed with an empty beer bottle, I will put a hole right between your eyes. I am an off-duty deputy sheriff from Dade County and I am armed."

Jack brought his hand around showing the pistol.

Number two and three backed away and returned to the bar. Number one just stood there, frozen in place. The color had left his face.

"Well. Are you going to use that bottle and get a hole in your head or are you going back to the bar too?"

As he backed away, he retorted, "I'm goin' t' call the cops on you."

After he left, Lucy put her hand on Jack's arm. Jack could tell that she was shaking.

"Jack, let's leave. I really don't like this place now."

"Finish your drink. We can't let them think they're running us off."

She downed her drink in one motion.

As they neared the door, badass number one yelled after them. "I called the cops. They'll be here soon so you'd better hurry."

When they left the club, two powerful six-cell flashlights were aimed at his eyes.

"You in the blue blazer, put your hands up."

Jack put his hands up. "I am a deputy sheriff from Dade County on holiday. My service weapon is in an ankle holster. My badge and ID are in my pocket."

"Get the weapon."

One of the officers approached and retrieved Jack's pistol.

"Got it."

The cop turned off the flashlight.

"Okay, slowly remove your wallet."

With glacial speed, Jack pulled his wallet.

"Check his ID Ernie."

Ernie shined his flashlight on the contents of the wallet.

"Looks okay to me, Jesse."

"What's your name, deputy?"

"Jack Wexler."

"Look, Jack, we got a call that a tourist was flashing a gun and scaring the customers."

"Three men, holding empty long-necked beer bottles like they were clubs, started hassling me and my girlfriend. I identified myself as a deputy sheriff, showed them my weapon, and told them to back off."

"Jesse, his story checks out as far as I am concerned."

"Yeah, we get a few complaints each week. Usually tourists call in with a similar story. So, what do you want us to do, deputy?"

"We're only in town for a couple of days. After all, it wasn't as though we swapped punches. Only words were passed. If you want to roust them till morning for public drunkenness, it's up to you."

"I don't know, Ernie. With the paperwork and all, it don't seem worth it. Oh, and, give him back his wallet and piece."

When the cop called his pistol 'a piece', it got Jack's attention.

"Marines?"

"Yeah."

"Semper Fi, buddy! I left the corps three years ago."

"Jack, can we please go back to the hotel? There's a chill in the air."

"Is that all, officers?"

"Yeah, sorry for the bother."

They walked the half-block to the light, crossed the street and returned to the hotel.

They left the hotel at ten o'clock on the morning of the third day. Lucy was bubbling with excitement over her experiences at Epcot and Disney World. She had several shopping bags full of souvenirs. As they traveled the highway, she reminded Jack of one thrill after another.

"Oh, Jack. I am so glad we didn't have the sex. We would have just stayed at the hotel and I would have missed everything."

"Are you hungry? There's an exit up ahead where we can get lunch."

"Yes. I want the hamburger."

Jack pulled into the Wendy's parking lot. They went inside and ordered.

The rest of the way back to Homestead, Lucy slept. Although Jack enjoyed her company, he was glad for the spate of quiet. As the traffic started backing up, Lucy woke.

"Where are we?"

"You'll be home in a few minutes."

"So soon?"

"You've slept for quite a while."

"Is this all, Jack?"

"What do you mean?"

"Will you leave me at the home of my aunt and never call or visit?"

"I'm afraid so. I was to escort you to Orlando and see you safely back."

"It's not fair."

"In a normal situation, I would gladly have made love to you but I have an obligation to Grace and Gordon."

"But, it's so hard to meet boys."

"Don't be so eager. You'll start college soon. Believe me, there'll be plenty of boys then."

"I will need the thingies?"

"Yes. You may buy condoms at any drug store."

She remained silent for the rest of the trip.

CHAPTER
24

Gloria Stein Gault and Roxie Stein Arnold

H E TOOK THE JOB but he wasn't looking forward to it. Mrs. Pinson from last year suggested that two of her friends from her apartment building in Manhattan hire him as escort to explore the Miami scene. So, the sisters, Gloria and Roxie, widows in their mid to late fifties, gave him a call. The job was for only a week and short hours, but he quoted two thousand dollars in an effort to scare them away. They didn't balk at the price. So now he was stuck with the job.

Jack met his clients at the airport and drove them to their hotel. They had a room at the *Atlantic Breeze*, a nice hotel but a cut below the ones on Miami Beach. He followed them and their luggage to their room to find out what his duties were going to be.

"Now, Jackie—is it okay if I call you that?"

Jack nodded.

"That's what our friend Mavis Pinson called you. Well, anyways, my sister Roxie collects seashells and those funny looking snails you have in the Everglades. And I like to do a little gambling—you know, bingo, dog and horse races and that funny game the Cubans like. What is that game? You know—they play it with baskets and bounce a ball off a wall. What is that game?"

"Jai Alai?"

"Oh, Jackie, you're so smart!"

Roxie mumbled something.

"What's that, Roxie?"

"Gloria, I'm ready for lunch. When do we eat?"

"We had that sandwich on the plane."

"But it was only a dinky little thing. It was a thin slice of ham and a smear of cream cheese on a small dinner roll. Two bites and it was gone. I ate my banana, though."

"Well, there you are."

"Mrs. Gault, can we settle on just what you want me to do for you."

"Just call me Gloria and call my sister Roxie. Oh, yes, back to your duties—we want to visit places and see things. Don't we Roxie?"

"The banana was really small and the bag of pretzels I could hide in my brassier. Well the whole bag lunch was too small if you know what I mean. Now in the old days you could get a really nice meal in coach when Eastern was flying those Electra planes. But Eastern went in the toilet, you know."

"Roxie, just answer the question."

"Oh, my goodness. What was the question?"

"Dear, Jack wants us to tell him what his duties will be."

"Oh, just tell him we want to go to some places. Isn't that right?"

Jack let out a sigh and settled deeper into the chair. This would be a long week. He would earn every dollar of his fee.

That afternoon they had an early dinner so they could visit the dog races. Their usual bet was five dollars. At the end of the night, Gloria was up twenty-eight and Roxie down fifty-five. But the value of the fun they had was a far greater win.

On the way back to the hotel, they stopped at Krispy Kreme for donuts and coffee. They both ate four—Jack just had coffee. He dropped them off and headed back to Homestead to get a good night's sleep.

They were waiting in the lobby when Jack arrived. They had done their homework. Gloria had a list of seashell stores. They started near the hotel and continued on until they neared West Palm Beach.

Roxie was hunting the shells of a large snail for her collection. Each hummock or island in the Everglades has a snail with a unique coloring. There are literally hundreds of variations. Her collection was scant with only thirty or so shells. Roxie tried to show Jack how they differed with their various color bands. But Jack failed to understand the attraction she had for such minor differences.

They turned south toward Homestead and Florida City traveling parallel to the direction they had taken north. It was only when they came to Florida City did Roxie find what she had been looking for. She was able to almost double her collection. As Jack drove back to their hotel, she continued to examine her treasure. Jack took a different route back.

When they passed by a Bingo parlor, Gloria squealed with delight.

"Here, Jack, stop, stop, stop! This is what I was looking for. When do they open?"

Jack had slowed the SUV enough so he could turn in the parking lot of the Bingo parlor. "Wait here. I'll check on their hours."

He came back in a moment. "It's open now. They start at ten in the morning and go until ten at night. Want to get something to eat and play until closing?"

"There's a burger place on the corner. How about you get a couple of sandwiches and Pepsi's and bring them to us?"

"Fair enough. Go in, get as many Bingo cards as you can handle and play on. Uh… Roxie. I think you can leave your shells in the car. They'll be safe, I promise."

Roxie put her shells back in the SUV and quick-stepped toward the door. She looked back to Gloria. "Hurry, we don't want to miss the start of the next game."

Gloria gave Jack a twenty for the food and followed her sister into the Bingo parlor.

Jack was back in ten minutes. There was a pretty girl on the door.

"How many?"

"What?"

"Cards. How many cards do you want to play? They'll be calling another game in a minute."

He pointed to the sisters. "I'm with them."

"Oh. Are you related?"

"No, just the hired hand."

"I'm Judy."

"My name is Jack. Have you worked here long?"

"Family business. I've been hanging around here all my life. Since our parents passed away, my sister and brother and his wife have kept the place open."

"Are you here all day?"

"Just got here. My sister opens the place up and stays until school lets out when she has to be home for her kids. Then I take over 'till we close up. My brother and his wife work on the weekends."

"That sort of ruins your social life."

"Except for Saturday night my social life is next to zero. It's not like I get to meet anyone my age working here. They're all over fifty at least."

They started calling the numbers for the next game. Jack took the two bags of sandwiches and Pepsis and set them on the table. They were so engrossed with the game, they didn't notice. Jack got a Pepsi from the machine and wandered over to talk to Judy again.

When a game was over, Judy handed out the prize and sold more game cards. It only took a few minutes. Many of the players took advantage of the break and headed for the restrooms.

The lady calling the numbers looked to be a hundred. Too much of the Florida sun will do that to you. He remarked as much to Judy.

"If you think she looks old, you should see the lady who calls the first shift."

The numbers droned on. As closing time approached, Jack made arrangements to meet Judy later. She had an apartment above the Bingo parlor.

On the way back to their hotel, Roxie was excited over winning a punch bowl set. Jack didn't have the heart to tell her that it would cost more than its worth just to ship it back home.

He picked up Judy and drove less than a mile to a Latin dance club that always had a mixed Anglo and Latino crowd. The atmosphere was genial and a lot of fun. They danced until two then spent the rest of the night in Judy's apartment.

The next morning, Jack had just enough time to take a quick shower at his aunt's house, get dressed and meet his ladies at their hotel. As before, they were waiting in the lobby for him.

Jack helped them into the Caddy, closed the doors and got under the wheel. As he drove away from the hotel he asked, "Well, what's up for today?"

"We had so much fun playing Bingo, we decided to do it again only this time we'll make a full day of it. And tonight we'll have a nice dinner at an upscale restaurant. How does that sound?"

"It's your vacation."

Judy had a smile for him and a complaint. "How do you look so fresh and alert? After all, you didn't get any more sleep than I did."

"I guess it's the Marine Corps training."

"Yeah, I bet."

Gloria was waving at him to get his attention. Jack walked over.

"How about you just pick us up here at three? There's no need for you to hang around. That is, unless you want to get lucky with that girl over there." She smiled and winked. "Oh, I know how you young people are."

He smiled and winked in return. "Gloria, whatever do you mean?"

"Get out of here. Do your laundry. Service the car. Buy a… whatever. We'll be ready at three or so."

As he left, he spoke to Judy. "They've let me go until three. Do you have plans for later?"

"Yes. I'll be catching up on my sleep you rat. Tomorrow night would be okay, though."

"Tomorrow night it is. I'll be here at ten."

He drove by the Sheriff Substation to check in with John Reynolds. It had been a few days since they had talked.

"Hello Jack. I was just thinking about you. Are you working?"

"Yeah. I've got this one-week contract ushering a couple of ladies around town. I will say this, they're really a hoot—can't get enough Bingo. Why? Do you have anything for me?"

"Yes, maybe in a week. Check by when you get free."

"Can you give me a hint?"

"Just come by—okay?"

Jack drove to his aunt's house and put a change of clothing in a small gym bag. She tried to feed him. He opted for a wrapped sandwich and coffee in a small thermos for later. He really couldn't refuse his aunt's beef pot roast.

He went to Shooter's Heaven and bought a box of fifty rounds. He hadn't shot his new weapon yet. He shot all fifty in the range just to keep in practice. His next stop was at a service station for an oil change. While there he had his tires rotated as well.

After he got all that done, he still had a couple of hours before he was to pick up the ladies. He stopped at a bookstore and picked up a couple of magazines. Then he drove to the Bingo parlor to wait outside and read his magazines. He really didn't mind the wait—they were paying him well for his time. Other than meeting Judy, the week was kind of boring.

He was relieved when the week was over. Jack helped pack all the prizes they had won at Bingo. Fed-Ex promised to have them delivered the next afternoon.

Jack took them to the airport and saw that their luggage was safely checked in. They said their good-byes at the ticket counter.

Candace Brock

"OKAY. Now what was the job you had for me when we talked last week?" Jack was standing at the door to Colonel Reynolds' office.

"Come in, Jack. I was going to call you. Take a seat, this'll take just a moment."

He dialed his phone, gave a few orders and cradled the receiver.

"Here's the deal, Jack. And, I should say, this comes from the Sheriff himself. His sister's daughter is married to Billy Brock. You may have seen the signs. He's big in real estate in the area. Specializes in housing developments, industrial parks and the like. A year or more ago, his wife Candace, separated and filed for divorce. The only thing holding up the divorce is the division of property. There have been several attempts on her life. Each time, Billy has an alibi. We believe he has hired the job done."

"I guess she'll need a bodyguard."

"Big time. The sheriff doesn't want anyone under his command to do this because he will be up for reelection this fall. His political enemies will try to make something of the family connection if he assigns deputies."

"How long?"

"The case has dragged on until the judge got pissed. He has taken proposals for property division from both parties. He will make final disposition himself and grant the divorce in… uh, ten days. After the divorce is finalized, half will be gone. There will be no need to have her killed then."

"Unless he wants revenge."

"Yeah. That's a thought."

"It's not a solo job."

"I have arranged for two female Miami PD officers to take vacation. They're with Candy now."

"Candy?"

"Short for Candace."

"Oh. And the pay?"

"There's the rub. You only get paid if she survives. She'll pay you out of the divorce settlement."

"Five thousand a week?"

"Hey, she's my boss's niece!"

"Okay, five thousand for the ten days then. That's five hundred a day or twenty dollars an hour. I could make that much as a bellboy."

John got out his calculator. "Oh, I see. You figured on a twenty-four hour day. I guess that would be fair."

"When do I start?"

"Now." He wrote the address on a post-it note and handed it to Jack. "The house is big enough for the four of you. Pack enough for ten days. Oh, yeah, I know your ways. Try to cut out the romance part, will you?"

Jack just grinned.

The house was in Coral Gables. Not quite Cocoanut Grove but close enough. From the front, it had to have at least six bedrooms plus servant's quarters. There were two cars in the circular driveway. Jack parked on the street, got his suitcase and made his way to the door.

He sat his suitcase down and rang the bell. He could hear the sound of loud conversation inside. Soon, the door opened to the extent allowed by the chain.

A husky voice came from behind the door. "Are you Jack Wexler?"

"Yes I am."

"Show some ID."

Jack got out his badge and ID card. He passed the card through the door opening. The door closed for a moment. He heard the chain rattle then the door opened wide.

"Come on in." She looked around. "Where's you car?"

"On the street in front."

"Good. I'm Charlene and my partner is Wendy. They filled me in on you. We're all back in the kitchen. Follow me."

She had a short haircut, broad shoulders and looked like she had been working out in the weight room. There were few feminine qualities about her.

In the kitchen, Jack met Wendy and Mrs. Brock. Wendy looked nothing like her partner. She was had a pretty face and nice figure. Mrs. Brock, however, looked like she hadn't slept in a week. There were dark circles under her red-rimmed eyes. He guessed Candace Brock to be in her mid-forties and probably attractive with a little makeup.

Charlene took charge. "What we'll do is sleep in shifts so there's always two awake at a given time." She caught herself and added, "If that's okay with you."

"Sounds good to me. Where do I bunk?"

Charlene frowned when Wendy jumped up. "I'll show him."

Mrs. Brock explained with a forced smile, "I had to let the housekeeper go when Billy emptied out my checking account. So we'll just pretend we're camping out."

Jack followed Wendy up the stairs to his room.

"Now, you'll use the bath next door and the rest of us will share the other two."

Tossing his suitcase on the bed, Jack asked, "I'd like to see the other rooms."

They went down the hall with Wendy pointing to each room and listing the occupant. Jack briefly looked in each of them. They went back to the kitchen.

"We'll have to cover all the windows. A shadow cast on the sheer curtains will give away the fact that someone is there. Don't want to invite a shooter to aim at the shadow, now do we? I'm going to look around the outside of the house to see if there's an easy access to the building. I see that only Charlene is armed. Wendy, you should be armed at all times as well. I noticed that one of the bedrooms has a pair of twin beds. Mrs. Brock, you ought to be in one of those beds with either of the female officers in the room with you at night. Place some pillows under the covers of your regular bed to suggest that you're sleeping there. Any questions."

He made eye contact with each of them.

"Wendy, get your weapon. And Charlene, lock the door behind me."

Jack slowly walked around the building. There were three entrances: The front door, the door from the kitchen, and a side door leading to a covered area that once was a carport now converted to a solarium with glass all around thus blocking in the side door. The flat roof over the solarium was a way to three second-story windows if the intruder had a ladder. He checked in the garage for a ladder—there was only a six foot one. There were a few tools scattered about on a workbench. Jack picked up two short pieces of two-by-four boards, hammer, drill motor with a set of bits and a small box of ten-penny nails. With his arms full, he went back into the house.

Charlene opened the door. "Good grief, what's all that for?"

Jack grinned. "Live and learn Charlene. I didn't spend almost three years in engineering school for nothing. You want to help?"

She grinned. "Sure, all us butch types favor power tools. Put me to work."

Jack first blocked the rear and side doors by nailing a two-by-four wooden block on the floor butting against the doors. Then he drilled holes in the windows at the point where the top sash overlaps the bottom one to accept the nails as locking pins. Now, the only way a window could be opened would be to pull the pins from the inside. Charlene caught on right away and helped by drilling the holes in the windows. When they were finished, there was only one entrance to the house. Also, in an emergency, all they would need to do is pull a couple of pins to open a window.

On their way back to the kitchen, Charlene confessed, "By the way, Jack, Wendy and I are not an item. We were talking when you went out. She's sort of attracted to you."

Jack grinned. "Hey, I appreciate the heads-up. Glad to know there's no competition."

She grinned back. "Don't bet on it."

"My job right now is the protection of Mrs. Brock."

"Yeah, first things first."

When they got to the kitchen, Jack noted that Wendy was armed.

"Mrs. Brock, I want you to stay out of the kitchen. You should spend as little time as possible in any first floor room that has a window. Just relax in the library. There's a TV, plenty of books and a couple of tables."

"I don't know about that. Who will cook? How will you find everything?"

"We'll make out just fine. Go to the library now. It's too dangerous here."

She grabbed her coffee and went down the hall muttering something about being a prisoner in her own home.

Wendy stood. "I guess I should go with her."

"Good idea."

Charlene and Jack sat at the table drinking coffee. A few minutes passed. Charlene broke the silence. "When they told me you were coming to help I really thought we could handle things without you. I was wrong, stud. I've been on the force for ten years but I've got to admit, you've taught me a few things."

"Charlene, can you think of anything more we need to do?"

"What we need to do is hide out someplace. We're a fixed target here, but she won't hear of it."

"Some people have a feeling of safety with familiar surroundings. It's the old 'devil you know' reasoning."

"Yeah, I'm like that too."

The doorbell rang.

"Charlene, I'll answer the door. You and Wendy keep out of sight. We don't want it known how many are here."

Charlene stationed herself just off the entry hall. Wendy stayed with Mrs. Brock in the library. Jack took his badge and hooked it on his pocket. Jack opened the door with the chain still attached. It was a Miami PD uniformed officer.

"Please state your business."

"I'm officer Browning. Who are you?"

"Deputy Sheriff Jack Wexler. Now answer me, what do you want?"

"I'd like to speak to officer Torres if she's here."

Charlene came from behind the door. "That's me, Jack. Joe is my riding partner."

Jack stepped back.

"Hey, hoss. What the hell you doin' here?"

"Just drivin' by and saw the Caddy at the curb. Thought I would check on you."

"Is the whole shift checking on me?"

"Well, uh… yeah, I guess so."

She laughed. "You ass holes. Didn't you think we could handle the job?"

"If you're okay, I'll scoot on out of here."

"Bye. Have a good shift."

She closed and locked the door.

"I really love those guys. I'd take a bullet for any of them."

Wendy came in. "Who was that? Browning, I'll bet."

"Yeah, he's like a brother to me."

It was getting dark. Jack rummaged around in the pantry for something for dinner. He found a jar of pasta sauce and a box of spaghetti. In the freezer he located a pound of hamburger. He started the water, put the burger in the microwave to defrost and found the Parmesan cheese—they would have everything but the garlic bread. When Wendy saw what Jack had gathered, she began putting together a salad.

After dinner, Jack and Charlene washed the dishes and put them up. They all gathered in the library den for television. Jack found a book he was supposed to read in High School and settled down to finally complete the assignment.

They had decided on three-hour shifts to take care of the hours between eleven and eight. Jack volunteered for the middle one—from two to five in the morning. So he retired at nine in order to be alert for his shift. He loaded the coffee maker so all he would have to do is turn it on.

Jack was up and dressed by the time Charlene knocked on the door. Other than having to make a new pot of coffee, his shift was uneventful. He would have to have a talk with Charlene about having the coffee ready.

He woke up Wendy at six giving her an extra hour of sleep. Jack took his shower and dressed for the day. In the kitchen, he mixed up pancake batter. Wendy joined him for the feast.

After taking a few bites, she put down her fork. "Jack, you're a woman's dream."

"How so?"

"Where did you learn to cook like this?"

"I'm an Eagle Scout."

"Are you serious?"

"Scout's honor."

Mrs. Brock took on the task of teaching Charlene, Jack and Wendy how to play bridge. For the first hour, they played with open hands. Candace examined each hand to help in learning the bidding process. After that, they dissected each hand with a review of the bidding and play.

After four or five days, their play improved to the point where they were evenly matched. The only difference in the scores was attributable to the luck of card distribution.

The sixth day, Jack went to the grocers. He was back in an hour. Nothing at all happened while he was gone. Jack had begun to think that the anticipated attempt on her life wasn't real.

During Jack's shift that night, the lights went out. This was not an unusual occurrence in south Florida where power failures are frequent. Jack put down his book and started to the door leading from the library to the main hall when he heard the sound of breaking glass coming from the kitchen. As he turned to go toward the kitchen, he heard the front door open, followed by a pop and ping as a bolt cutter severed the safety chain. He immediately knew that someone had entered by the front door.

The glow of a flashlight shined down the hall. Jack stuck his head around the door opening for a moment then pulled back. A shotgun boomed, then again. Jack heard the shells being ejected from a double-barrel shotgun. In response to the moment when the shotgun was being loaded, he squared up in the hallway and shot five times. He quickly jumped back into the library.

From the kitchen he heard the sound of a thud and breaking wood. Someone had forced the kitchen door open. Mentally he counted the rounds fired. He replaced the near-empty clip with the full spare.

He heard a scream from upstairs followed by two shotgun blasts. Jack headed for the stairs. Halfway up, he heard the sound of a handgun. He counted six rounds fired. He took the remaining steps two at a time.

The hallway on the second floor was dark except for the glow of a partially covered flashlight at the far end. Jack called out. "Is anyone hurt?"

Charlene answered. "We're okay. That is, I think we're okay. Candace? Wendy?"

Candace entered the hall with a flashlight. "I'm okay. Where's Wendy?"

"I'm here. Damn, what a way to get awake."

Candace aimed the light down the hall. The figure of a man with a shotgun was lying in a heap on the floor. His flashlight was a few feet away with the lens very near the wall casting a small spot of light.

"Let's go downstairs. I believe I shot the other one."

Wendy took a sharp intake of breath. "You mean there were two?"

Jack took Candace's flashlight and led the way. The body was in the foyer.

"Jack, I think that's Billy, my husband." She stepped closer. "Oh, my God. It is Billy!"

Jack ushered them into the library. "I'll check on the power. Maybe all they did was pull the meter."

Jack exited through the kitchen doorway looking for the meter panel. The power wiring was underground so it took a few minutes to find the box. Jack plugged the meter back in and returned to the house. In the distance he could hear the sound of a police siren. Before he got back into the house, he heard another.

On his way in, he flipped on the kitchen light. The others were still in the library. Charlene was on the phone—Candace and Wendy were crying.

"I told them where the bodies are located. They know we're all in the library. The Crime Scene van is rolling so we're going to be covered up in cops in a minute."

The lead detective kept them in the library until eight the next morning. They were still processing the crime scene when they loaded the four of them in two cruisers and drove to the station. Four interviewers took their statements then, after they compared notes, they repeated the process. When it was all completed, the Chief of Police himself came by. Jack kept in the background letting Charlene and Wendy take all the accolades.

They fired a test round from Jack's weapon since he was carrying a different weapon than before. They returned the pistol to him when he left. He was placed in the car with Mrs. Brock for the trip back to the house. The officer accompanied them as Jack packed his clothing and Candace packed enough for several days at a hotel.

She apologized as they left the house. "Jack, I'm sorry you had to kill him. I pray that his death will not bear on you too much. Just remember that he came to kill us all."

"They didn't tell me who the other shooter was."

"It was his damned business partner. Should have known. He fired both barrels into the pillows on my bed. I'll be forever grateful for you putting me in the room with Charlene. By the way, I'll pay you as soon as I can tap into Billy's bank account."

"Thanks. I prefer cash, you know."

"I'll always appreciate your protection."

CHAPTER
26

George and Betsy Callahan

H<small>E RETURNED</small> to his Aunt's house with a little more than two months left before he was due to return to Auburn for the Summer semester. So he made the rounds of several hotels looking for a client. He wound up at the Coral Palms to speak his friend Carl.

Jack tried Carl's office first. He recognized Juan.

"Seen Carl?"

"Carl is in the coffee shop."

He walked over to the coffee shop where Jack slipped into the booth across from Carl.

"Hey, Carl, how come I always find you hiding here? Is there some babe you're after?"

"Jack, my man. You're looking good. How are you doing since the Brock thing?"

"They were out to kill us all, you know."

'You got anything going work-wise?'

"No. I'm looking, though."

"We've got this nice couple that checked in this morning. He asked me for someone who could show them the sights. He's had a stroke or something. He can use a walker for support but moves very slowly. He can't speak too clearly, either. Most of the time, he moves about in an electric wheelchair. Stay here, I'll make a call."

Jack ordered a Danish and coffee. The waitress served him just as Carl returned.

"I told them about you. You're just what they need. Room 363."

The door to room 363 opened to his knock. He was surprised by the appearance of the woman. She looked to be in her early thirties, quite trim and beautiful. The warmth of her smile and greeting welcomed him into the suite.

It was a three-room suite with a small sitting room and two bedrooms. The man was sitting in his wheelchair with drool seeping form his partially open lips.

"I'm Jack Wexler. I believe that Carl spoke to you about me."

"Yes, I'm Betsy Callahan and this is my husband George. George had a stroke a year ago and is not able to talk in a way that others can understand, but I'm able to understand him."

George extended his left hand and muttered something. Jack took it as a greeting and shook his hand.

Betsy continued. "We're here for a vacation and need someone to show us some of the sights. We would have need of you from mid-afternoon until after dinner and dancing at a club."

"There may be a problem with transportation."

"Oh, we have a chair-lift van. I drove us down here from Ohio."

"Now, about my fee…."

"I was going to ask about that."

"From what you describe, my fee would be eight hundred a week plus expenses. If I'm expected to be on call 24/7 the fee is two thousand a week and I'll need a room at this hotel. Oh, uh… and I would like to be paid in cash."

George mumbled something.

"Yes, I agree. He is perfect."

George mumbled again.

"Well, if you think so."

She turned to Jack. "He said that we want you full time. As for the cash, I'll need to find a bank nearby so I can convert some traveler's checks. We usually use plastic for all our purchases. I'll get a room on this floor for you. Can you start today?"

"I'll need about three hours to get my things and return. If you'd like to ride along, I'll find a bank for you."

She glanced at George who mumbled something.

"You say it'll take three hours?"

"Maybe less. I have to drive to Homestead. With reasonable traffic, we can be back in two."

George mumbled again.

"Okay, I'll go with you. Maybe we can get better acquainted on the way."

She stopped at the front desk and got a room across the hall from their suite.

They were back in two hours.

Betsy insisted on carrying Jack's garment bag while the bellboy carried the two suitcases into the room. She put the bag on one of the beds while Jack turned on some lights and pulled back the curtains. She tipped the boy before Jack had a chance.

She sat on the bed. "Jack, we need to talk."

Jack sat down on the other bed, facing her.

"Okay."

"I just want to get a few ground-rules out of the way first."

"I agree."

"When we have sex, it will be in this room. Even though George is fully aware of…"

"Now, just a minute…. I must tell you that it can't be a condition of my employment to have sex with you. That is against the law. It is also against my moral code to have an affair with a married woman."

"Oh, this is getting complicated." She took a deep breath and continued. "It's like this, George and I haven't had sex since the stroke. Now, with his full knowledge and permission, I seek comfort with others. We have two children together and I love him dearly. The children, by the way, are with my mother while we're on vacation. In light of this, I hope you can reconsider."

"I'll need to think about it."

"George and I both chose you, you know. We'll be very disappointed if it doesn't work out."

Jack's instincts told him to give the money back, take his suitcases and run. But she seemed to be so sincere.

"Oh, the concierge said you were available for bodyguard work. Are you armed?"

"Yes, I'm a deputy sheriff on released duty. That means I can carry a gun and have a badge but I'm not presently on the department's payroll."

"Do you have the gun with you?"

"Yes. Why?"

"You hear stories about Miami, tourists and carjackers. I like to feel safe."

"What do you want to do first?"

"Dog races this evening. Then I'll get George ready for bed. After that, dinner and dancing. Then…."

"Don't plan on it."

With the handicap license plate, they were able to park close to the entrance of the Flagler dog track. Betsy pressed a button and a ramp extended from the side door. George was able to move the wheelchair with ease using a joystick control with his one good hand.

Jack stood back while George and Betsy discussed the past record of dogs in each race before placing their bets. At the end of the evening, they were up over three hundred dollars from their wagers. He seemed to thoroughly enjoy the experience. It was obvious that his mental agility hadn't been harmed by the stroke.

As Jack studied them together, he was impressed by the way they both coped with his disability. They had a happy, loving relationship in spite of his handicap.

Jack slowly became able to understand some of George's speech. He even began initiating conversation with him. Jack found him to be an intelligent, clever, humorous and engaging person.

As they made their way back to the hotel, George continued speaking from his wheelchair. Jack heard him clearly say:

"I had a good time. We must do this again."

They paused before the door to their suite.

"Jack, please dress a little more formally. We'll meet in say, forty-five minutes."

"Tuxedo or suit?"

"Tux would be nice."

"Will do. Goodnight George."

George mumbled something incomprehensible.

Jack opened the door to his room. He kept thinking about George's last comment. He hadn't been able to decipher it.

He showered and dressed quickly—he was ready in a half hour. When Betsy knocked, Jack checked his watch. She was five minutes early. They took the elevator to the Starlight Supper Club.

In the elevator, Betsy stood in one corner with Jack in the other. She avoided eye contact.

She broke the silence as they approached the top. "I'm hungry, how about you?"

Jack replied, "I could go either way. With my aunt's cooking, I could afford to miss a meal or two."

"She seems to be a really nice woman."

"Yeah, she looks a lot like my late mother."

Betsy put her hand in his and squeezed. "Sometimes we must make the best of our loss."

The elevator door opened with the sound of a forties style swing band. They were seated far enough from the band so that conversation was easy. They decided not to order food but made for the dance floor. For the first numbers, there was a polite distance between them; however, they gradually got closer until she molded her body to his. Jack was pleased and surprised when she ordered the same as Jack—-ginger ale over ice.

By two, the band stopped playing and the pair left with the last remaining customers. They took the elevator to the lobby for the coffee shop. Both ordered an omelet with coffee. Between bites, Betsy gazed intently into Jack's eyes. Her look was disconcerting. Jack tried to avoid returning her stare but couldn't quite pull it off. When the check came, she signed with her room number and stood. They walked to the elevator holding hands.

When they got to their rooms, they stood for a few moments.

"Well, are you going to invite me in or not?"

"Not tonight. I still have a morality dilemma."

Smiling, she turned toward her suite. "It's your loss."

"Goodnight."

When Jack closed the door behind him he remembered an old Marine Corps saying: Don't ever turn down any because once you do you'll be behind and you'll never catch up.

27

J ACK WAS UP at eight after only five hours sleep. He ordered room service before taking his shower. He just finished dressing when his breakfast came.

After breakfast, Jack spent an hour reading both papers and doing the crossword puzzles. He turned on the television but couldn't find anything worth watching when the call came. It was Betsy.

"Are you awake?"

"I've been up since seven, how about you?"

"Just got out of the shower. Have you had breakfast?"

"Hours ago."

"Come on over."

When Jack left his room, Betsy was holding the door open to their suite wearing her dressing robe.

George, however, was dressed and sipping from a can of *Ensure* while reading the paper.

Jack was able to understand George when he said, "Good morning, Jack."

"Good morning, George. What do you want to do today?"

He mumbled, "Everglades."

"You want to visit the Everglades? Would you like to ride in one of those air boats and see the alligators?"

"Yes, alligators."

Betsy came in fully dressed. "What are you two planning?"

"George wants to ride in an air-boat and see the alligators."

"If that's what he wants—then that's what we'll do."

They drove out highway 45, stopping at every alligator wrestling attraction. When they spotted a sign advertising air-boat rides, they stopped.

Jack could tell that George was excited. He charged ahead in his chair leaving Jack and Betsy behind. They got in a short line to buy a fifteen-minute ride in one of the boats. There were three boats parked and idle with another four or five in constant use.

The ticket sales lady took one look at George's wheelchair and emphatically declared that he wouldn't be allowed.

"No way. We ain't got 'nuff inshorance for him ta ride. Might fall gettin' on. Ain't takin' no chanct. Iffn' you two wan'sta ride, it'll be twenty dollar for each of you."

George was really dejected. Jack looked to Betsy—she shook her head in disbelief. They had no recourse but to get back in the van.

George muttered something when Betsy started the motor.

Betsy turned the van around and started back to Miami. Jack tried unsuccessfully to involve George in conversation. Jack glanced back and noticed he was crying.

At the hotel, they quickly exited the van and went directly to the elevator. There were no words of conversation. Jack could tell that George was deeply depressed over not being permitted to ride the boat. George and Betsy went to their suite—Jack to his room.

Jack turned on the television. He began channel surfing—not being able to settle on anything, he would watch a few seconds of first one program, then another. The phone rang. It was Betsy.

"George isn't feeling well, I've put him to bed. I thought we could go swimming in the hotel pool."

For Jack, it was an excellent suggestion. He had been idle for too long.

"I'll be ready in ten minutes. Is that okay?"

"I'll knock on your door."

He opened the door to her knock. She was wearing a terry robe the hotel furnished and carried a bath towel. Jack grabbed the matching terry robe from his closet and reached for his pistol.

"Do you really think you'll need that?"

He put the pistol back in the drawer. "I guess not. It's just that I'm accustomed to having it around. There've been a few times that it's saved my cookies."

After spending about thirty minutes in the pool, they found a shaded table where they ordered orange juice over ice.

When the drinks were served, Betsy confessed, "I have a friend back in Dayton. We met during a support group meeting at the hospital for spouses of the seriously disabled. As a result of diabetes, his wife has kidney failure, is blind and has had her feet amputated. He would no more abandon his wife than I would abandon George. I rented a furnished studio apartment near Dayton University. We meet three or four times a week. It helps us maintain our sanity."

"Have you had other lovers?"

"No, but George knew about Charlie."

"Charlie?"

"Yes, that's his name. He offered to find someone for me when we arrived in Miami. That's when we hired you. In a way, I am still pleased we found you. You have a pleasant calm manner that we both enjoy. The sex would have been good but I'm okay without it."

They gathered up their things and drifted toward the elevator. When they got to their floor, they were met by a crowd of police and EMS technicians.

"Sir, you can't go any further."

Betsy surged forward. "But, that's my suite."

"And I'm across the hall."

"Please stay here. The detective will talk to you in a minute."

"Is it my husband?"

"Someone will be with you in a moment."

"Oh, God. It is my husband. Let me by."

The detective came over.

"I'm Detective Ellison. Are you Mrs. Callahan?"

"Yes. Has something happened to my husband?"

"And who are you?"

"I'm Jack Wexler. I'm a deputy sheriff on released duty hired as bodyguard for Mister and Mrs. Callahan."

"Folks, Mister Callahan has been shot. It looks like it's self-inflicted but we'll know better later on when all the lab boys get through."

An hour later, they let Jack and Betsy get dressed before being taken to the police station. They were driven in separate cars and placed in separate rooms.

Jack looked around the room. It was sparsely furnished with a table and five chairs. At one end was a large mirror. Jack had seen enough television that he knew it was a two-way mirror.

The door opened, Jason Ellison entered followed by a female officer.

"Well, Jack, I talked to your Colonel on the phone. He gave me a good report on you. The gun belongs to you. Can you tell me how Mister Callahan got his hands on it?"

"When I left for the pool with Mrs. Callahan, I put my piece in the drawer. I didn't see any need to take it with me to the swimming pool. It's as simple as that."

"We'd like to have you take a polygraph test just to make sure we're on the right track here. Would you have any objection to doing that?"

"Of course not. Hook me up."

The female detective spoke. "It'll take another half-hour. Mrs. Callahan is in there now."

"I could do with a cup of coffee."

"Sure, how do you want it?"

"A little cream if you have it—no sugar."

The female detective left.

"I would have asked for a cup myself but she gets all pissed when I do. You been doing bodyguard duty long?"

"Five months last year and almost three months this year. Mostly bodyguard work with some industrial loss investigation. I'm trying to earn enough to pay for engineering school."

"Where, FSU?"

"No, Auburn."

"Good school. My vet graduated from Auburn."

"Yeah, lots of vetmed students there. My roommate from last year was in vetmed."

The female detective came back with the coffee. Jack stood and took the paper cup from the tray. She had brought one for Ellison and herself too in ceramic cups.

"We haven't met. I'm Jack Wexler."

"I'm Mona Bernstein. I remember you from that shootout a couple of months ago. Weren't you working bodyguard then too?"

"Yeah, bullets were flying all around."

"Sure made a mess of that new Lincoln Town Car."

A uniformed officer stuck his head in the door. "Jason, there's a Sheriff's Department Colonel out here. He want's to talk to your subject. Should I send him in?"

"Yeah, bring him on back."

John Reynolds came in with a worried look on his face. "Jack, how's it going? You need anything? You want a lawyer?"

"Thanks for coming by John. I really don't need any help. I'm here to give them information on the suicide of my client. They're going to hook me up to the machine in a few minutes."

"You don't have to, you know."

"I know, but it'll let them close the case sooner."

It was ten that night when they were finally finished with their questioning. Detective Ellison drove them back to the hotel and accompanied the pair to their rooms. There was still a crew from the crime lab at work.

"I'm sorry Mrs. Callahan, you may not get to use your suite tonight. However, I will allow you to get whatever you need. They'll be finished in a few hours, though, if you want to wait."

"When will I be able to get my piece back?"

He reached into his suit side pocket. "Oh, I forgot, here it is. We fired a test round and took gunpowder residue tests. Looks like he got your spare key card, took your weapon and… uh…. Well, you know the rest."

"Jack, would you go in for me? I don't think I can do it right now."

"Sure, what do you need?"

"Everything in the top drawer and everything in the bathroom."

Jack inserted the key card and opened the door to his room.

"You can call the desk from my room. They'll send up someone with the key to another room."

Detective Ellison beckoned to one of the technicians. "Connie, escort Mister Wexler to Mrs. Callahan's bedroom. Make sure he puts on a set of gloves. He'll get the contents of the top drawer and personal things from her bathroom."

"Okay, we're finished in those rooms anyway. Please follow me, Mister Wexler."

Jack had to make three trips. He put all her things on the spare bed in his room. She was in the bathroom.

After the bellboy came with the key card to her room, Jack knocked on the bathroom door. "The room key is here."

When she came out, Jack could tell she had been crying. She took the key and opened the door to the adjacent room. Then they opened the connecting doors between the two rooms. Jack helped carry her things over and went back to his room, leaving his side of the connecting pair of doors unlocked. She was talking to her mother when he left.

Jack checked to see if Ellison was still across the hall. He found him at the doorway to the suite talking to the tech.

Jack interrupted. "Do you have any idea when the body will be released? I figure Mrs. Callahan will want to know. There are funeral plans to be made, I'm sure."

"Tomorrow afternoon by two is a reasonable guess."

"You know, it was triggered by not being allowed to ride on one of those swamp buggies. I could tell he was feeling low, but I thought it would pass."

"Yeah, that's what his wife said."

"I guess he was just feeling useless and a burden on his wife and everyone around him."

"Hell, Wexler, sometimes I feel that way myself but I don't put a pistol in my mouth."

Jack went back to his room and listened to the connecting door. He couldn't hear anything so he knocked. She opened the door wiping away her tears.

"You want something to eat? We missed dinner."

"No, I really don't want to be alone this evening."

28

T HEY ORDERED room service breakfast the next morning. Afterwards, she went to the suite and started packing. Jack lent a hand with George's things until all was ready to go except for the wheel chair.

"We'll just take it to the van. Perhaps I could give the van and chair to the Red Cross, Salvation Army or Disabled Veterans. Jack, if you would, please take care of that. Just have them contact me for the title to the van. I'll be flying back with George as soon as possible."

She started to cry again. "Oh, God, there's just too much to do. I need to contact someone locally to handle the shipment of the body. How will they do that? Will they embalm him first or what?"

Jack picked up the telephone book and turned to Funeral Directors. "Do you want me to call?"

"Please."

Within a half-hour a woman from the funeral home came by. While she was speaking to Betsy privately, Jack drove the wheelchair to the van. He checked the glove box for any personal things before moving the van from under the canopy to the hotel's parking lot.

Back in his room, he called the Disabled Veterans office. They sent a volunteer out for the keys to the van. Betsy was finished with the funeral home woman so she talked to the man about the van. He left with the keys, her address and phone number.

"They're getting reservations for me on the same flight as George. Also, they'll contact the funeral home in Dayton my family used in the past. They'll meet the flight to pick up George. My brother and mother will meet my plane to take me home. Oh, I called Charlie. He said his wife could pass away at any moment."

"How do you feel about that?"

"I don't believe I want to marry him if that's what you mean. I think I'll just stay single for a while. Who knows, I may take a vacation to Miami in a couple of months."

Jack didn't tell her that he would be in school then.

"Jack, could you leave me alone for a while. I didn't get enough sleep last night."

Jack returned to his room and flopped down on his bed. He should have put the 'Do Not Disturb' sign on the door handle. He had dozed off for no more than twenty minutes when the housekeeping lady came by. He went out to the hall, put the sign on Betsy's door and quietly entered her room via the connecting door. She was still asleep when he lay down on the spare bed.

He was jolted awake by the ringing of the telephone. He checked his watch—it was eleven thirty—he had been asleep for a little over an hour. Betsy stirred as the phone continued to ring. Jack grabbed the phone first.

"Hello, this is Jack."

"May I speak to Mrs. Callahan?"

"I'm sorry, she's asleep."

"No, I'm awake. I'll take the call."

It was the lady from the funeral home. Betsy rummaged around in the drawer of the small table for a pen. She wrote the flight number and time.

"Well, Jack. Tomorrow at 3:15. I guess we should get there an hour or so before. Don't you think?"

"Betsy, do you have plans for the rest of today?"

"Any suggestions?"

"Before you go back to Ohio, you should at least see the keys. I was thinking about a glass bottom boat ride to see a real coral reef. Later we can have a nice seafood dinner. How does that sound?"

"Sure, It might take my mind off things. How should I dress?"

"Shorts and blouse or tee and jeans—something casual. It's your choice."

They were away from the Hotel by twelve thirty, stopping for a burger on the way to Key Largo. The boat left with only twelve aboard. They headed for the coral reef of the John Pennycamp State Park—the only park that's completely underwater. With the help of black-lights, the coral formations glowed with iridescent colors of pink, green, orange and blue.

For a while, Betsy was occupied with the beauty of the coral formations. At least it was something other than the death of her husband. When the boat reached the dock, there was plenty of afternoon left.

So Jack kept going southwest to Islamorada and the great food of the Coral Grill. Their early dinner took almost three hours. They talked, joked and laughed through every course.

It was dark but not late when they started north. Betsy was quiet on the trip back, deeply in thought. Jack knew she was reliving the stroke, paralysis and death of the father of her children. So, he didn't intrude in her quiet and solitude.

He had been surprised over the sex of the last evening. Instead of being somewhat mechanical—wham, bam, thank you Maam—she was definitely an active and inventive participant each time.

After Homestead, the traffic picked up. When they got to the hotel, they wordlessly entered their respective rooms. Through the connecting door, Jack could hear her replying to phone messages.

He took a shower, put on a clean pair of boxers and went to bed. She came to his bed early in the morning. The digital clock next to the bed glowed three.

She had been crying. "Just hold me, Jack. I really need someone to hold me."

They made it to the airport a good two hours early. Jack parked in the police parking spot and found a luggage cart. After checking the luggage and getting her ticket they proceeded to the gate. Betsy went through security, Jack was able to bypass using his ID and badge.

They held hands until the flight was called. The line formed but they still sat waiting. As the last of the travelers entered the jetway, they stood. Betsy faced Jack and kissed him.

"Jack, you have been a good thing in my life. I'll never forget you."

She turned away and boarded the plane. She didn't look back.

CHAPTER

29

CLIENT: Kristin Lingstrom

J ACK WAS BUSY pruning back the rank growth in the back yard when his
aunt shouted from the back door. "Jackie, you have a phone call. It's
Colonel Reynolds."

"Okay, thanks."

He put up the shears in the shed and picked up the phone. "Hi, John,
what's on your mind?"

"Jack, you're going to owe me big-time for this. You remember Kristin
Lingstrom?"

What a bomb he dropped. Of course he knew of Kristin the super-
model. His roommate of last year had a poster of her pinned on the wall
above his bed.

"Sure, I've heard of her. What about it?"

"Got a call. They're looking for a bodyguard for her. You have an interview at two. You know where the West Wind Hotel is?"

"Yeah, I know where it is. Who do I see?"

"One of her associates, Gary O'Hara. Just ask at the desk."

"Did he mention the money?"

"No, you'll have to negotiate on price. Oh, yeah, since she's a fashion
model, maybe you should dress appropriately."

"What did you tell him about my background?"

"Oh, I spread it on pretty thick. You'll have a hard time living up to
your reputation now."

Jack could hear him chuckling.

"I was afraid of that, Colonel."

"Gotta go, Jack. Let me know how you make out."

He went to the kitchen. "Aunt Emily, I've got a job. I'll need to leave
in an hour or so. I won't be here for lunch."

"That's okay, Jackie, I'll just put it all in the refrigerator so you can have a nice snack when you get back."

"Now, Em, don't go to all that trouble."

"You should know by now that it's no trouble at all. As a matter of fact, if you weren't here I don't know what I'd do. It's been so lonesome here since my husband died."

Jack showered and dressed in one of his 'Miami casual' ensembles that Wilma had picked out. Powder blue slacks with a pink linen jacket over a flowery silk shirt would not have been his first choice at all but it seemed to please the ladies. He had two other similar outfits. At the last minute, he decided to go armed with the 380 in his ankle holster.

He left in time to make it a few minutes early if traffic was normal. It was. He circled the parking lot without finding a space. So, he parked under the canopy at the lobby entrance. The bellboy opened the door for him.

"May I get your luggage, sir?"

Jack flashed his badge. "I'm not a guest. I'll just leave the car here, okay?" Jack pressed a five in the bellboy's hand.

"Yes, sir! And I'll make sure no one parks in front and blocks you in."

The girl behind the counter greeted him with a smile. She looked Cuban. When she spoke, she sounded Cuban. "Good afternoon, sir."

"Mister O'Hara, please. Tell him that Jack Wexler is here."

"He is in the lounge. Look for a man with no hair."

The lounge was empty except for his man. Gary O'Hara was sitting at a table reading the sports page.

"Gary O'Hara? I'm Jack Wexler."

"Yeah, figured you were when you walked in. Grab a chair and I'll order a drink."

He motioned for the bartender. He fumbled around pretending he was doing something more important than waiting on a customer, then he tossed a bar towel across his shoulder and sauntered over to their table.

"Wha' can I getcha?"

"Another vodka rocks and club soda on the side." Looking at Jack, "And whatever he wants."

"Diet Seven-Up in a can and a glass with two ice cubes."

"No diet of any kind."

"Club soda, then."

"What's the matter, guy, not drinking today?"

"I don't drink."

"Never heard of an ex-marine that didn't drink. But, to each his own."

He kept reading the paper until their drinks arrived. He wadded the paper up and tossed it in the adjacent chair.

"You've got quite a reputation, you know."

It didn't seem like a question so Jack didn't reply.

"Kristin has the final say-so, but I know how she thinks. I've talked to a half-dozen guys who could do the job but all are too fat or too old. So, finish your drink and we'll go visit Her Highness."

"Her Highness?"

"She's been at this far longer than the usual run-of-the-mill model. She is now what you could call a personality. Because of her popularity and the fact that she still has a great face, she is now what you would call a personality. Did you know that her poster sold about two million copies last year?"

"Yeah, I've seen them around."

Jack took a sip from his glass. O'Hara downed the vodka and sipped on his club soda. He picked up the paper and returned to his reading.

He tossed the paper aside when Jack put down his drink. "You ready?"

Jack stood, and then followed O'Hara as he made his way to the elevator. He pushed the button for the top floor. When the elevator stopped, they stepped down the hall to the door. He knocked and waited. The door opened slightly, then closed while the safety latch was lifted.

The woman who answered the door looked to be in her late thirties. "She's asleep but wanted to wake up when the bodyguard arrived."

They found chairs in the sitting room while the lady fetched Kristin. In what seemed to be a few minutes, The Kristin Lingstrom, herself, breezed in as though she had been up and awake for hours. Her makeup and hair were perfect. She lit up the room with her smile. She approached Jack as he rose from his seat with her hand extended.

"So, this is the new man."

"I'm Jack Wexler. Nice to meet you, Miss Lingstrom."

"Oh, please, call me Kris and I'll call you Jack."

O'Hara kept his seat. "I've checked all his credentials. He's the very best available."

"Jack, are you armed?"

"Yes, I am."

"Funny, it doesn't show. Button your jacket and turn around slowly."

Jack grinned and complied.

"Still doesn't show. By the way, I like the clothes. Very Miami. Now, where's the gun?"

He pulled up his pant leg.

"Oh, very clever. I understand you have a badge as well."

"Yes, I am a sworn Deputy Sheriff. I'm on release assignment. That means I don't receive a salary."

"Speaking of salary, what are your rates?"

"Depends on the hours. If I'm to be available twenty four-seven, I get two thousand a week plus expenses. If it is an eight hour, five day, it's eight hundred a week plus expenses. And I prefer being paid cash in advance. This is my regular rate and I have no problem getting clients. I will not do anything illegal or against my moral code."

"Have you ever shot someone?"

"Yes, I have."

She motioned for Jack to sit on the couch. She sat on the floor in front of him, leaning against the Ottoman.

"Are you seeing someone?"

"Sure, various female friends from time-to-time. No one serious."

"Do you dance?"

"Of course. This is Miami, after all."

"Okay, let me tell you the problem. I've got a guy stalking me. He's been at it for well over a year. Every where I go, he's there. Lately, I've been getting threatening letters and notes pushed under my door. They're a mixture of declarations of love and hate. I really don't want to go into the details, but Gary has a whole file of them."

"Yeah, I'll get them for you tomorrow."

"Your bedroom is over there. Get your stuff and be back by five or so. Is that possible?"

Jack looked at his watch. "Be more like five-thirty or six. Will I need to bring formal wear, you know, a couple of tuxes or tees and jeans, clothing like this, or what?"

"Bring a mixture. Do you have a car?"

"Yes. The new Caddy SUV."

"We'll use your car. Just report your expenses. Oh, and Gary, get him a key to the door, also pay him for the week, will you?"

On the elevator, Jack asked, "Who's the lady?"

"Oh, that's my assistant, Monica. She'll be leaving in a few minutes.

"I need a description or a picture of the stalker."

"No can do. Never got a look at him. All we got are the letters and notes. We don't go on location for the shoot until Monday. We'll take a 'copter ride to the island."

"Where do we get on the helicopter?"

"Some place called Opa-Loca."

"Yeah, north on 27th Avenue and left on Gratigny Parkway."

"We leave at five Monday morning."

At the desk, Gary got a box from the hotel safe. He counted out two thousand. After making out a receipt for Jack to sign he put the receipt in the box. He had the clerk get an extra key for the room. Gary followed Jack to the car.

"Let me give you a little advice. She'll want to get in bed with you tonight. My advice is to wait for a couple of days or else she'll think she owns you. If you don't wait, you're in for a tough time. She'll ridicule, demean and insult you at every opportunity. If you wait, she'll be putty in your hands. Take my word for it. I was married to her. I had hair then. It lasted only a couple of months. Now, I really don't know why she keeps me around. But, then, that's another story."

On his way to his aunt's place, he thought how strange the relationship between Kristin and Gary was. But, it was a job for at least a week.

CHAPTER
30

H E HAD JUST STOWED AWAY his clothes when Kris came into his room. To his surprise, she was wearing only bra and panties. For a woman nearing thirty, she had the body tone of a teenager.

"Let's see what you have."

"How's that?"

"Your clothing, silly."

"Oh, help yourself."

She went to the closet and began pulling out items. "Yes. Oh, yes. This is good. This is too. Hmm, I don't know." She continued to examine without comment. Finally, she turned with a quizzical look. "Are you gay?"

"Why do you ask?"

"I've never found a straight guy that had any sense of color or texture, that's all."

"Oh, I didn't pick out these clothes, a chick did."

"Well, that explains it. Wear the Armani tux. Versace sent over a loaner dress for me. Gary alerted the paparazzi so I should get some good press out of it. You do dance, don't you?"

"I can do any dance or make a good impression of faking it. Where are we going?"

"Rudolfo's."

"Yeah, mostly Latin music. I've been there but they wouldn't let me in."

"Bunch of snobs if you ask me, but it is an 'in' place to go."

When they entered the elevator, Kris continued, "I had Gary get a limo for us. Although your Caddy would have been okay as far as I'm concerned. But, the paparazzi would be more likely to shoot up film if I were to arrive by limo."

"Hey, it's okay by me. I do feel somewhat handicapped not knowing what your stalker looks like, though."

"Is your weapon on your ankle?"

"No, under my left arm." He pulled back his jacket showing his shoulder holster. "This coat was specially made to conceal a weapon."

When the elevator door opened they were greeted with exploding light from photo-flashes. Gary cleared a way to the limo. They quickly entered the rear compartment; Gary rode up front with the driver.

The scene was repeated at Rudolfo's. The flashes continued to the entrance door. They paused when someone shoved a microphone in front of Kris.

"Kristin, who's the new boyfriend?"

"He's not new at all. He's just an old friend of mine."

"What's his name?"

"Just say he's a mysterious friend, okay?"

Kris turned and entered the club with Jack and Gary following.

After they entered, Kris turned on Gary with venom. "Damn, Gary, whatever were you thinking? The interview was supposed to be about me. Where did you get that jerk?"

"The magazine sent him over with two photographers. Want to invite him to your table for a sit-down?"

"Hell no! He had his chance. But before we leave, you prepare him. Better yet, go outside and tell him right now that I don't want a bullshit story about my new boyfriend. The story is me and don't you forget it. Now scram while I make another entrance because here comes the owner."

A Spanish looking man, well dressed, approached with his arms wide preparing for an embrace.

"Ahh, Kris. Welcome, welcome."

He embraced her with a fake, non touching, kiss to each cheek.

"Rudolfo. Let me look at you. You have such a beautiful tan. Have you nothing to do but play on the beach?"

"A few hours a day at my pool only. My, what a lovely gown."

When they were finally seated, Rudolfo spoke in a fake whisper to the two waiters so that anyone near could hear,

"These people are my special guests, everything is on the house."

Since it was the dinner hour, a guitar trio was playing forties ballads. Loud enough to be heard but soft enough for comfortable conversation. In a moment, first one, then another would awkwardly approach for an autographed picture. Jack could see Gary over to one side handing out the photographs and regulating the flow. The parade stopped when the waiter brought the bar order. After they had taken a sip or two and put their glasses down, the flow of admirers began again. Only when the appetizers were served did Gary call a halt. He disappeared to the bar until after dinner.

After the dinner service had been cleared away, Kris rose to go to the lady's room. Discretely, Jack followed and waited quietly to one side. He scanned the room, looking for anyone with an interest in her activity. From his vantage point, he could see Gary, seated at the bar. The guitar trio was busy packing their equipment with the arrival of members of the main band.

When Kris exited the lady's room, Jack quickly walked to the table. He remained standing at her chair to seat her.

She smiled, "My, aren't you the considerate one."

Jack took his chair. "I looked around while you were away. I looked especially for someone looking your way."

"Unless every man in the house was looking, I'm really losing my touch."

"Well, they weren't." The band started with a cha-cha. "You want to dance?"

"Sure, we'll see if you can keep up."

They stayed on the floor for every number. Finally, it was Kris who called for a rest. Gary then set up his station, handing out photographs for Kris to sign. After a few minutes, she raised her hand and the signing ended.

She got her face close to Jack and whispered, "I'm convinced. You are a good dancer. Now, what else do you do well?"

A flash went off. The photographer quickly disappeared. Kris fired an icy glance toward Gary.

Gary shrugged his shoulders and mouthed, "It wasn't me."

"We're leaving." She beckoned to Gary.

"Get the limo, we're leaving."

"It'll take a few minutes. I'll come back for you."

"I can imagine what that one shot will do to my career. My fame is dependent upon appearing available. For me to be photographed in a pose like that will bring nothing good."

Jack was at a loss about what to do next. It would certainly do no good to point out that the pose that caused her so much distress was one of her own making. So, he kept quiet.

Rudolfo came to their table. "Oh, Kris, Gary tells me you're leaving."

Jack rose politely as a courtesy to their host.

She turned on the smile and charm. "Rudolfo, I must rise early tomorrow. We've had a lovely time. Thank you so much for your hospitality."

"Yes, we so appreciated your presence as well as your talented escort."

"Oh, I didn't introduce you. Rudolfo this is my good friend Jack Wexler."

"Ah, Mister Wexler. I noticed that you dance well indeed. If there is ever an occasion you wish to return, please tell the booking clerk that you have received an invitation from me. Or, if you just want to attend after dinner for dancing, show this card to the man at the door." Rudolfo pressed a business card in Jack's palm.

Jack could see a hardening of Kris' smile. She was not pleased with the attention given to Jack.

"I'm afraid you're mistaken concerning my dancing ability. Anyone with a partner like Kris couldn't help but look well."

She brightened slightly as Gary came near.

"All is prepared. You can leave now."

Kris led the way to the lobby with Rudolfo, Jack and Gary following. At the lobby, Rudolfo bowed and kissed her hand.

"Adieu, Kris, please return soon."

"Goodbye Rudolfo. Again, thank you for a lovely evening."

Gary whispered to Jack. "We need to make a way for Kris. There's quite a crowd outside."

They led the way through the double doors. The limo was at the curb with the driver holding the back door open. Half way across the sidewalk, a slender man dodged between the people at the front and made a lunge for Kris with an open pocket knife.

Jack stepped between them and fended off the blade with his left forearm. Jack grabbed his long hair with his right hand and spun him to the ground. His left foot pinned the knife hand to the sidewalk. He released the man's hair and pulled his pistol. Kneeling at the man's side with his left foot still on the man's wrist, Jack put the pistol to the man's head.

"Open your hand and let the knife fall away. If you struggle, I will put a hole in you. Do you understand?"

The man started crying. "I only wanted to talk to her. I wouldn't have hurt her."

Security from the club arrived to make the arrest. They were off-duty Miami PD officers. When they had him in cuffs, Jack showed his badge.

"Okay, take your client and leave. We'll take it from here. There'll be someone calling on Miss Lingstrom tomorrow."

"Thanks, sounds like a plan."

Jack got into the car. Kris was crying hysterically with Gary trying to comfort her. He checked on his arm, there was blood. Jack asked the driver to take him to the hospital emergency room.

At the hospital, Jack got out and spoke to the driver. "I'll take a cab. Get her to the hotel, I'll be there as soon as I can."

Dripping a trail of blood, Jack went to the desk.

"What can I do for you this evening?"

"I have a knife wound in my left arm. I am an off-duty deputy sheriff. I'll call my Colonel later."

"Do you have insurance?"

"No, I'll pay cash."

She finished typing and gave him a folder. "Second room on he left."

He entered the room, took off his jacket and rolled up his sleeve. It had mostly stopped bleeding. The cut looked superficial. He really didn't think the knife went too deeply. A young woman entered. Her white jacket had J. Simms MD' embroidered over the pocket.

"Well, what have we here, sheriff?"

"I have this bodyguard job. I'm on released duty for awhile. This creep jumped out of the crowd trying to knife my client. I got in the way."

A nurse came in. "Clean up the wound and get me a suture kit. Oh, yeah, tetanus shot as well."

The doctor picked up the jacket. "Wow, good label. Bet this set you back a couple of thousand."

"I get paid expenses. Maybe they'll cover the tux, shirt and your bill."

She pointed to the shoulder holster. "You ever have to use that?"

"A few times."

The nurse came back and began cleaning Jack's arm. The doctor stepped in and placed eleven tiny sutures, closing the wound. She finished by bandaging the site and gave him a shot in the rear.

Jack asked, "What does the 'J' stand for?"

She wrote on a prescription pad. "Janet. Call me sometime, we'll have coffee."

Jack glanced at the script. She had written her home and cell phone numbers.

"How do you know I'm not married or seeing someone?"

"Oh, you're not married. But seeing someone? Maybe, we'll see."

He rolled down his sleeve, retrieved the cuff link from his pocket and put on his coat. Other than the small quarter inch cut in the sleeve, the coat looked whole. He thought he would try to see if the cleaners could re-weave the cut and sew up the lining.

When he went to pay the bill, he found he didn't have enough money with him. With his promise to pay and a Xerox of all his identification cards, they let him go.

It was slightly after one o'clock when he got back to the hotel. Expecting everything to be quiet, he inserted his key card and opened the door. The room was filled with cops, reporters and photographers.

Kris spotted Jack and shouted, "There he is, the man who saved my life."

CHAPTER
31

I T WAS WELL AFTER THREE when Jack was finally able to go to bed. He tossed and turned thinking over every little detail. He felt he would be able to go to sleep if only he could take a shower. Janet said not to get the bandage wet so he ruled that out. His thoughts turned to the shirt soaking in cold water. Then, he tried to reason how such a small cut, really less than a quarter-inch, in the jacket could yield a slice through his skin an inch and a half long. Only if the knife was dull could the point enter through the jacket, lining and shirt and pull the cloth with it as it raked his arm. Satisfied with his reasoning, he slept.

He woke with Kris kissing and putting her tongue in his ear. "Wake up, Jack, we have breakfast ready in the sitting room."

"Uh, what time is it?"

"Ten thirty. Rise and shine!"

"Okay, okay."

Only wearing his shorts, he got out of bed and headed for the bathroom.

"Nice tush."

He closed the door and rummaged about in his shaving kit looking for a plastic plaster to go over the cut. He carefully removed the bandage. The wound looked clean so he applied the water-proof plaster over the cut.

In the shower, he tried to keep the force of the water from that arm. While still in the shower, he shaved. When he stepped out of the stall, Kris was standing there with a towel.

"Hey, I'm taking a bath here."

Smiling, "With your wounded arm, I thought I would help you with the drying off part."

"Well, you thought wrong."

Her face drained, the smile was gone. She turned and left the bathroom.

He finished drying off, dressed and joined Kris in the sitting room.

"We need to talk."

She acted embarrassed and angry. "What about?"

"Just what are the conditions of my employment? I thought you needed a bodyguard and escort. If I am required to perform sexually, I must tell you that is against the law. I will escort you, protect you and be a friendly, comfortable companion but anything else is not for hire. There may indeed come a time when we become intimate but it will not be at your command or mine but by mutual consent."

She burst into tears and left for her room. Jack poured a cup of coffee and began eating breakfast. He started reading the paper. The page was open to the article on the events of last night. He was especially interested in the history of the attacker. All the article said was that he was a former mental patient. They got Jack's name wrong. He was listed as Jack Welker. That was fine with him. At least his aunt wouldn't be worried.

A small voice came from Kris' room. "I'm sorry Jack."

"Come on back to the table and have coffee with me. No hard feelings on my part, I assure you."

"My shrink tells me that I try too hard to please the men I come in contact with. I should have just told you how very much I appreciate you taking the knife instead of me."

"Kris, listen to me. Make eye contact with me and really listen. I would do it again. Not because you hired me but because that's the kind of person I am. I promised to keep you safe and that extends to not taking advantage of you as well. You can depend on that."

"Oh Jack, you're going to make me cry."

"If that's what you feel like doing, just let it go."

She picked up a napkin and dried her tears. "Right now, I'm really glad we didn't. I think I'd much rather have a friend than a lover right now. Maybe, at some time, we could be both."

"What do you take in your coffee?"

"I'll fix it. Oh, the fruit looks good. Have you tried the melon?"

"You read the paper?"

"Sorry about them not getting your name right."

"Suits me. I wouldn't want my aunt to worry. Since my parents died, she's the only family I have."

"I apologize again, Jack, I never thought of you as having family. My shrink tells me that my shallowness is the result of a narcissistic nature. I usually think only of myself to the exclusion of others."

There was a knock at the door.

"I'll get that. It's probably Gary."

"No you won't. I'll do it."

Jack stepped into his room and got his gun. He peeked through the viewer and let Gary in.

"Hey, fella, what's with the pistol?"

"It's my job."

"How's the arm?"

"A little sore. It was only skin deep, you know."

"You'd get a little more sympathy if you didn't tell that part. A dozen stitches is still quite a gash."

Jack asked, "What's scheduled today for Kris?"

"Just laying around. Tomorrow is Sunday so we lay around then too. Got anything in mind?"

"The hotel has a nice swimming pool."

Gary frowned. "That'd be too much like work."

Kris objected too. "If I get sunburned, I can't do my job on Monday."

"Tell me about Monday."

"Okay, we take this 'copter to an island. Islands around here are mostly mangrove without a beach, but this one has a nice sandy beach with an old shipwreck and lots of nice background. I was there four years ago when I did a swimsuit catalog for Vera Alliston."

Gary piped up. "That was good money."

"It's even better now that I have my own company."

"So, we just sit around and veg."

"Veg?" Asked Gary.

"You know, vegetate. We could go to the hotel's spa and work out. A little time on the Nautilus, Stairmaster and treadmill would do us good."

"You know Jack, when you're right, you're right. I have a few Spandex outfits to chose from that look really cute. Be ready in five."

"You're on."

Gary begged off. "I think I'll just vegetate in the lounge downstairs."

"It's your loss."

They took the elevator to the lower level, the one below street level. They wore hotel terry robes over their gym wear. To be safe, Jack brought his badge and weapon in one of the large pockets of his robe.

The room was well equipped with machines and free weights. They had the room all to themselves. Jack started on the Stairmaster, Kris on the Nautilus. She was familiar enough with the machine to be able to set the resistance herself. She finished all stations with a reasonable number of reps and started on the treadmill. Jack switched to the Nautilus then to free weights. When Kris finished the treadmill, she threw herself across the weight bench.

"Enough! I'm ready for the steam now. How about you?"

"Later, maybe. I'll just wait for you here. I'm still on duty you know."

"Don't tell me you're armed."

"I don't go out without it."

"Somehow I'm comforted by that."

He followed her to the ladies sauna but stopped short of entering. He went back to the spa for a chair and one of the magazines left by people using the Stairmaster. He had his choice between *Newsweek, Elle* and *Redbook.* He took *Newsweek* and a folding chair back to the sauna and started reading.

When the door to the sauna opened, he glanced at his watch. It had been a half-hour.

"Hey, you look loose and rested."

"I know the cold shower is supposed to pep you up and close your pores but I could sleep for a month. As far as releasing tension, the sauna is almost as good as sex."

Jack punched their floor after they entered the elevator. Kris leaned against the back of the car with the bundle of Spandex under her arm and closed her eyes. In the apartment, Jack went directly to the shower, Kris to her room.

After taking his shower and putting on jeans and a tee, he went to the sitting room.

"Kris, want to watch some TV?"

"Jack!"

He raced to her room. Kris was huddled in a corner, crying. "Someone has been here. Look!"

Drawers were pulled out of a chest with lingerie tossed here and there.

"Anything missing?"

"I don't know. I was frightened. I thought he might still be here. I was afraid to shout, so I tried to hide. Who would do such a mean thing?"

"He may be harmless. Perhaps he was looking for a souvenir. In any case, we need to alert hotel security."

"Don't leave."

"I won't. I'll call security on the phone."

"Don't leave now!"

"I'm just going to call, that's all. I'll be right here in the sitting room. Get dressed, they'll probably send someone up."

She looked down. She then realized the robe was open to reveal her nakedness.

Jack looked on the directory card for the number and dialed.

"Security, how may I help you?"

"This is Miss Lingstrom's suite. We've had an intruder. Please send someone up."

"Right away, sir."

Jack cradled the phone. He went to his room to retrieve his weapon. If he was going to answer the door, he wanted to be armed.

Soon, there was a knock at the door. Keeping the chain fastened, he opened the door.

"Let me see some identification."

The man showed a laminated photo ID card. His name was Steven Crofter. He looked absolutely ancient.

"Okay, come on in Mister Crofter."

"I'm Jack Wexler, off-duty deputy sheriff doing bodyguard duty for Miss Lingstrom. We just returned from the spa on the first floor and found drawers in her room pulled out and things strewn about."

Kris entered, "Hello, I'm Kristin Lingstrom. So glad you are here. Come, look what someone has done."

Crofter followed and viewed the mess.

"Someone got in here, that's for sure."

"Well, are you going to take any prints or something?"

"No, that'll be for the police to do."

"You will not call the police. What you will do is find out which person on the hotel staff with a master key card has come into my rooms."

Backing away toward the door, "Yes Miss Lingstrom, I'll get right on it."

Jack interrupted, "Is there any way with these electronic locks to restrict access to just the two of us and the maid?"

"Well, let me see. I don't rightly know. I just fill in on weekends. I'm retired, you know."

Jack bolted the door. As he walked over to the couch, he had one of his flashes of insight. With Kris busy putting all her things away, he picked up the phone and dialed the operator.

"Bar please."

"Lounge, this is Louie."

"Louie, don't tell Gary I'm calling but answer something for me."

"Sure. What do you want to know?"

In the past hour-and-a-half, has Gary left the lounge? Just say yes or no."

"Yes."

"Okay, good. Now answer if he was gone for a period of ten to twenty minutes."

"Yes."

"Thanks Louie."

"Don't mention it."

He cradled the phone and wondered why Gary would do such a thing.

CHAPTER
32

HE REMEMBERED HIS TUX. He picked up the phone book to look up the number for Armani and dialed. When the clerk answered the phone, he explained the situation.

"I am employed as a bodyguard. My client was attacked last night. As a result, I have a small knife cut in the left sleeve of the jacket. Can you recommend someone who can repair the cut cloth?"

"Yes, we have someone who can re-weave it. Would you like us to send a messenger to pick it up?"

Jack gave them the name of the hotel and the room number. The clerk promised to have someone over within the hour. After Jack cradled the phone, he remembered he hadn't asked the price. Whatever it will be, he thought, it won't be as much as a new one.

Kris returned from her room. "It doesn't look like anything is missing. I don't understand it."

"Are you sure he didn't swipe a pair of panties? Some of these creeps get off on that sort of thing."

She sat down on the couch next to him. "What do you get off on?"

"Are you asking me or telling me?"

"Please. Pretty please. Will you please?"

Taking her in his arms, he whispered, "That's more like it."

The kiss was long and full of passion. When they parted, it seemed that steam was rising.

"Now?" She asked.

"Later. Someone is coming over from Armani to pick up my tux jacket for repair."

"I knew it was too good to be true." Smiling, she returned to her room.

He debated whether to tell her about Gary. Instead, he began thinking of ways for her to come to the same conclusion on her own. He really didn't relish being the bearer of bad news, especially since she and Gary had so much history together. Now, he had to decide whether he was a real threat or was keeping up a charade for some other reason. He decided to ask Gary for the threatening letters and notes. He would then ask Colonel Reynolds to have the handwriting analyzed. Reynolds had to have access to that kind of expertise. However, the number one need would be to find a true example of Gary's writing for comparison.

There was a knock at the door. Surely, he thought, it's not the person from Armani.

It was Gary.

"Hey, I heard from security that someone got into her room and messed up her clothing."

"Yeah, it was a real panty raid. It upset Kris."

"She in her room?"

"She may be asleep."

"Oh."

"Look, Gary, I need you to do something for me."

"Just ask, my man."

He pulled some of the hotel writing paper from the small desk.

"Please list the schedule for Monday. I want you to tell me as much of the detail as possible. Also list the people involved and indicate how long you have known them or been associated with them."

"Sure, I'll just sit over here."

He cleared a space at the desk and began to write. After filling up three pages he sat back. "There, that ought to do it. Let me know if you need anything else."

"I've been thinking, I should take a look at the notes and letters she's been getting from the stalker."

"They're in my room. I'll get them now if you want."

"Please. It'll give me something to do the next couple of days."

Gary brought the letters back just as the guy from Armani was leaving. "Who was that?"

"Armani. I'm getting my jacket repaired from the knife attack."

"Turn in the bill, her company will pay for it."

"How about the emergency room bill?"

"Yeah, that too. Oh, did you hear? They're committing him to the loony bin. He's done that sort of thing before. As a matter of fact he had been out only a few days. They'll probably keep him forever now. He was some kind of Hinkley nut, you know, the guy who shot Reagan."

"So, he can't be the one writing all these notes. Also, he isn't the one who entered Kris' room and messed her things up today."

"Yeah, it must be someone else."

He started to press the issue but thought better of it.

"What's all the noise?"

"Hey, Kris. How are you feeling?"

Kris was dressed in jeans and a tee shirt. "Okay, I guess. You heard about the intruder?"

"Yeah, security told me."

"Kris, you want to go for a ride with me. I want to see my aunt for a few minutes. It'll do you good to get out for a while. Let you see Homestead."

"Sure. Am I dressed okay?"

"You look fine. We're wearing the same uniform."

Jack threaded the holster through his belt so it was at his side while Kris threw a few things in a tote bag. They left Gary in the sitting room watching TV. Jack had both the hand-written schedule and the stalker notes.

As they entered the freeway to Homestead, Kris fiddled with the radio. Finally, she found a station she liked.

"I've got to stop off at the sheriff's substation for a minute or two. It's just up ahead. Then we'll find somewhere to grab a bite to eat. If we go directly to my aunt's place, she'll insist on cooking for us. My waist-line can't stand too much of her cooking. I always overeat."

Jack and Kris entered the building together. Jack went back to talk to the Colonel while Kris waited in the lobby.

"Hey, Jack. How did you know I'd be in this morning?"

"You always keep your shoulder to the wheel, John."

"So, what can I do for you?"

"My client has been getting notes and letters from a stalker. I think I've figured out who he is but I need to be sure."

He tossed the large envelope containing the notes and letters on his desk followed by the three-sheet schedule.

"The notes are in the envelope and a sample of my suspect's writing is on the three pages. How much trouble would it be to have the writing analyzed?"

"No trouble at all. We have this woman on retainer. How soon do you need an answer?"

"Early next week, if that's possible."

"How's the arm?"

"So, you found out, did you?"

"Yeah, guess who had your name spelled wrong for the report?"

"Thanks, I wouldn't want my aunt to worry."

"The arm?"

"Just superficial. Took a few stitches. Here, take a look."

"Make a nice battle scar. Who's guarding your girl?"

"She's in the lobby. Want to meet her, maybe get an autograph?"

"Lead on."

In the lobby, Kris was surrounded by four deputies.

"Oh, Jack, back so soon?"

"I want you to meet my Colonel. Miss Kristin Lingstrom this is Colonel John Reynolds, my sometimes boss. John, this is my friend Kristin."

"So nice to meet you, John. I really appreciate you finding Jack for me. You heard how he saved my life last night?"

"Yes, if you don't mind, could I have an autograph?"

"I'd be honored. I have a few photos in my tote." Looking around, "How about your other officers?"

Almost in unison they answered.

That she wasn't wearing makeup was more than compensated by her not wearing a bra. She made small talk with each of the deputies as she made personal comments with her signature.

When she finished, Jack asked the colonel, "We're going to have lunch at Harry's Crab House. Want to join us?"

He looked to Kris. "Are you sure?"

"Love to have you with us."

"Okay, deal. I'll drive my car and meet you there."

After they were seated and their order placed, John started the conversation, "So, who is this guy you suspect?"

Well, Jack thought, the fat is in the fire now so he might just make the best of it.

"I really don't want to place the blame on just my hunch. I'd rather let the evidence speak first."

"Who is this you're talking about? Do you have someone in mind who's doing this to me?"

"Nothing hard, Kris, I just added up some of the facts, that's all."

"It's Gary, isn't it?"

"So, you had suspicions about him?"

"It was just so convenient. At times when I felt free to do as I wanted to, here would come a note that caused me to isolate myself for a while. So, tell me what you have."

"Don't mind me," The Colonel said, "I'm just the fly on the wall."

"When I realized that only Gary knew we would be at the spa for an hour or so I put it all together. He has a keycard to your suite and we saw no one on our way to the first floor workout room and sauna. By simple reasoning, it had to be him. Further, I called the bar and was told that Gary left for fifteen minutes in the interval when the room was wrecked."

"And the evidence you spoke of...."

"I got a sample of Gary's writing to compare with the threatening notes Kris has been receiving. If that comes back true then it's proof positive he's our man."

The food arrived so they immediately turned to making a mess of the pile of steamed crabs before them. When they had finally reduced the crabs to a mound of empty shells, Kris returned to the subject of Gary.

"What you don't know, John, is that a few years ago I was married to Gary for all of two months. He wanted family and I didn't so we mutually ended it. I kept him on as manager, though. With this revelation, I really think he hasn't changed his earlier plans. He's doing what he can to interrupt my career with the stupid idea of starting where we left off six years ago."

"If Jack does prove he is the man, do you want him arrested?"

"Good grief no. I'll just fire him as manager."

The bill came. Jack grabbed it first. "This is on me, John."

"I'll treat you next time." He tossed a ten on the table. "I will get the tip, though."

In a few minutes, Jack was pulling up in his aunt's driveway.

"Come on in and meet my aunt."

They walked around to the front door. His aunt met them.

"Oh, Jackie, you've brought a friend. Will you be staying for supper? It'll be no bother."

"Aunt Emily, this is my friend Kris. Kris this is my Aunt Emily."

"I am so glad to meet you. Please come in and sit."

They took their seats in the living room. Emily raced to the kitchen for refreshments.

Jack raised his voice so he could be heard. "Have there been any messages?"

"Yes, Dotty, Mona, Cathy and Rosemary called. They all want you to call them when you get a chance."

Kris grinned and held up four fingers. Jack just shrugged.

"If anyone else calls, tell them I'm tied up for a while. By the way, any bites on my car?"

She returned with a tray with glasses of iced tea and cookies.

"Yes, one man was interested if he could make payments to you. He suggested twenty dollars a week. I told him no."

"Did you post a note on the bulletin board at the Senior Center?"

"Yes, but the asking price of eight hundred scares them away."

"The book value is eleven."

"I know. Just have patience."

"Honey, haven't I seen you before?"

"Maybe, I have done some modeling work."

"I know you. You were the one the man with the knife was after." She took a sudden fast intake of breath. "Jackie, it was you the guy stabbed wasn't it? Here, let me see your arm."

"It isn't bad, really."

"Oh, Jackie, I worry about you so. You do be careful."

Somehow Jack and Kris were able to change the subject. They visited for another twenty minutes and rose to go.

"Be careful, both of you. There are mean people in this world."

Back in the car, Kris confessed, "I like your aunt. She's a lot like my own mother."

Jack turned on the stereo but pressed the CD button. It was a guitar trio.

"This is my kind of music."

"It's so old fashioned."

"But it's so good."

In the elevator, going up to her suite, she was passionate with her kisses. Jack broke them apart.

"You know they have a camera in this car, don't you?"

"I don't care and I don't want to wait."

"We'll be there soon enough. Look, the door is opening now."

"I'll race you." She took off running to the door, inserted her key card and held the door open for Jack as he walked a normal pace.

She made for her bedroom while Jack fastened the chain and flipped the deadbolt.

"Hurry, don't make me wait."

CHAPTER

33

THREE HOURS LATER, Jack left the sleeping Kris to take a shower. After he finished bathing and dressing, the phone rang. It was the Colonel.

"Hey, Jack, I knew you were in a hurry so I took the material to our expert personally. She dropped everything in order to give me a preliminary finding."

"It's him, right?"

"She said that it's a no-brainer. Quite obvious, she says he's our man. She'll have a formal written report within a week. You might have your client come to some sort of decision about the prosecution of this jerk."

"Okay, I'll let her know. By the way, thanks for having lunch with us."

"It was my pleasure. The guys at the station are still talking about her. I heard an offer of fifty bucks for one of the autographed pictures."

"Did he take it?"

"I think he's seriously considering it."

"I appreciate the call, John."

"Glad to help, son."

When he cradled the phone, he looked up. Kris was up but still undressed.

"Was that the Colonel?"

"Yes, he had news concerning Gary."

"He did it, didn't he?"

"Yes, John rushed the documents over to the expert. She said that there's no doubt about it."

She came into his arms. "Want to fool around some more?"

"I think I'll have to give it a rest for awhile. Get dressed, we'll go out."

"Let's look at you. Hmm, Miami casual. I can do that."

They didn't return until two Sunday morning. Gary was waiting in the sitting room.

"Just where in the hell have you been?"

She flounced past him to her room. "Out," she commented over her shoulder.

"Out. What the hell does that mean?"

She stuck her head out. "It means that it's none of your damn business," then slammed the door.

Jack said, "I think you should leave now."

He was hot. "I'll leave when I damn please. You're fired, get out."

Jack grabbed his shirt front and twisted. "I don't work for you. Give me your key card to this room and leave. If you want to enter, you will knock. Is that understood?"

Gary was surprised at Jack's decisive action. He fished in his pocket for the keycard, then left.

Kris came out of her bedroom. "What's next?"

"We need to get him in jail before he can empty your bank accounts. If you're willing, we can get him arrested tonight."

"Then do it."

Jack looked in his address book for John's home number, lifted the phone and dialed.

The sleepy voice answered. "'Lo."

"John, this is Jack Wexler. I apologize for waking you. Kris wants him arrested as soon as possible."

"Jeez, Jack, you know what time it is?"

"Will you do it?"

"Tonight?"

"That's what she wants."

"You know, this is a Miami PD jurisdiction case."

"Well?"

"And he's registered at your hotel?"

"Yeah."

"Okay, I've got a pen. Give me the spelling of his name."

Jack gave him his name and room number.

"I'll go to the magistrate myself and swear out the warrant. He'll be arrested before morning."

"Can you lose the paperwork until Tuesday? She needs to get his name off all the accounts and cancel his company credit cards."

"I'll do what I can. We have to transfer him to the Miami PD anyway. Should be a snap to lose the paperwork since he'll be locked up at our substation first."

"Thanks, John."

"Don't mention it."

Turning to Kris, "You heard?"

"Yes. When I think of all the grief he has caused me I just want to wring his neck or something worse."

"Does Gary have an assistant?"

"Sure, Monica really does all the work. All Gary does is sign the checks. Most of the crew are theater union local but my own people are at the Gold Crest Motel."

"Get Monica to call all your crew together for a meeting tomorrow. I believe you can still salvage your photo shoot on Monday. You also need a lawyer on board as early as possible."

"My company has a New York firm on retainer. They have an office here in Miami."

"Now we sleep. We will wake at seven with breakfast at seven-thirty. I'll call the desk for the wake-up call and room service now."

She moved in close to Jack and purred, "I would sleep so much better if I were relaxed. You know that sex is relaxing, don't you?"

"You forgot the secret word."

"Oh, yeah, I remember. Please, pretty please."

"How can I resist?"

The next morning, a phone call to the legal firm's local office got a recording. It was only after a call to the New York office did someone local respond. He sounded peeved but agreed to meet Kris at ten.

Monica took charge and arranged all the other details including securing a meeting room.

Jack and Kris arrived five minutes late. She went directly to the lectern.

"First of all, I want to apologize for interrupting your weekend. I wouldn't have called you in if it wasn't necessary. As you know, I've been getting threatening letters from a stalker for over year. I have hired a bodyguard, Mister Jack Wexler. He saved my life Friday evening by stopping a recently released mental patient who attacked me with a knife. Mister Wexler, please raise your hand so we can see you…. Yes, go ahead and applaud…. In the course of his work, Jack has discovered evidence that my former business manager Gary O'Hara is implicated in the stalker note crime. This evidence was presented to law enforcement and an arrest has been made. I hereby name Monica Exum to that position. I want you to know that when she speaks, it is my voice. We have a photo shoot tomorrow so if there is some detail you were to get from Gary, let Monica or myself hear about it now."

She paused for a moment before continuing.

"Take charge of your own job. If you have any questions, just ask Monica."

After the crew filed out, Kris and Monica met with the lawyer. He listened, taking several pages of notes. He decided to generate some documents for Kris' signature to be ready at five that evening. He would have them sent to New York by courier so they could be delivered to the bank when their doors opened on Monday. A simple phone call to American Express canceled Gary's company credit card. With Jack's badge and the presence of the attorney, the hotel released Gary's safe box with its cash.

In the elevator to her room, she confided, "What a relief. I really didn't think it would be so easy. Thanks Jack."

"Don't mention it. What do you want to do for the rest of the day?"

"Go with you wherever you want. Just surprise me."

Jack drove south past Homestead to Florida City. After picking up a picnic lunch, entered the Everglades National Park. They stopped at every chance to view the wildlife and scenery. Finally, they had their lunch at Flamingo on Florida Bay, the end of the road. The restful afternoon ended back at the hotel in time to meet the lawyer.

To their separate beds at nine and up at five, rested and ready. They arrived at the island by eight. Kris disappeared into her trailer. The hum of the diesel generators filled the air. Jack walked around the area looking to the preparations.

"Hey, get off the sand."

Jack backed up.

"Sorry, but we need to keep the sand unmarked by people tracks."

"Tell me where I can go to be out of the way."

"See that tent over there? Get a cup of coffee, a Danish and take a seat. We get the best light in a few minutes. There are thirteen swim suit changes before the sun is too high. Then we continue at two-thirty for another session involving seven costume changes. If we don't get it done today, we'll have to be back tomorrow. We know what we're doing so just keep out of the way."

Jack did as he was told. He watched the work and marveled at their efficiency. There were three men changing lights and large shiny reflectors. One man operated the generator, two women took care of hair and makeup while another handled costumes.

The photographer had two assistants loading film into six cameras. As he shot, he kept on a continual line of talk as he cajoled, threatened, verbally caressed, and browbeat Kris into revealing more of herself for the camera. As the morning progressed Kris took to changing bathing suits right on the beach. The makeup girl and the hair girl held a large towel as the costume lady assisted Kris in changing.

The last shots that morning featured Kris in the water with her body, face and hair wet. With the small waves rolling over her body. After this, they called it quits as everyone charged the caterer's table.

Kris and the hairdresser were tied up in the trailer as Kris took a shower and had her hair shampooed and blow-dried. They exited the trailer with Kris wearing a robe. She got a banana and a glass of cranberry juice then returned to the air conditioned trailer.

Monica revised the schedule and called the crew to work at two. Some of the men tried to cite union work rules but Monica knew better. They quieted down and went to work as instructed. A short spate of rain came at three-fifteen, lasting for all of five minutes. Soon, they were shooting again. They wrapped at four. Everyone was relieved. The helicopter came at five for Kris, Jack and four of the crew. The pilot would make three more trips to get them all. Tuesday, they would haul the equipment out by 'copter as well. By Wednesday only a single small scrap of paper remained.

Kris and Jack left the airport in Jack's car. The rest of the crew in a fifteen passenger minibus and personal cars. Wearily, they entered the elevator and punched their floor. As Jack inserted the keycard to Kris's suite, a familiar voice spoke behind them. It was Gary.

"You think you're so smart, don't you?"

Jack stepped between Kris and Gary. "You're drunk."

"You damned straight, I'm drunk! You know, you really did a number on me. My credit card won't work now. I've been arrested for something I didn't do and now I find I'm out of a job. You know, I ought to shoot you. By God, I will shoot you."

He reached in his back pocket but the hammer of the revolver hung on the pocket opening. Jack pulled his weapon first.

"Just let it be and you'll live. If I even see what you have in that pocket, I'll put a hole in your head. Do you hear me?"

Gary continued to tug at the pistol. Jack grabbed his arm with his left hand and brought his pistol flat against Gary's temple. He wilted to the floor. Jack turned him over and removed the revolver.

"Go in the room and call the police. Tell them there is a man with a gun who attempted to assault a sheriff's deputy. I'll keep him here."

Gary started to 'rouse up. He turned over, propped up on one elbow and vomited.

"Boy, am I drunk. You know that Jack, old boy, my buddy who just screwed me over with the police? Now you've fixed me good haven't you?"

"I will not tell them you pulled the pistol only that you tried to remove it. That changes the charge of assault with a weapon to attempt. Big difference."

"Thanks for small favors."

"Why the threatening letters to Kris?"

"She'll be at the end of her career in a year or two. I just wanted her to think about getting out earlier, that's all. I have never really stopped loving her, you know."

"Oh, Gary, I didn't know."

Jack turned around; Kris was standing there crying.

"Kris, I wanted us to have children together, grow old together, get fat and flabby together. I've never stopped loving you no matter what you did."

She started sobbing. "Oh, Gary, what have you done to yourself with all this?"

"I ran out of ideas."

Jack flipped the cylinder open and emptied out the cartridges. He put them in his pocket as two uniformed cops exited the elevator. Jack flashed his badge.

"Please charge him with D&D and possession of an unloaded weapon. There was no assault. We were mistaken. Watch your step, the vomit is his."

"We'll put him in the tank and keep the pistol. They'll ROR him in the morning with a misdemeanor charge."

They grabbed his arms, lifted him up to a standing position and cuffed him. Soon the elevator door closed and they were alone. Jack followed Kris into the suite and closed the door.

Kris plopped down in a chair. "I feel so sorry for him. I wish now I had never had him arrested."

"I did what I could for him out there in the hall."

"I know, I saw."

"Since your photo shoot is over and the stalker is arrested I guess you don't need me any more."

"Oh, but I do. At least for tonight."

Emily and Earl, the Townsend Twins

34

T HE CALL CAME on Monday morning. Jack had been waxing the Honda trying to make it more appealing to prospective buyers. He had cleaned under the hood, vacuumed the trunk and interior and applied Son-Of-A-Gun to the dash, vinyl seat covering, and door panels. The car was looking pretty good. He momentarily thought about selling the new Caddy SUV and keeping the Honda.

He was just finishing the job when his aunt came to the door making the thumb and pinkie sign of 'telephone call'.

"Hello, this is Jack Wexler."

"Clark Townsend here. You have been recommended to me as a very capable person who can be trusted. Are you free for the next two weeks?"

"Yes, I'm free. I appreciate your confidence. May I ask who you spoke to?"

"Yes, one of your clients from last year. Do you remember Mrs. Allero?"

"Of course."

"If you could meet with me this afternoon at my home in Bal Harbour we can discuss my needs."

"Sure, give me the address and your phone number in case there's a problem."

Jack clicked the point out on his pen and wrote on the cover of the phone book.

"And the time?"

"Let's say threeish, okay?"

"Three it is."

Jack located his address book and transcribed the information.

After his shower, he dressed and packed enough clothes for a couple of weeks. He anticipated getting the position so he wanted to avoid making the round-trip back to Homestead to get his stuff. If he was mistaken, no harm would result.

He took the Broad Causeway off I95 and turned left on Collins. He missed his turn so he had to double back. The house was on the bay side. As he entered the circular driveway he could see a run-about and a yacht that looked to be at least seventy feet long docked at the slip.

The garage had bays for five cars, all of them occupied. He parked to one side. A man dressed in black met him. Jack took him to be a servant but wasn't sure.

"Mister Wexler?"

"Yes."

"You're expected. Follow me."

They entered the house through a side door. Jack followed the man to a richly paneled office.

"Please be seated, Mister Townsend will be with you in a moment."

Townsend, a very fit man in his fifties, came in wearing a tennis outfit with a towel around his neck. He was covered in sweat.

"I know, hand ball outside at this time of day is a little much but I like to work up a good sweat. How about you? Do you work out?"

"Yes, I run and do weights. I like to spend time on a Nautilus if one is at hand."

"Ah yes, machines."

He picked up a manila folder from the desk. After flipping through a few pages, he tossed it back.

"Marines, part-time engineering student, bodyguard, escort, great dancer, doesn't drink, absolutely trustworthy and deputy sheriff. Have I missed anything?"

"That about tells the story. Looks like you had a good investigator."

"He works for me in my business." He picked up the file again. "Many love interests, most on a sexually intimate basis. None of his ex-girlfriends hold any animosity. He is fondly remembered by all."

Again, he tossed the folder to the desk. "That's quite an accomplishment. All my ex-wives and girlfriends hate my guts. How do you do it?"

"Total honesty, perhaps."

Townsend studied Jack intently. "You know, I think I believe you. Now, as to the task I want to present to you, I will require the ultimate in discretion. From this moment on, I want your assurance that none of this will be told to another."

"I agree with one exception. If a crime has been committed, I will report it to the authorities."

"I accept that. Now to the job: Mister Wexler, my son James is a drunk and a drug addict as was his wife until her death by a drug overdose. Their twin children are now my own children by adoption. I love them deeply and will protect them from harm no matter what. About a year ago, my son completed a rehabilitation regime and remarried. He now wants to take custody of the twins. Knowing his past, I will not even consent to a visit. Since he knows all sorts of low-life types from his drug days, I fear the worst."

"How old are the twins?"

"Nine. We have a nanny to care for them. She's also their teacher. Emily and Earl are quite a handful but she's able to shepherd them. From all indications, she loves them as if they were her own. Now, my wife and I will be gone twelve days on the Friendly Mistress with some close friends and business associates."

"I take it that Friendly Mistress is your yacht."

"Yes, we leave Wednesday and return on Sunday a week and a half later."

"I assume you have provided the nanny with written parental authorization to act in your stead while you're away."

"Good point. I'll call my lawyer. I'll authorize you as well. Now, let's discuss your fee."

"Since you require me to be resident and on call twenty-four-seven, my fee is two thousand a week plus expenses."

"Is this what you regularly charge?"

"Yes. For this fee, I have received eleven stitches from a knife wound, was run down by a car and shot at several times in the line of duty. But no client has been harmed."

"Done."

"May I be paid in cash? I don't trust banks or the IRS."

"Done and done. Anything else?"

"I have my things in my car. I can start now."

"That's a good idea. It'll give you time to familiarize yourself with the house and grounds. By the way, are you armed?"

"Of course."

"If my dope fiend son gets in the way, don't hesitate to use it to protect the twins."

A young woman entered the office. She appeared to be in her late twenties and very attractive. Jack arose from his chair. "Oh, I'm sorry, Clark. I didn't realize you were occupied."

"Beth this is Jack Wexler. I have engaged him as bodyguard for the children. Mister Wexler, this is my wife, Beth Townsend."

"Pleased to have you in the family, Mister Wexler. Funny, you don't look like a bodyguard."

Jack smiled, "Just how should a bodyguard look, Mrs. Townsend?"

"Touché. I'm sure you'll do fine."

"Dear, would you show Mister Wexler around? There's some pressing business I need to tend to."

"Of course, please follow me."

She took him to all the rooms on the ground floor, introducing each servant as they were encountered.

"Stairs or elevator?"

"What?"

"We're going to the second floor. Would you like to take the elevator?"

"Stairs, I think."

At the top of the stairs, she pointed to the right.

"There is the suite used by Clark and me. We have our own elevator to the main floor and basement. The other elevator is at the end to our left. There are six guest bedrooms as well as the suite used by the children and Miss Cuervas, the children's nanny. Come, I'll show you your room."

He followed her to the left.

"This room is adjacent to the children's suite. I thought it best if you were nearby."

"Good idea. I'll get my luggage from my car."

"No need, Smith has taken care of that. Your luggage is in the room, Estelle is putting away your clothing now."

"Hey, I can tend to my own things."

"Tonight we'll dress for dinner. We will have the children as well as Miss Cuervas and of course you present. We consider you and Miss Cuervas as members of the family rather than of the household. Mind you, we only dress formally on Mondays and Thursdays as a custom. Most of the time we are quite casual. Miami becomes a habit, you know."

She knocked on the door next to his.

"Come in."

She opened the door.

"Hello, Linda. How are my children doing?"

"They should be up from their nap now. I heard them giggling a moment ago."

She walked a step or two toward a set of two doors.

"Children, your mother's here."

They came bursting out of their rooms, excitedly running into their mother's outstretched arms. As the children shared details of their day, Jack glanced about the room. It was obviously that the room served many purposes. On one side, there was a stack of library shelves on either side of two computer stations on child-sized tables. On the other side were toys of every sort scattered about. On still another wall was a bulletin board with samples of their drawings displayed. Next to the bulletin board was mounted a white board for dry markers. He studied the white board. They had been studying Algebra. He thought it advanced for nine-year-olds.

"Oh, I didn't introduce you to our friend Jack Wexler. This is my precious Emily and this is my handsome young man, Earl. And this is their teacher, Miss Linda Cuervas. We are so pleased with Miss Cuervas; she has a Master's Degree in Childhood Development from Miami University. We are delighted to have her in our family."

Earl spoke up, "Are you going to live here with us, Mister Wexler?"

"Yes, I'll be here for a few weeks. Perhaps we can see if we can catch any fish in that bay."

Emily chimed in, "You'll not go without me, will you?"

"Of course not. How about if we get a picnic lunch and invite Miss Cuervas along with us."

The children readily agreed with Miss Cuervas nodding a smiling approval.

They walked back to the stairway. "Mister Wexler, as is our custom, after we have had a meal together and you have spent the night here in our home we will begin addressing each other by our first names. As to the servants, our head butler is called by his last name, the other servants by their first names. They will refer to me as Mistress Beth and my husband as Master Clark. You will be called Mister Jack. I know it's old-fashioned but my husband insists."

They reached the bottom of the stairs.

"Now to the basement. I must warn you that it's quite musty there even though we have a forced cross-ventilation system. We've spent a rather large sum to keep it dry but have yet to be completely successful. There are six sump pumps at work trying to keep the water out. Now watch your step, the stairs are rather steep."

They descended a stairway that was more like a ladder. Jack thought he could do better if he turned around, but he noticed that Beth had no problem even in her high-heels.

"I'll show you the technical stuff first. I know their names but little of their function. The tank over there is gasoline for the garage. It holds fifteen hundred gallons. On the other side is diesel fuel for the emergency generator. It is slightly larger at twenty-five hundred gallons. The building code would not allow these if the house were being built today but when this house was built, there was no code."

Jack had a good nose but he couldn't detect vapors from either tank.

"Over here is the generator. I used to know how many watts but I forgot."

Jack took a peek at the record plate. Two hundred kilowatts, enough to power everything with no need to conserve on usage.

"Now we'll retrace our steps back to the stairs and go the other way."

As they passed the stairs, Beth continued, "Back here is the wine cellar, pantry and laundry ending in the elevator to the first floor and to the master bedroom suite. Follow me and we'll take the elevator to the first floor."

After the elevator started, Jack could sense that it was operated by a hydraulic piston rather than by steel cables. Out on the first floor, Beth led him through the main front door to view the outside.

"Over there are the swimming pool, handball and tennis courts. On the other side is the garage are living quarters above the garage for some of the servant staff with Smith, the cook, and her husband living in rooms to the rear. All other staff lives off grounds. However, there are quarters in the gate house in case we need to provide for more guests or staff."

Jack had seen the gatehouse as he drove in. It didn't look large enough for more than a couple of people. They took a path to the boat dock.

"Well, here she is, the Friendly Mistress. I hate it. We're gone days on end with stupid business associates and all of them drinking."

Jack could see her chin quiver. She brushed away the hint of a tear.

"Never mind, my husband likes it. As for me, I'd much rather be here with my children. We adopted them shortly after we were married. They were only a year old then. I truly love them as my own."

"What's next?"

"I'm afraid that's all there is to see. I'll walk you back to the house."

CHAPTER
35

B EFORE GOING TO BED, Jack checked the lock on the children's room. Satisfied, he turned in after setting the alarm for five the next morning, Tuesday.

It was still dark when he finished his run. He wandered into the kitchen for a cup of coffee and a superb waffle with the cook and her helper. He had just finished eating when a buzzer sounded. The cook glanced up to a series of lights over the door. The first one was lit. The cook and helper jumped into action preparing a tray. Within a few minutes the helper was wheeling the cart toward the elevator.

Carrying his coffee cup, Jack wandered outside to view the sun as it rose casting shadows of the huge palm trees across the lawn. He liked the morning with it's silence. Across the bay he heard the buzz of boat motors as fishermen left for their morning catch.

He heard a noise behind him. It was Mister Townsend.

"Good morning, Mister Townsend."

"Jack, just call me Clark. Yes, this is a great time of the day. Have you been up long?"

"Yes, I got up two hours ago. I checked around the house. You know, locks and such. You really should have an alarm system."

"Good idea. I'll get a quote today. We'll have it installed as soon as possible."

"Another thing Clark, we're operating in the dark here. It would be an advantage if we knew the what and when of your son's planning."

"Suggestion?"

"I worked briefly as a bodyguard for a woman who had hired the Jefferson Agency for investigation work last year. They have guys who can blend in with the drug scene. They can also plant bugs in your son's house on the sly."

"Isn't that against the law?"

"Misdemeanor charge with a small fine if they get caught, that's all."

"I'll get them on it today. Anything else?"

"Can you get all this rolling in time before you to leave? We're talking about less than two days."

Clark laughed. "Really one day. We sail early tomorrow. Just watch me, Jack, it'll get done."

By ten, a crew from the alarm company was puttering around the house. Jack sought the foreman and introduced himself.

"Has Mister Townsend given you any instructions?"

"He asked us to provide an alarm system for the building. I guess he figured we knew our job and trusted us to do it."

"If you want the contract, I have a couple of suggestions that will cinch the job for you."

He stepped back a half step and examined Jack's expression.

"What are you saying? Are you looking for a piece of the job?"

"No, nothing like that. My job is to protect the children. That is my only interest."

"Fair enough. Tell me your suggestions."

"You should present your alarm system in two stages. The first one is to rig the children's rooms with detectors serving an alarm in the master suite and my bedroom. This you do immediately so that the system is in service and working while you install a more extensive system."

"Thanks, Mister Wexler. That's just what I'll do."

"Have the proposal ready in an hour for installation by this evening."

"Now, I don't know about that."

"You'll get the job if you do."

At lunch, Clark was beaming. "I told you I could stir up some action. These people are really on the ball. They suggested two alarm systems with the children's room set up first with the remainder to follow. And, listen to this, they'll get the first part installed by this evening."

"Were you able to contact the Jefferson people?"

"I meet with them at one."

"Do you want me to be there?"

"Yes, since I will be away for the next two weeks, I want the agency to report their findings to you. Now, eat up. Your soup is getting cold, your salad is getting warm, and I don't know about your sandwich."

"I was sort of waiting until the rest of the family got here."

"Oh, they take lunch in the children's suite. Sometimes I have to pry my wife away from the children, you know."

Jack wondered why she wasn't raising her own, but it wasn't his business. Could be any of a number of reasons.

Two people from the Jefferson Agency arrived promptly at one. The man, Sid Graham, was in his fifties. The woman, Jerry McHone, he guessed in her middle thirties and quite pretty. Jack figured they were hitting them with the sexy girl eye-candy as well as the trustworthy mature expert angle.

Clark did all the talking, Jack just listened, as he outlined his fears and suspicions concerning his son. He summed up with, "What I need is information on two fronts. What are his plans concerning my children? And is he really off drugs and booze? I need answers quickly about my adopted children. He is my son and I love him as a father. But I hate what he has become. I want to believe he has truly reformed."

Jerry McHone looked up. She had been taking notes. "We'll need to bug the place and tap the phone."

Sid picked up her hint. "If our operative is caught and convicted, we need a promise of five thousand a month for the period of incarceration plus reimbursement of the fine to be paid to the family."

Clark turned to Jack. "What is the prison and fine possibility?"

"Could be a felony if he breaks in and takes something. More than likely a misdemeanor with a fine and no jail. Is that how you read it, Mister Graham?"

"I can just tell you of my past experience. We haven't had anyone go to jail yet. We've had two cases where a small fine was paid, but that's all."

"Then do it." Clark said firmly.

They got up to leave pausing as Clark continued. "Make all spoken reports to Mister Wexler with written reports weekly to me. I want nothing in the report that identifies either your firm or any of the real names involved. Refer to my son as the subject. Keep no records of this in your files. There is to be no paper trail."

"How do we bill you?"

"A simple note with the amount will do. Just say that it's for services rendered. Miss McHone, tear up your notes, please."

Jack and Clark followed them out to their car. When they left, Clark looked at Jack for a few moments. "They'll get the job done for me. You were right to recommend them."

Beth came outside to meet them. "Clark, we've got to talk."

"Inside."

"No, right now, right here!"

Jack continued on inside but waited by the door.

"Is this act two of the argument we had this morning?"

"Clark, I'm serious. If she's going, I'm staying here."

"But, she's already invited."

"She's an employee, you're the boss."

"She is not my mistress. How many times do I have to tell you?"

"Some things are proven by actions. Tell her to stay home."

"Okay, you stay here. I will do what I promised."

Jack quickly left his hiding place near the open door. Mounting the stairs, he took two at a time so as to enter his room before Beth could see him. He found one of the alarm people stringing wires along the baseboard.

"Be out in a minute. Soon's I run them wires to that box over yonder and hook 'em up."

"When do you think this part of the job will be finished?"

"'Nother half hour or so. All's we has to do is test 'er out."

Jack inwardly cringed at the guy's grammar.

"Do you do many of these installations?"

"Yep, ever day, all day. Been doin' this for 'most four year. They give me insurance for my family too. Made a big difference when we had the baby last year."

Jack left his room in time to see Beth get to the top of the stairs. She was crying.

"Beth, what's wrong?"

"Never mind me."

"Is there anything I can do?"

"I'm not going on the trip tomorrow. I'll be staying here."

"Oh?"

"I want to be here to see after my children."

She quickly entered her room.

Before the alarm company left, they demonstrated the system to Jack. With the windows and doors all wired, glass breakage sensors, motion detectors in the hall and IR heat detectors on the grounds, an intruder would be unable to keep from triggering the alarm. The only hitch was that the sensors had to be set or armed when the last one went to bed using the controls for the system in Jack's bedroom and in the master suite.

The night was uneventful. Jack rose at an early hour, turned off the alarm system and went for his usual run. This time, he limited his circuit to running laps around the house. He was still running when the first of the guests arrived.

The first group consisted of three men. The car drove around the garage to the slip. Two crewmen assisted with the luggage. As soon as the men and luggage were unloaded, the driver left.

Jack continued his run another twenty minutes. He was ready to take his shower when the same car returned. This time, four women exited. Again, the crew helped them aboard with their luggage.

Jack jogged back to the house in time to meet Clark.

"Up early again, Jack?"

"Yes, I try to get in my run before anyone else stirs. I looked at your yacht. Really beautiful. How long is she?"

"Seventy-two feet. We have a crew of five including the cook. Five staterooms with each having their own head. The head is the restroom, you know."

"Being an ex-marine, I'm aware of naval terminology."

"We're going to visit a few islands and do a little gambling."

"Well, bon voyage."

"Thank you. Just keep everyone safe until I return."

Later that afternoon, Jack took the twins fishing. The children caught a few croakers to their delight. They kept Smith and Jack busy baiting their hooks. After catching a dozen or more, Jack told them they had caught enough for their supper. On the way back to the house, Jack offered to clean and scale the fish. The children insisted on watching.

Smith found a knife, water hose and a bucket. Right there on the dock, Jack scaled, gutted and filleted the fish. When Jack finished, Smith hosed down the dock.

The cooperation of the cook, however, was another matter. She had her menu planned and mostly prepared. But the pleading of the children won out. After the children left for their room, the cook had much to say to Jack.

"Don't you know how bony croakers are? How do you expect these kids to pick out the bones and not get choked in the process?"

"But, I filleted them."

"Sure, you got out the large bones, but there are zillions of small ones. I'm going to have to fake it, you know."

"Fake it?"

"Yes. I'll send Smith to the market for something more appropriate for the kids. They'll never know."

"What'll we do with the croakers?"

"We'll wrap them in plastic and let the garbage man take them away. Is that simple enough?"

During dinner the children made sure everyone knew that they caught the fish. They even argued about which kid caught a particular fish. After dinner, all they could talk about was how Jack took them fishing.

Linda took the children back to their room with Beth lingering at the table talking to Jack.

"It's been quite a while since the children were this excited. Thank you for your fishing adventure."

"I enjoyed it as much as they did."

"You're not married, are you?"

"No, perhaps when I graduate from Engineering School. That's a year and a half away.

"You'll be some catch."

"That's what my aunt says."

"Aunt?"

"Yes, she's the only family I have now."

"Oh."

"You're an orphan, then?"

"I guess you could say that."

"Well, it's time to read to the children. Goodnight."

"Goodnight."

CHAPTER
36

A FTER HE HAD MADE his morning run and while he was eating breakfast in the kitchen, the call came. Smith came into the kitchen with a pained look on his face.

"Mister Jack, I think you should take this call. It's the Coast Guard about Master Clark."

"Hello, I'm Jack Wexler in charge of security, how may I help you?"

"This is Lt. Ruth Conway of the Coast Guard Information Office. I'm sorry to report that Mister Clark Townsend is feared lost at sea. As near as we can tell, he fell overboard last night. We are mounting a search by sea and air, but expect the worst. According to testimony from the passengers and crew, he may have been intoxicated."

"Is the Friendly Mistress returning to Bal Harbour?"

"She should be back by nine tonight."

"I'll tell Mrs. Townsend."

"Please write down this number. Call me anytime for an update on the search."

Jack pulled out his address book and wrote the number.

"Okay, thanks."

Jack turned to Smith. "Did she tell you?"

"Just that it was bad news. I really didn't want to hear it so I gave the call to you. He's dead, isn't he?"

"He fell overboard last night. They're searching for him now. Please tell the staff."

Smith wiped away a tear. "I appreciate you taking charge, Mister Jack. I don't think I could tell Mrs. Townsend."

Jack looked at his watch as he slowly climbed the stairs. He knocked at the door to Beth's room.

"Just a minute."

Jack waited until the door opened.

"Good morning, Jack."

"The Coast Guard called. Clark fell overboard last night and is missing. They're searching for him now."

Her legs weakened as she clung to the door for support. Jack grabbed her and lifted her to his arms. He carried her to a large chair.

"Thanks, Jack. I still feel faint. Just give me a minute. How did it happen?"

"Just the bare facts for now. I was told that he fell overboard last night. The crew and passengers say that he had been drinking heavily."

"That sounds like something Clark would do. He only drinks when he's on that boat."

She started to cry. "Damn him. How could he be so reckless? He has children to raise. Now they'll have no father."

"Listen to me, Beth. You have to take charge now. It is a fair conclusion that Clark is dead. It is also a reasonable conclusion that his body will not be found. In the next few days, you need to be named conservator of his estate. Call the lawyers after you have found your strength. There will be reporters as well as investigators here when the boat returns tonight. I'll call the Jefferson Agency about getting additional security. We need someone on the gate full time."

By the time the Friendly Mistress docked, there were eight cars from various agencies in the driveway and parked on the lawn. The Jefferson Agency people were keeping the press and curious out.

Jack and Beth met the ship but were turned away by the FBI, Coast Guard and Miami PD investigators. Jack flashed his badge but was told that the Sheriff's Department would not be involved. They returned to the house and waited. By two the next morning, all the cars were gone. There was yellow tape across the gangway to the yacht marking it as a crime scene with a Miami PD uniformed officer standing or rather sitting guard.

Since the entire household was up, Jack had coffee sent to the policeman before they all retired for the night. The next morning, Jack was visited by Jeraldine McHone.

"I thought I would come by to check on the people we have at the gate. The police are there as well. Don't know how long they'll be there so we may as well keep our people here just in case."

"Any word on our subject?"

"We placed the bugs and tapped the phone. The only thing we've found out is that he is dealing crystal meth."

"Felony dealing?"

"Felony big-time."

"Listen in for a few more days, pull out the bugs, and call the police. Surely you have someone you can call at the Miami PD or DEA, don't you?"

"Yes, that can be done. So, you want him charged and jailed?"

"Miss McHone, right now we need him away and out of Mrs. Townsend's hair."

"Please call me Jerry and I'll call you Jack. Okay?"

"Thanks Jerry, I appreciate anything you can do for the family."

As she left, she smiled, "Give me a call after this is over, okay?"

Jack smiled back. He was not at all surprised when overt, aggressive flirting occurred. He really didn't have a clue that he was unique and women normally waited for the guy to make the first move.

After he saw Jerry to her car, Beth met him at the door.

"Did she have any news?"

"Not really. She did say that Clark's son, James, was dealing in drugs and that an arrest was coming soon. I asked if she had heard anything on your husband's situation. She had nothing new on that."

"It's been so hard. I try to keep up a bold exterior but it's only an act. By the way, I called the law firm Clark uses. They thought it a good idea to petition the court to have me named as conservator rather than having him declared dead. The only thing is we will not be able to access the life insurance. However, Clark was… My God, I'm already thinking of him in the past tense. I was going to say, we are really quite wealthy so the insurance has little consequence."

Jack noticed that her lower lip had started quivering. He knew she was on the verge of breaking down. He reached out and took her in his arms.

"I know it's hard. I could hardly keep myself together when my parents died. I tell you truly that almost every new day will be better. Sometimes it's one step forward and two steps back."

She clung to him tightly, softly weeping. Finally, she kissed him on the neck and slowly backed away.

"If you have a minute, Jack, I'd like to tell you something."

"Sure. What's on your mind?"

"Come, sit down over here."

Pointing to a couch, she sat in a facing chair.

"Clark and myself have been married for eight years. For the last seven, we have not been intimate at all. Clark had taken a mistress. He named the yacht after her, you know. I asked for a divorce several times during the early years but we couldn't come to an agreement. The adoption of the twins changed all that. They are now my life. I love them as my own. I tell you all of this to explain my lack of emotional feeling about Clark's loss."

"I appreciate your confidence. Knowing your situation helps me do my job."

"If you would, please show me how to set the alarm thing. They put a box with lights and buttons in our suite and I haven't a clue what they are for."

"Come, I'll show you."

They mounted the stairs and entered her suite. On a wall in the sitting room he found the box. It was identical to his own.

"Here, you see this amber light? This tells you that the system is off. Now we push the button marked ARMED and the amber light goes out and the green light is on. Please open the door."

She opened the door. A pulsating alarm sounded.

"Now look. The green light is out and the red light is lit. This means that there was something that triggered the system. In this case, one of the motion detectors in the hallway saw the door open."

"Please, stop that nasty sound. It's driving me mad."

"Now, when I push the off button, the alarm goes off and the amber light is now on."

"I think I know how it works. Would you please come back tonight and show me again."

"Good idea."

He had started to say 'It's a date.' but thought better of it. She might have thought he was flirting.

Jack spent the rest of the morning calling the Coast Guard, FBI and Miami PD. All he could get was what he already knew. The only real news was that an inquest was scheduled for a week from next Tuesday. He figured Beth would want to attend so he made arrangements for someone from the Jefferson Agency to be at the house to guard the children.

He thought about the outcome of the inquest. The most logical finding would be that Clark accidentally fell overboard and was presumed dead. At least he and Beth would hear the testimony of all the ones on board.

After lunch, Jack lingered over a cup of coffee reading the Herald sports section. Smith rushed in.

"Mister Jack, Mister James Townsend is at the door. Mister Clark instructed that he not be admitted and to call the police if he were to appear.

Mister Clark had a restraining order against him. What shall I do?"

"I'll tend to it Smith. Where is he now?"

"Outside, at the main door."

Jack put the paper aside and followed Smith to the front door. Smith stepped aside for Jack to open the door.

"Mister Townsend, I am Jack Wexler. I am the resident security officer. Please state your business."

He smiled. "Well, the old man hired a goon. How very like him. Look, I want to see my kids so get out of the way."

"No, you will not enter the house. You, sir, are under arrest for trespass. I believe an order of restraint has been placed against you. Smith, please get some rope in case we need to restrain Mister Townsend and then call the police."

"Hey, no need of that. I'll just get in my car and leave."

"No, you're under arrest. Just sit down on the steps until the police arrive."

"Be damned if I will. I'm leaving."

He turned to go. Jack twisted his arm and brought him to the ground. Smith arrived with a length of rope. In spite of a flurry of curses, Jack quickly had him hog-tied.

"Smith, do you think you can find a copy of the restraining order?"

"Yes. Do you want me to fetch it?"

"If you can operate the Xerox machine, just bring a copy."

James had stopped his stream of invective and was trying to loosen the rope.

"Now, James, I don't know too much about rodeo work but I really believe the knots will hold until the police get here. If you do happen to get loose, I'll just tie you up again."

Jack heard the door open. It was Beth. She stood there angrily with her arms folded.

"James, what are you doing here?"

"I just came to pay my respects. He was my father, you know."

"You must realize that the children are no longer yours now. In addition, I don't ever want you around here under any circumstances."

"Look, just let me go before the cops get here. I'll get out of your life and you'll never see me again. I was planning to split for New Orleans in a couple of days anyway."

She turned to enter the house. "Jack, don't let him loose."

As soon as she entered the house, Smith returned with the copy of the order.

"Thank you Smith, that will do nicely. I'll handle it from here."

Two hours later with James arrested and his car towed away, Jack joined the family at the pool. Linda and Beth were at the shallow end with the twins. Jack dropped his towel and dove in. It was just deep enough so that he missed the bottom. He surfaced and started doing laps. Back, breast, butterfly and free. Each time he came to the side edge, he switched stroke. The pool was tee shaped with his end seventy-five feet long. He could barely establish a stroke when the edge of the pool signaled a turn. He kept going until his arms tired. He dragged himself out, breathing hard.

As soon as his ears cleared of water, he could hear the applause. All four were clapping. He made a mock bow and raised his arms in a victory salute. He jumped into the shallow end, making a large splash to the delight of the children and to the annoyance of the women.

Jack played underwater tag with the children letting them easily win by moving slowly. Beth and Linda moved out of the way. It was evident they didn't want their hair wet with all the roughhousing going on. When the twins tired of the play they all got out of the pool.

Jack grabbed his towel and started for the house.

"Wait a moment, Jack. I'll walk with you."

Jack turned back to see Beth slipping on her shoes. She soon caught up with him. The children ran past with Linda running with them. She put her arm in his as they walked the winding path to the side entrance to the house.

At the top of the stairs, they parted. "Don't forget, Jack, we dress for dinner."

Jack started to say something about Clark not being here but thought better of it. He figured she wanted to keep up the routine for the children's sake. In his room, he pulled off his swimsuit and hit the shower to get the chlorine off.

The phone was ringing when he exited the bathroom. Smith was calling him.

"Sir, a gentleman from the newspaper is on line number one. He wants to speak to Mrs. Townsend. However, no one answers in her suite."

"I'll take the call."

"Very well, Mister Jack."

Jack pushed the line one button.

"Hello, I'm Jack Wexler. How can I help you?"

"Joe Hennessy with the Herald. Do you have any comment concerning the arrest of an employee of Mister Townsend a Miss Gladys Turnbull?"

"An arrest, you say?"

"Yes. She confessed. As I understand it, she pushed him overboard."

"Since we have just now heard of this, we have no comment. Perhaps tomorrow."

AFTER NOTIFYING SMITH not to take any further calls from the press, Jack started searching for Beth. Since Smith had told Jack he had rung her suite with no answer, the suite was the last place he checked. She came to the door dressed in a terry robe, towel-drying her hair.

"I just got off the phone with a reporter for the Herald. He wanted to get a statement from you concerning the arrest of Gladys Bullock for Clark's murder. It seems she confessed to pushing him overboard."

She dropped her towel and put her hand over her mouth. "Oh my god, what did you say?"

"I said we have no comment."

"What else did you say?"

"Nothing. We're going to have to put someone on the gate. It won't be long before we're under siege."

She leaned against the doorjamb. "I'm getting a little light-headed. Help me to a chair."

She was trembling as Jack took her hand to lead her to a nearby chair. He knelt beside the chair. "Can I get you some water?"

"No. Really, I'll be okay. It's just that this is the final shocker at the end of a succession of shockers. I know it seems naïve, however, I really thought he would be found alive on some island or something. I still hold a sliver of hope."

"If you are really okay, I'll call the Jefferson agency now."

She nodded.

Jeraldine McHone answered. "Jerry, this is Jack Wexler."

"Oh, Jack. I really didn't expect you to call so soon. How about my place at eight?"

"Sounds good but this is business."

"And you don't believe I mean business?"

"Hey, for myself, I really can't wait. But enough of this. We need the around-the-clock guards on the gate and at the boat dock again. Three armed men with handcuffs and badges. Arrest anyone who enters the grounds for trespass."

Jack quickly left the house and walked to the gatehouse. He found the control panel and closed the massive iron gate. As he settled down, he found some old magazines to read. He really didn't get a chance to read them, as he had to turn away several reporters. Instead of leaving, they camped on the street. Soon a television truck parked nearby and extended its satellite dish.

Smith came running up. "Mister Jack, there is a launch at the dock. People with cameras are at the door."

Jack quickly ran to the house, shouting as he caught up with the intruders. "You are all trespassing on private property. If you do not immediately leave, you will be arrested. You will be put in handcuffs and carried off by the police. Is that understood?"

The camera lights came on. The well made-up lady stuck a microphone in Jack's face. "Do you have any comment on the arrest of Gladys Bullock?"

Jack looked at his watch. "You have just two minutes to get into your motor launch and leave."

Again the microphone was thrust forward. "What is your name and how are you connected to the Townsend family?"

"One minute to go."

The female reporter with the microphone gave the cameraman the finger-across-the-throat gesture. "We're through here. Back in the boat."

Jack waited long enough for the launch to leave then went back to the gate. On the way back, he met two reporters walking toward the house.

"Who are you people and what are you doing on private property without permission?"

The guy in the lead answered. "We're here to interview Mrs. Townsend."

"You are under arrest for trespass. Get on your knees and place your hands over your head."

"Like hell I will."

Jack grabbed his collar and pulled him down. "I said you are under arrest. If you do not obey my order, I will shoot you. Is that understood?"

The second man quickly went to his knees.

"Now, take off your neckties."

"Why?"

"So I can tie your up your hands. Now, do it!"

As each took off his tie, Jack tied their hands together. When they were both bound, he escorted them to the gatehouse.

"Smith, please call the police. I have two under arrest for trespass."

Placing two reporters under arrest had a chilling effect on the ones waiting outside the gate. They weren't so eager to argue about entering the grounds. The police arrived at the same time as the Jefferson people. The Jefferson operatives were evidently either off-duty or retired cops, as they knew each other by name.

They set up a command post at the gatehouse with Smith bringing out an urn of coffee and sandwiches. Jack returned to the house and trudged up the stairs.

Beth met him at the top of the stairs still in her terry robe. She slowly walked toward him with her arms outstretched. Jack took her in his arms and held her for a long time. She started kissing him slowly on the neck.

She pulled away and held eye contact. "In here."

She held his hand and led him into her suite. As soon as the door closed she turned and kissed him passionately.

"Make love to me."

He turned to leave.

"Please."

"I'm going to my room for a condom."

"Stay. I'm on the pill." Seeing his expression, she added. "It keeps me regular."

As they made love, Beth's tears flowed with a smile on her face.

During the next two weeks Beth and Jack were routinely together in the afternoons in her suite and after ten at night in Jack's room.

Their days were filled with routine. Jack became involved with the children with various adventures and games. Their favorite game was 'Gulliver's Travels' where Jack as Gulliver would be subdued by the children and tied up. Beth and Linda would help out when Jack resisted a little too much.

The inquest was scheduled for two in the afternoon. Attendance was restricted to those invited and the press. The press would be admitted only after the others were seated. Therefore, there was a gauntlet of reporters and cameras that all had to endure.

The officer in charge of the hearing was a Coast Guard Commander. The statements of crewmembers were entered first. The first officer testified that he was employed by Sullivan Yachting Services and had served on the ship several times in the past. Meticulous detail was presented of the exact course the yacht took that night. A printout and a digital data disk of the GPS plot of position data taken every five minutes was entered into evidence. However, the only data that mattered was the time Clark went overboard. On this there was a discrepancy window that was one and a half hours wide.

Then written documentation about the Coast Guard search patterns as well as charts showing tides and current was entered into evidence by the presiding officer himself.

Next came the testimony of the guests. Each of the men were represented by an attorney. Their statements were guarded at best offering little in the way of information. The three women each gave their occupation as unemployed office worker though all knew they were call girls. Gladys Bullock, dressed in prison garb, declined to answer any questions on recommendation of her lawyer.

After all were heard, the presiding officer shuffled through some papers until he found what he was looking for. "The complete published report of this hearing will be available in approximately two months. However, I am prepared to offer the following finding of fact. That, Clark Henry Townsend, an adult citizen of the United States, as a result of accident or foul play by person or persons not named herein has entered the waters off South Florida unaided by life vest or other flotation gear and is therefore presumed dead."

He banged the gavel and quickly left. Jack looked at his watch. The entire hearing took only slightly over an hour.

As Gladys was escorted out, she glanced toward Beth and silently mouthed, "I'm sorry."

Beth started crying as they walked out of he hearing room to the glare of the camera lights. Six or seven microphones were shoved in front of her with reporters shouting questions. Jack ran interference as they raced at a fast walk to Jack's car with the reporters following. As he pulled away from the parking lot, both breathed a sigh of relief.

"Jack, I really didn't think this hearing would be so tiring and emotional to me. I should have stayed home; after all, here was no new information given that meant anything. In a way, I feel sorry for Gladys. She loved him, you know. She was just tired of waiting."

"Yeah, I figured that was the case. With a good lawyer, she may even get probation with no prison time."

"I wanted a divorce for several years but I wanted my adopted children too. It was obvious that I couldn't have both so I stayed."

"I guess we all make compromises of one sort or another in life."

"Oh, Jack. Up ahead is a drug store. Please stop, I need to pick up a few things. Just wait in the car, I won't be but a minute."

Jack found a space near the door and waited for her return. When she got back to the car, she placed the plastic bag with her purchases on the seat beside her.

"Don't forget to buckle up."

She snapped the belt on and settled back in the seat.

"You know, Jack, this is a very comfortable car."

"Do you want music? There's some jazz on the CD changer."

"I know it sounds elitist, but I like classical myself."

"Yeah, me too. All except grand opera—if I could understand the language it would be different."

"But the singing is so beautiful."

A dog ran out into the street. Jack slammed on his brakes, just avoiding hitting him. The plastic bag tumbled to the floor emptying its contents. Jack quickly pulled to the side while Beth struggled against the seat belt trying to put it all back in the bag. Finally she unhooked the belt and finished the job. Jack couldn't help note the labeling on three particular boxes.

When Jack saw the shocked look on her face, he returned a relaxed smile. "Sorry. Did you get everything from the floor?"

"I think so."

They were both silent for the remainder of the trip back to the house. Beth was hoping that Jack had not seen the purchase whereas Jack was thinking about the importance of the presence of the three boxes.

After dinner, Jack found Beth in the office. She had the safe open, counting money.

"Clark always was able to get money from the safe. I never knew how much he kept here. I've counted over a hundred and twenty thousand and still have this to count." She pointed to a smaller pile of cash.

"We need to talk."

"Your money? I believe the fee was two thousand a week, wasn't it? I'll make it an even six so you can leave whenever you wish."

She picked up six stacks of bills and pushed them toward Jack.

"That's not what we need to talk about. When were you going to tell me?"

"Tell you what?"

"I saw the three pregnancy test kits."

"Oh."

"I repeat, when were you going to tell me?"

"I wasn't. My plan was to name Clark as the father."

"Are you pregnant?"

"I'll know in the morning."

"But you're fairly sure, aren't you?"

"I should have started my period four days ago."

Jack picked up the money. "I'll leave as soon as I get my things packed."

She came around the desk and kissed him. "I'll never forget you."

"Nor I you."

CHAPTER

38

LaVerne Hollings

H E RETURNED to his Aunt's house with eight weeks left before he was due at back at Auburn for the summer term. So he made the rounds of several hotels looking for a client. He wound up at the Coral Palms to speak his friend Carl.

Jack tried Carl's office first. He recognized Juan.

"Seen Carl?"

"Carl is in the coffee shop."

"See you later."

Jack walked the few steps to the coffee shop and spotted his friend.

"Carl, how's it going?"

"Same old rut, my man. But it's a rut I chose so I have no complaints. Say, I read about the shootout at the Brock place. You okay with that?"

"Yeah, the trouble came to me. I had no choice in the matter."

"You looking for work?"

"Yeah, keep a lookout for me. I'm going crazy hanging around my aunt's place."

"We're having a convention here starting Thursday, the day after to-morrow. Security will need extra help if you're interested."

"What kind of convention?"

"Cosmetics. They were here last year. These gals really kick up their heels. We've got a new security head now."

"Anybody I know?"

"You're going to be really surprised." He waved toward the waitress. "Hungry?"

"No, I had a burger a while ago."

Carl led the way to the security office. Jack was expecting to see an old, fat, retired police officer.

Carl knocked and opened the door. "Mrs. Cotton, I'd like to introduce a friend of mine."

Jack followed Carl into the office. Mrs. Cotton looked to be in her late thirties. She was trim and good looking. On her desk were family pictures. He saw a ring on her finger.

"This is Jack Wexler. He has worked security and bodyguard for several guests here at the hotel."

She stepped out from behind the desk and shook his hand. "I've heard of you. Please call me Charlotte."

"Thanks. I was just checking with Carl about any prospects. I'm between clients now."

"Would you be interested in working security this next weekend? I have a few openings."

"I usually work for private clients. The pay is much better. Anyone coming in that needs that kind of help?"

"As a matter of fact, yes. LaVerne herself wants private security."

"LaVerne?"

"Cosmetics mogul. Pyramid marketing making millionaires out of housewives. It's really somewhat like a religion for these people. Their color is violet. You'll see them in violet dresses and driving violet cars."

"I appreciate the lead. Who do I see?"

"The advance man, or should I say lady, is here in the hotel now."

She picked up her phone and made a call. After hanging up, they had a bit of small talk until a very tall, beautiful blond lady entered the room.

"Patricia Hollings, this is Jack Wexler, my recommendation as security bodyguard for Miss LaVerne."

All business, Miss Hollings began by asking for references. Jack excused himself while he went out to his car, bringing back a manila envelope with all the information.

"This package of information should be all you need. These are copies of course. You may see the originals if you like. A previous client, Colonel Robert Fossgrave is still a resident at this hotel. If you wish to inquire of him, I'm sure he would be happy to furnish any further details."

"Where can I reach you?"

"It's in the envelope. I live with my aunt."

"Then you're not married?"

"No."

"Gay?"

"Hardly."

"You would need to be on hand 24-7 and live in LaVerne's suite for the entire time. Is that okay?"

"That's what I usually do."

"Armed?"

"Of course."

She turned and opened the door. "If all this checks out, I'll call. We'll discuss your salary then."

Mrs. Cotton smiled. "Well, that was easy. It had slipped my mind. She asked for a bodyguard yesterday. You just did me a great favor."

"I'm the one in debt to you."

When Jack pulled into the driveway of his aunt's house, she came to the door making the thumb and pinkie sign of a telephone call. It was Patricia.

"Quite impressive, Jack. Oh, may I call you Jack?"

"Sure."

"And please call me Pat. Only my best friends call me Pat. I made a few calls and I spoke to Colonel Fossgrave. As I say, quite impressive. I called Mrs. Ellman. She couldn't stop gushing. Told me about saving her life. Is your rate still five thousand a week?"

Jack realized Wilma had exaggerated his fee. "Since the contract is for Thursday through Tuesday, I think four would be fine. Expenses will be extra, of course. And I expect to be paid in cash in advance."

"Can you move into the suite tomorrow?"

"Sure. Say, tomorrow afternoon at two. I'll ask for you at the desk."

"I'll be expecting you."

Since in South Florida everything grows so fast, Jack spent the rest of the afternoon working on the yard. After mowing, trimming the shrubbery, weeding the flowers and edging the driveway and curb, he took his shower.

After he watched television with his aunt for a while, he went to bed. It wasn't like him to sleep so much.

He was packed and gone by noon the next day. The suite was the same one that Wilma had rented when they were forced out of the condo. It brought back memories. He chose the small bedroom he had used before. It seemed to him an eternity since he had made love on that bed.

For a moment the thought of Allison flashed. He felt guilty as he tried to remember the details of her face. He knew it was a healthy mental trick.

His mind would continue to keep pushing hurtful memories into the background until he could function normally again.

He was stowing the last of his things away when Pat came in.

"I see you're settled in. You may have to move across the hall if LaVerne's latest boyfriend is with her."

"We need to agree on how to handle my expenses."

"I'll get your fee out of the hotel safe on the way to pick up LaVerne. Most expenses will go on my company credit card. Anything else, just keep receipts or a record."

"Okay, glad we got that cleared up."

"I just got word a few minutes ago on my cell phone that LaVerne will be arriving this afternoon. I have to meet her at the airport. Want to come along?"

"Okay, you want me to drive?"

"Oh, no. We have a stretch limo rented for the week."

"Fine, I'll tin us a good parking place."

"Tin?"

"With my badge. Since I'm a deputy sheriff on released status, I just flash my badge so we can park in a tow-away zone."

"Wear something less casual than tee and jeans. If anyone near her is less than the best, she takes it as reflecting on her."

"A tux?"

"No, nice casual shirt and jacket will do." She walked over to the closet and pointed to a few things. "Something like this, or this."

"What time?"

"Her flight arrives at 4:30. But you know about flights. I have never, ever, arrived early. The limo will pick us up at 3:30 just to be on the safe side."

"Plans for the evening?"

"Me or her?"

"Both."

"LaVerne will take a tour of the convention hall and the hospitality rooms, then we'll have dinner. You will be present through all of this."

Jack was in the lobby when Pat exited the elevator. She wore a dark violet leather micro-miniskirt, leather bolero jacket to match with light violet silk blouse. Even her hose and shoes were violet. As she walked, it was obvious she wasn't wearing a bra.

At the airport, Jack met the traffic policeman as he approached, showing him his badge. "Hi, I'm Jack Wexler, deputy sheriff. I'm doing VIP escort duty. Will it be okay to have the driver stand here until we can leave?"

The cop stopped. "Sure, Jack. It'll be okay as long as the driver stays with the car. Since the car is so long, we may need to move it a few feet. But it'll be here when you get back."

Looking at Pat, he remarked, "Man, what a beauty. Her legs, man, look at those legs. Damn, Jack, how did you catch this duty."

"Just luck, my man. Just luck."

LaVerne didn't just exit the plane; she made a grand entrance to the airport. They were whisked away on an electric cart to the escalator leading to the baggage claim area. Jack took the baggage checks and loaded all the violet colored luggage on a cart. Pat and Her Highness were in deep conversation, paying no attention to Jack at all.

After stowing the luggage in the trunk, Jack waited for the ladies to be seated before taking the front seat next to the driver.

"No, Jack. Back here. I want to introduce you to LaVerne."

He sat facing the ladies. It was his first chance to look at LaVerne up close. She appeared to be in her middle to late forties, but with cosmetic surgery, he knew she could be a lot older.

"This is Jack Wexler. He will be your personal bodyguard for the week. For now, we have him occupying a small bedroom in your suite. He will be available every day at all hours. He comes highly recommended."

"Oh, Jack. I just know well get along famously. I am so glad you will be sharing the suite with me and Patricia."

When they arrived at the hotel, there were twenty or more ladies dressed variously in violet waiting for the appearance of LaVerne. Jack left the car first, keeping the door open for her.

She put on quite a show. Like a queen greeting her subjects. Out of the corner of his eye, Jack spotted the man. He had an angry, purposeful look on his face. He was focused on LaVerne to the exclusion of anything else.

The man shouted at LaVerne. "It's your fault she left me. It's your fault and you're a goin' t' pay."

He attempted to pull a pistol out of his jacket pocket but the front sight snagged on the lining. Jack lunged at him, bringing him to the ground. Jack's body smothered him, keeping the hand with the pistol bound and unable to move. Jack reached under, finding the hand with the gun.

"Let it go. It's over now. No one got hurt. Everybody is safe."

Weeping now, the man blurted out, "You don't understand. My wife left me because of her."

LaVerne and Pat had gone before the first officers arrived to put the man in handcuffs. Jack was delayed with giving his statement to the arresting officer and later to the officer's sergeant.

He took the elevator to his floor, inserted the key card and entered to a darkened suite. He looked into every room, and then left taking the elevator to the lobby. He eventually found LaVerne, Pat, and a lady in the hotel uniform examining the décor of hospitality rooms.

Smiling, Jack asked, "Does that happen often?"

"What's that, dear?"

"A deranged man with a pistol blaming you for losing his wife?"

"Oh, he wouldn't have used it. Would he?"

"Well, it was loaded."

LaVerne turned to Jack with color drained from her face.

"You mean he was really going to kill me?"

CHAPTER

39

WHEN THEY LEFT the hospitality room, reporters and photographers accosted them. The strobe flashes filled the room. Jack took charge and escorted LaVerne and Pat to the elevator.

"I would recommend that you hold a press conference as soon as possible about the incident this evening. That way, you can get it over with. The main thrust of your convention has to be business and not this nut that tried to kill you."

"Quite observant of you, young man. And thank you for saving my life. I had no idea he was armed."

"I suggest we call the *Herald* and the television stations and set up the conference this evening. Let's see, it's 5:50 now.... What time do you want to have dinner?"

LaVerne glanced toward Pat. Pat shrugged. "How about nine?"

Jack suggested, "Press conference at 8:00 or 8:30 and then dinner at the hotel. Will that work for you?"

"Pat, would you please make the calls? The hotel should be able to provide a room and lectern. Just make sure there's a back door."

The elevator door opened at their floor. A videographer and reporter were waiting.

Jack took the lead. "Please, guys. There'll be a press conference at 8:00 downstairs. You'll have plenty of time for the 11:00 news."

The press conference went without a hitch. LaVerne was all business. She was able to turn the whole thing to a commercial for free enterprise. On how a woman can gain financial independence by just being friendly to her neighbors and co-workers—and selling cosmetics in the process.

They had dinner at the hotel restaurant. At 10:30, LaVerne was ready for bed but Jack and Pat insisted on going dancing. So, Jack made sure LaVerne was safely in her suite before heading out on the town. They took the company limo after locating the driver in the coffee shop.

Jack checked his wallet and found the business card for Rudfolfo's—their ticket in. When they got to the door, they were stopped.

"I'm sorry, but you need a reservation."

Jack handed him the card.

"Just a moment." He picked up the phone. It wasn't ten seconds before Rudolfo came to the door.

"Ah, Mister Wexler. How good it is to see you again. Is this lovely lady with you? Dear, how beautiful you are. Have I seen you in the cinema? On the television? You must tell me where I have seen you."

Pat extended her hand and offered a super smile. "My name is Patricia Hollings, perhaps I have appeared to you in a dream."

He took her hand and kissed it. "I apologize, Jack. I have given my private table to some special friends. If you could please wait at the bar, I will have you seated at the next empty table."

A couple walked past out the door.

Rudolfo whispered to Jack. "Give me two minutes and I'll have their table cleared."

He clapped his hands twice. The maitre d' quickly left his station. "Alexander, this is my very good friend Jack Wexler and his lady friend Miss Hollings. They are my personal guests this evening."

He turned to Jack. "I'll never forget your selfless act in protecting Miss Lingstrom. Was the wound severe?"

"No, I had excellent medical attention."

As they were escorted to their table, Pat inquired, "What's this about being wounded?"

"I was working as bodyguard for Kristin Lingstrom. Someone attempted to knife her."

"Oh, my god, the model? You really saved her life? So the business with the man with the gun wasn't a new thing for you, was it?"

"Really, Pat, I don't look for trouble."

They ordered their drinks and hit the dance floor. Surprisingly, Pat was a little clumsy. Jack kept the steps simple so she could follow. Soon she became accustomed to the movement of Jack's body and was able to follow with increased confidence.

By one, both were fairly well spent. Rudolfo again met them in the lobby entrance way. This time he gave Pat an air-kiss a half-inch away from each cheek. They had to wait a few minutes for the limo to arrive since the driver had to park a couple of blocks away.

In the car, Pat was quite uninhibited as she and Jack mugged it up. Neither came up for air the entire trip back to the hotel. They only unclenched when the driver opened the door for Pat.

"Miss, will you need me again tonight?"

"No. If you could have someone on duty by eight in the morning, that will be okay."

As soon as the elevator closed they began kissing. Her hand started massaging Jack's crotch.

After they entered the suite Jack led the way to his room. When he turned on the light, he heard the voice of LaVerne.

"Pat? Jack? Is that you?"

Pat answered, "Yes, mother. We're back."

"Well, come in here and tell me all about it."

She shrugged and silently mouthed, "I'm sorry."

She didn't quite close the door so Jack could hear some of their conversation. Pat began with their royal reception by the owner of the club; how Jack was a recognized patron and that their tab was on the house. At this point, Jack began to get undressed. He decided against having a shower, opting to hear more. Their words began to get muffled so Jack turned off the light and opened the door a little wider.

He heard LaVerne say, "Well, I don't think you should just jump in bed with him."

Pat answered, "Mother, I haven't been a virgin for quite some time. Furthermore, you're a fine one to caution me on sex. I can't count the number of men you've been to bed with."

"Shush, Patty dear, he'll hear you."

With that, Jack could hear nothing else. So he went to his bathroom, brushed his teeth and took a shower. He put on a clean pair of boxers and went to bed. He strained to hear something but all was quiet.

He had been asleep less than a half hour when she came to his bed. She whispered, "Shhh, we don't want to wake her."

Jack answered in a whisper. "I'll get a condom."

"I brought one with me. I'll put it on you."

After they had made love, Jack remained awake until he could sense her slow deep breathing. He then fell asleep himself.

At six-thirty with only a few hours of sleep, Jack got up to take a leak. Sometime after he fell asleep, she had gone to her room. He decided to stay up so he ordered room service breakfast for three to be delivered at eight. He took his morning shower and dressed.

There were two morning newspapers, the *Herald* and *USA Today* on the floor outside their suite. Jack made coffee in the small kitchen and settled down to read. He turned to the metro section of the *Herald* and found a nice treatment of the arrival of LaVerne and a short paragraph on the attempt on her life. Thankfully, his name wasn't mentioned. They named the Miami PD officers who actually made the arrest, though.

Pat exited her room first. She was wearing a remarkably sheer night-shirt.

She smiled, "I had a lovely evening, Jack."

"My pleasure, I assure you."

"Is there any coffee?"

"Yes, in the small kitchen over there. I think they call it a butler's pantry. I ordered breakfast for three. They'll bring it in fifteen minutes or so."

"Coffee will be fine for now. Can I have some of the paper?"

"Sure, *USA Today* or the *Miami Herald*?"

"*USA Today*. I work the crossword."

They turned to reading the paper for a few minutes. Pat put her paper down. "I forgot. The hairdresser will be here in a few minutes. I need to see if LaVerne is awake yet."

At that moment, LaVerne left her bedroom. "Of course I'm awake. I'm not like some people who spend their nights on the town."

Pat looked at Jack and smiled.

"I saw that smile."

The doorbell rang. Jack glanced at his watch.

"That should be breakfast."

"Or Glynnis." Remarked LaVerne.

"Who?"

"My personal hairdresser."

Jack was at the door looking through the peephole. "It's breakfast."

The door was still open for the breakfast cart delivery when the purple clad hairdresser, Glynnis, arrived with her kit. Jack thought it better if he were not around for a while.

"Miss LaVerne, I think I'll make a tour of the convention spaces and have a conference with the director of security, Mrs. Cotton. Please look through the peephole before you open the door."

Jack was glad to be out of the suite. When he got to the lobby, the size of the crowd of purple-wearing ladies surprised him. The conference wasn't supposed to start until ten.

He headed for the auditorium. Mrs. Cotton was there with some of her security people. They appeared to be a mix of retired cops and college students. Jack followed the group as Mrs. Cotton explained their duties.

Jack wandered into the grill, sat at the counter and ordered a cup of coffee and a Danish. He had taken a few bites when he felt a hand on his shoulder. It was Charlotte Cotton.

"Hey, Jack. I wondered where you ran off. Did you want to speak to me?"

"I just wanted to find out about the security plans. I'll be escorting LaVerne down when she's ready for her entrance."

"So there you are!" Pat exclaimed, as she sat down next to Jack.

"So, how is security shaping up?" She squeezed his leg."

"Looks like Mrs. Cotton has everything taken care of. When does the program start?"

"I start the meeting at ten and introduce several of our top generals. Each of these ladies will give a half-hour pep talk. Laverne will welcome the army at eleven-thirty. We then break for lunch to return at two for three simultaneous workshops. We switch attendees twice so that all have the opportunity to experience each of the three sessions. Then tonight, LaVerne will do her magic."

"How about tomorrow?"

"Tomorrow is for the officers of the army. We have scheduled *Brunch With LaVerne* at ten. The whole thing is over after that. I will be so relieved."

CHAPTER
40

JACK WAS AT THE CONCIERGE DESK TALKING WITH JUAN.
"Mister Wexler?"

It was one of the bellboys.

"Yes, I'm Jack Wexler."

"Mrs. Cotton sent me to find you. She's in her office."

Jack walked the few yards to the hotel offices and entered Charlotte's room.

"Jack, I'm glad they found you. We've got a problem. They turned that damned psycho asshole loose. Lawyer got a magistrate to set a low bail. So, he's in the wind."

"Damn, Charlotte. He could be anywhere. Or, on the other hand, he could be on his way back home. This really makes my job a lot harder."

"Are you going to tell her?"

"Damn right! She, of all people, needs to have this information."

Jack took the elevator up and entered the suite. The hairdresser was just finishing up. LaVerne was wearing only bra and panties.

"Uh. Excuse me. I'll come back in a few minutes."

"Don't be silly, Jack. I'm sure you've seen a woman partly dressed before. I don't mind if you don't."

Pat came from her room fully dressed.

"How are things below?"

"I have some disturbing news. They let the psycho out on bail. God knows where he is now."

Glynnis returned from LaVerne's bathroom with a terry robe for LaVerne. LaVerne stood and put it on.

"My God, Jack. Do you think he'll try again?"

"We have to believe the worse. If we don't, you can be very dead."

"He's right, mother."

LaVerne quickly looked to Pat. Her eyes shot daggers. "I told you not to refer to me that way in front of others."

"LaVerne, for the next two days, I suggest that you go nowhere without me being at your side. At least until they locate the nut."

"Within reason, of course."

"How's that?"

Laughing, "Well, you aren't going to follow me into the powder room, are you?"

"You want'a bet!"

The doorbell rang. Jack pulled his pistol and looked through the peep-hole. It was Charlotte. Jack opened the door.

"Miss LaVerne, this is Charlotte Cotton the chief of security here at the hotel."

"A female security chief. How delightful and so twenty-first century."

"I've called the Jefferson Agency. They will provide a pair of off-duty policewomen around the clock until you get on your plane. After that, you're on your own."

"When will they report for duty?"

"Jack, they're on their way now. Should have them here within fifteen minutes."

"We need to get a copy of the guy's mug shot. Surely they took a photo of him when he was booked."

"I'll make a call and have them fax or e-mail it."

The photo of the kook arrived. The quality of the fax was so poor that Charlotte had to send a messenger to obtain shots of better quality.

Jack looked at his watch. "Pat, it's almost ten. You have to open the meeting, don't you? I'll stay here with LaVerne until it's time for her to leave. Let's see, that would be eleven fifteen or so, right?"

The female officers from the Jefferson Detective Agency arrived soon after Pat had gone to conduct the start of the convention. Glynnis scav-enged violet blouses from some of the LaVerne officer corps. At least the female operatives would be able to blend in.

Hazel, one of the female officers, took the elevator to the lobby first. Then Jack, LaVerne and the other officer, Audry, took the elevator to the lobby. At every stop on the way down, Jack stood in front of LaVerne with his pistol drawn. His arm was positioned behind his back so the pistol was hidden.

When they exited, Jack led the way. Hazel was positioned at the side and Audry bringing up the rear. Charlotte wearing a hotel blazer met them.

Jack could tell she was armed by the bulge at her right hip.

"Jack, follow me. We're going to the rear of the auditorium. There's a service hallway used when we cater for a large group. A doorway leads to the dais."

Jack entered first. He scanned the crowd looking for the face. Hazel followed.

"He may be dressed as a woman so don't let the clothing fool you."

Hazel nodded and quickly walked behind the dais to the other side of the stage riser.

When the introduction was made, LaVerne entered to a standing ovation. Several women in their violet outfits came forward with their flash cameras. Jack and Hazel focused on these in particular.

After sending Audry to the rear of the auditorium, Charlotte joined Jack.

"Short of running everyone through a metal detector, we've done about as much as we can."

Charlotte drifted to the side of the auditorium. From time-to-time Jack would check on the three women. Each time, he was satisfied when he found their attention focused on the audience.

LaVerne finished her rousing speech of welcome to her army. She was interrupted several times with standing applause. The army was hypnotized by her every word. Jack couldn't believe anyone could have that effect on a group of independent women.

When she finished, she held both fists high in the air like a football player who had scored the winning touchdown. The women clapped and yelled with no indication of slowing down. She left the dais and the platform escorted by Jack and the three ladies.

This time, Charlotte led them to the service elevator going directly to their suite. Thus they were able to avoid any contact with people in the lobby. Charlotte, Audry and Hazel left them at the door. Jack entered the apartment first, motioning for LaVerne to wait at the entry alcove. He quickly inspected each room and closet.

"All clear. You want to order room service?"

"Yes, there should be a menu in the desk drawer."

Jack noticed that she seemed tired and emotionally drained.

"Are you okay? You seem to be tired. You want to lie down?"

"I don't know, Jack. I'm scared to death of that crazy man. I guess I should eat something or else I'll be a little jumpy later from low blood sugar. Order a b-l-t with plus a beer—make it a New Castle."

Jack picked up the phone and ordered.

After they finished eating, LaVerne's mood changed. She was happy and obviously flirting with Jack. Jack reciprocated and flirted back.

"Oh, Jack. I'll bet you're something in the sack."

"All I can say is modesty prevents me, Miss L."

"Would you like a little tumble in the hay?"

"Pat may return. Would you want that?"

"Just latch the door with that chain thing."

Later, Jack made coffee using the small pot in the butler's pantry. LaVerne was still asleep. He closed the door to her room, turned on the television with the sound muted and watched a soccer game on the Cuban station. In a few minutes, Jack fell asleep.

He was wakened when the noise of door opening to the extent of the chain. He checked his watch. It was five-thirty. He got up and unlatched the chain.

Pat breezed in. "Well, the workshop sessions are over, thank goodness. How's LaVerne?"

"Asleep. She was spent when we came back to the room. Also, she's really scared of that crazy guy, you know?"

"I'll just check on her."

Pat opened her door and looked in. She softly closed it again.

"Sex. I knew it!"

"What?"

"You provided a service for her, didn't you?"

"I don't think I'll answer that."

"Don't get me wrong. She really needed it. Otherwise, she wouldn't now be getting the rest she needs. Did she have lunch?"

"Yeah, a b-l-t and a beer."

"She ordered a New Castle, right?"

"Yeah."

"You don't drink, do you?"

"Nope."

"I admire that in you?"

The routine for escorting LaVerne to the evening program differed. This time, they took the service elevator, exiting to the hallway behind the stage and dais.

The auditorium was crowded with hardly a vacant seat. LaVerne, Jack and Charlotte sat in folding chairs in the service hallway. The sound system was loud enough for them to follow the advance of the program. Every few minutes, LaVerne would stand, stretch, pace back and forth then plop back into her chair. Jack reached out to hold her hand. She squeezed tightly.

"I don't know how I could have endured this without you, Jack."

"It'll be okay. I'll do my best to keep you from harm."

The loudspeaker blared the introduction. LaVerne stood. Then, with her palms she pressed imaginary wrinkles from her violet suit, put on a huge smile and entered the room.

Jack quickly moved ahead of her. A heavy-set woman with a flash camera moved from the crowd. From behind the camera, Jack saw the pistol. Instinctively, he moved in front of LaVerne. He realized this was not a woman but the crazy man from the previous day. Two shots rang out followed by two more.

CHAPTER
41

WHEN HE AWOKE, he was in bed with the room lights dim. A nurse pulled back the curtains.

"Well, Mister Wexler. Glad to see you awake. How do you feel? Any pain?"

"Yeah, my side."

"That's where you were shot."

"Yeah, I remember the ride to the hospital but very little afterwards. How long have I been here?"

"You were shot yesterday evening. It's now Sunday afternoon."

"Anybody told my aunt?"

"She's outside with Mister Reynolds and two women, Pat and LaVerne Hollings."

"My Aunt Emily first. The others later."

She came in dabbing tears from her eyes. "Oh, Jackie, I was so afraid you would die. You've just got to find different work."

"I know, I know. I have enough money now to finish college if my hospital bill doesn't take it all. But, I promise, no more bodyguard jobs."

"If you do, I'll just take you over my knee. You aren't too big for a good spanking, you know."

"Oh, come on. I'm okay now so don't worry so much. Did you drive your Buick?"

"No, John Reynolds drove me. He's a nice man. He's worried too."

"Please send him in. Tell Pat and LaVerne I'll see them in a few minutes."

John came in with a serious look on his face. "Damn, son. You've got to take better care of yourself."

"Yeah, like I planned taking a bullet or was it two."

"One, the other shot found a wall. The shooter's dead, you know."

"Yeah, I thought I heard four shots."

"Charlotte Cotton got him twice. Either would have been a kill shot. I knew her when she was on the Miami PD—she was a good officer."

"Have you been told what was hit? You, know, anything important?"

"He was using a lousy .22 automatic—in and out through the side. Hit the gut, though. They sewed it up. You'll have to be here a few more days until they can take the drain out. At least, that's what your doctor says."

"Could you send in Pat and LaVerne? Then, I think I'll take a nap. I'm not feeling so good."

Pat and LaVerne came in. Both had been crying. LaVerne came to his side, Pat held back.

"Are you alright?"

"I think I'll live. How about you?"

"You saved my life then you saved my life again."

"That was my job, you know."

Both started crying again.

"Bob Fossgrave told me you don't have medical insurance. I just wanted to tell you that your hospital bill will be taken care of. Also, I'm tripling your fee. I gave a check for eight thousand dollars to your aunt. Jack, you have my deepest appreciation for your sacrifice. I will be forever in your debt."

Pat stepped up and gave him a kiss. Over her tears she promised, "I'll never forget you." Both women left the room crying.

Jack was just falling asleep again when he heard a familiar voice.

"You keep getting hurt and I keep patching you up. When will it end?"

His eyes focused on the name on the white coat.

"Doctor Sims. Oh yes, Janet wasn't it?"

"So soon you forget someone who put a tube in your… uh."

"I remember now. How have you been?"

"You were going to call. What am I, chopped liver?"

"We meet again. This must be fate."

"No, it's just your reckless ways. You need to stop what you're doing and get into some other line of work."

"So, how much longer do you have before you can get into private practice?"

"Actually, four weeks from now. How about you?"

"I have another three semesters plus a summer term to go before I finish in Mechanical Engineering. You want to get married? I'm a really nice guy, you know."

Laughing, she replied, "That's the best proposal I've had all day."

"How much longer will I have to stay here hooked up to these tubes?"

"Your bowel was pierced by the bullet. That let some nasty bacteria into your abdominal cavity. The surgical team did their best to clean you out but you never are able to get it all. So, you have a tube to help the process. At least, the surgeon didn't have to make a large incision. How long? My guess is two to three weeks."

The nurse came in so Janet waved bye and left.

That afternoon, Janet popped in again.

"Hey dude. How you doing?"

"Not bad, considering. I had a little fever so they added something to the drip."

"Yes, I expected that. If you make it another week without major infection, you'll coast the rest of the way."

"When will I be on solid food?"

"Ask your doctor."

"Janet, you look tired. Are they treating you mean?"

"No it's the usual treatment they give interns, even the senior ones. I'm pulling eighteen hours today."

"I appreciate your visit. You really bring in the sunshine. Hope you can come by before your shift is over."

"Be glad to. Bye."

She continued visiting Jack as many as six times during the day. Occasionally she would kiss him on the cheek when she said good-bye.

"Look, Janet. Meeting you every day can't end when I'm finally released. Would you consider seeing me socially?"

"You mean like, on a date?"

"I would really like to date you and get to know you better if that's okay."

He was released sixteen days after his surgery. Jack lost no time adapting his schedule to match hers. On her days off, they spent almost every hour together. Movies, dinner and dancing, walks on the beach and mugging it up in Jack's car but nothing more intimate.

Jack and Janet enjoyed being together at the ocean front park near Homestead. Janet would pick up Jack at his aunt's house driving her Miata convertible with the top down. Every day, it became obvious to them both that they were falling in love.

The real test of their relationship came when Jack took Janet to a jewelry store to pick out a ring. Though there was no proposal yet, they both knew it would be soon. Jack picked up the ring after it had been sized the same day. He wore a tuxedo and bought a dozen roses for their evening date.

Janet's roommate answered the door to her apartment.

"Come in, Jack. She'll be ready in a second. Oh, this is so exciting!"

"She told you?"

"Are you kidding? She told me a week ago."

Janet breezed in wearing an evening dress.

"Oh, Jack. Flowers!"

She took the flowers and handed them to her roommate.

"Audry, please put these in a vase for me. We need to go now."

When they were in Jack's car, she asked: "Can you tell me where we're going or is it to be a surprise."

"You'll find out soon enough."

When Jack pulled up in front of *La Petite Cheri*, Janet was delighted. On their way in, she could hold it no longer. "Tonight's the night, isn't it?"

"You'll find out just before the dessert."

"Have you already ordered?"

"Of course. I've left nothing undone."

They were seated near a jazz combo consisting of guitar, drums and bass. The soft ballads weren't intruding on anyone's conversation. Every fourth song, a lady would approach the microphone and sing a sultry number.

They didn't have to speak to the waiter. He had received his orders earlier in the day.

"Oh, Jack, I need to tell you something that'll expand your sweet over-inflated ego even more. The first time I saw you, I knew you would be the one for me. I know love at first sight is for the movies, but it happened to me. Then, when you told me you loved me last week, I knew this would be next."

"For me, my emotions can't switch that fast. I needed time to express my love to you. But the end result is the same. Now, let's delay the mushy stuff and concentrate on the salad."

She punched him on the shoulder. "You rat!"

During the remainder of the meal, their conversation skirted the reality of the occasion. When they cleared off the remains of their meal, Jack moved his chair back and stepped to her side.

"You're not getting down on your knee, are you?"

"You bet."

Jack knelt and took the small black box out of his pocket. "Janet, I want to spend my life with you, have children with you and grow old together. I promise always to cherish you with love and kindness. Will you marry me?"

"Oh, Jack. This is so hokey. Of course I'll marry you."

Jane and Jack stood and kissed. The other patrons applauded as the singer belted out a really sappy love song.

They sat down again. Janet put her arm out to get a perspective on the ring.

"It looks so much larger than it did in the store. Did you switch to a larger diamond?"

"I love you."

"I love you too."

CHAPTER
42

THE STUDENTS WERE AWAY so Auburn was nearly deserted. Jack had made a lightning trip to rent the apartment when Janet and her mother were busy with the hurry-up wedding plans. The schedule was extremely short with Janet finishing her internship and the start of the summer term at Auburn.

The Caddy pulled up to a duplex apartment towing Janet's red Miata. The couple, hand-in-hand, walked to the apartment, pausing at the door. Jack took a key and opened the door. He swept Janet up in his arms and carried her inside.